Part II:

Dawn Breakers

A novel by
Lebron James Bond

This is a work of fiction. All characters, organizations and events portrayed in this are either products of the author's imagination or are used fictitiously.

Editing and Design: Rochelle Levy

Digital Painting and Texturing: Luther Berry

Cover Art: Oluwole Olubadewo

ISBN 978-0-9970782-3-7

COV dot PUB, a division of The COV, LLC
7001 S. La Cienega Blvd - Unit 302
Los Angeles, CA 90045

www.shadowprecinct.com

shadowprecinct@gmail.com

@ShadowPrecinct

2

Rochelle, Luther, and Olu. Thank you for seeing the vision.
Thanks to my family and friends for their continued support.

Inspired by Notorious BIG's Life After Death

CHAPTER ONE

May 1995

Cyrus sat slightly shifting in his seat as he waited to be retrieved from the industrial-style waiting room. The neutral hues of everything, the walls to the tile floor to the small coffee table at the center, seemed to be purposefully chosen to dull the senses. Or at least numb them. The only splash of color was from the various science magazines strewn about the table. He was in the middle of another observatatory trip hoping to find something worthwhile. Months bouncing around the Northern Hemisphere had yielded nothing besides promises of weapons to be shipped at a later date and a few manuscripts about techniques that he already had.

This particular excursion brought him to a facility in Thailand, after an excruciatingly long flight followed by an hour long drive into a sticky green cloud of trees damp from the humidity. He continued to wait as patiently as he could considering his mind was still in the corridors many thousands of miles away. Everett's graduation. Cyrus could close his eyes and instantly be in his backyard with Everett as a child. He fought off the encroaching guilt by telling himself he was there for the greater good: to continue the work that he had started and build upon the legacy that his son had helped to solidify at Mount Z. With that newfound resolve firmly in place, he patiently continued to wait. A sliding door opened and a beautiful European woman in a lab coat and glasses gently marched out.

"Mr. Santeaux?"

"Yes."

"Please, follow me. He is waiting for you."

Cyrus rose from his chair dreading the fact that he would be in the same position in a couple hours on the return trip back home, with considerably less leg room and food that was downright disrespectful. Their feet pinged against a metallic floor as they went side by side down a long hallway, her heels and his hard bottoms making for an annoying duet. There were doors with blacked out windows that presumably lead to rooms lining either side.

"What's with the windows?" Cyrus inquired.

"Just a precaution. The work that we do here is...confidential in nature Mr. Santeaux. A man with your reputation should understand such circumstances, yes?"

Cyrus silently nodded in agreement. They methodically twisted through the hallways in lockstep. The rhythm in the footfalls produced a more favorable noise. Just as Cyrus was beginning to wonder when the hell they would arrive at their destination, the woman, who still hadn't introduced herself, stopped at a door that looked like the many that they had passed.

"He's in there," The woman said as she slid a keycard pulled from the breast pocket of her lab coat into a door mounted locking mechanism. Cyrus nodded in her direction again, and proceeded towards the door. As he came within a few steps, it slid open abruptly releasing a slight rush of air. He took a large step through the threshold and let the door seal behind him. A man sat at what appeared to be an interrogation table with his back to Cyrus.

"Welcome Mr. Santeaux. I have been anticipating your arrival for some time now."

"Is that so?" Cyrus replied, seemingly surprised.

"Indeed, that is so. To say that I am a fan of what you have achieved in the United Corridors with your training facilities is an understatement. Truly remarkable."

"Thank you, I'm actually kind of flattered that my name has preceded me here, of all places," Cyrus said slowly, cautiously, taking in his surroundings, "We still haven't been formally introduced, you are?"

The man chuckled lightly, "If I were to tell you all the things I've been called over time, we'd be here for a long while I'm afraid. You can call me Tozen."

Tozen rose from his seat and turned to face Cyrus. Cyrus analyzed him. The man's ethnicity wasn't immediately identifiable, nor was his age. Cyrus himself looked younger than he actually was but this was different. There wasn't a wrinkle on Tozen's pale face. Odd because he wasn't a young man, he couldn't be. His eyes seemed old, like they had seen more than his perceived age might suggest. He was bald with a scar above his right eye that chopped his eyebrow in two. He definitely wasn't from anywhere in Thailand. He also wasn't dressed like a doctor of any sort. Every part of his skin was covered, save for his face. Even black gloves covered his hands.

Tozen stepped away from his seat and revealed that they were not alone in the room. A dark-skinned Asian boy of no more than seven years of age sat across the table. Cyrus could tell that he had been crying. His eyes were puffy and his small chest jerked sporadically as he hyperventilated, trying to keep his tears from returning. Cyrus's heart began to thump a bit faster than normal. There was something very uncomfortable about the proceedings he had just joined. Upon closer inspection he saw the boy's hands outstretched on the table with a small wood saw in front of him.

And just what in the shit did I just walk into?

He was lost in his own thoughts when the gravelly voice of Tozen jolted him out of it.

"How rude of me to keep you waiting. I know a man of your stature is quite busy, so I will get on with our little demonstration."

Cyrus was silent as he tried to decipher the man's definition of, "demonstration".

Tozen paced slowly back over to the table where the child was sitting. Without saying a word, he picked the saw up off of the table. The child's face was filled with restrained terror. Clearly, the boy had been conditioned not to show any emotion, but he couldn't hide the obvious fear that began to dampen his face along with the beads of sweat that were sticking to his forehead. Cyrus cringed as he watched Tozen gently grab the child's wrist and place the saw right above his pinky finger. The child began to whimper like a wounded puppy, which caused the man to glare at him. Cyrus saw the look on the child's face as Tozen stared into his eyes.

He knows something worse than this will happen if he doesn't cooperate.

The boy bit his quivering lower lip and tightly closed his eyes. With one ferocious initial thrust, Tozen began to saw at the boy's pinky. The pain caused every ounce of restraint that the boy had shown up until this point to immediately dissipate like smoke in the wind. The sound of the serrated edge slicing through skin and muscle seemed to echo louder in the confines of the room, mixed with the shrieking of the young boy. Cyrus felt his stomach turn. Not from what he was witnessing, but rather at the realization that he was no different that this man sawing a young boy's finger off. They were two sides of the same coin. Cyrus spent the better part of his adulthood crafting a training regiment that some would say is equally barbaric as what was playing out before him at this very moment.

Blood pooled on the table in the shape of a prehistoric continent. It gradually swelled until it dripped to the floor; the gradual plop of blood hitting metal added the snare kick to the disturbing soundtrack of the events taking place. Tozen pressed down forcefully as he sawed through bone. The pain was so intense it sucked all of the sound out of the boy's chest. Cyrus forced himself to continue watching. With one final thrust, the boy had four fingers. Tozen wiped his brow with his sleeve and looked over his shoulder smiling like he had just completed a carpentry project. He turned back to the child.

"Keep your hands outstretched, boy. And keep still, please," Tozen said coldly as he gently placed the now bloody saw on the table. He looked over his shoulder back to Cyrus, "Come closer, before you miss it."

Cyrus slowly stepped towards the mess of a table. It looked like the cutting board of an inebriated surgeon. Pieces of meat were still clinging to the teeth of the saw.

"It should start any moment now," Tozen noted.

Cyrus looked at the bloody nub where the boy's pinky used to be. He stepped closer to ensure that his eyes weren't playing tricks on him. The bloody nub began to pulsate and throb. The blood flow slowed to a stop. Seconds later, Cyrus looked in amazement as blue blood started to bubble from the wound. A small bone slowly jutted out from the bloody space where the boy's finger had been. Cyrus's eyes darted towards Tozen, who had a satisfied smirk on his face. Cyrus looked back at the boy's hand.

The process was moving exponentially faster, the bone began to push out like toothpaste being squeezed from a tube, slowly taking the shape of a finger. Blood began to surround it. Nerves endings began to fan out. Muscle fibers began to wrap around the bone. Skin began to rapidly grow up from the knuckle on the child's hand, covering his newly grown extremity. The finger nail of the boy's pinky was the last thing to appear. It was perfect, as if the grotesque performance that had taken place minutes before had never happened.

"What in the hell did I just see?" Cyrus asked, shocked.

Tozen stood up and walked Cyrus towards the door, "You have seen the future Mr. Santeaux."

Cyrus immediately forgot about Everett's graduation. He walked out of the room and promptly canceled his return flight home.

CHAPTER TWO

March 9th 2004, 6:00 AM

Everett inhaled the fresh air of the early morning as he sat in the courtyard of his home. It was a place that he usually came to meditate, read, or practice the numerous katas that he committed to memory. A perfectly landscaped square of emerald green grass shrouded in trees. A man-made stream with smooth stones lining the bottom outlined the perimeter. Sometimes when he returned from the depths of his meditative state, he would be surprised at the surroundings.

It was a noticeable improvement over the high rise apartment he shared with Simone years ago. Not to say that the previous abode was a shack, but this, as it turns out, was one of the perks of being a member of the Metropolitan Corridor Tribunal. You get the fly shit. Everett was about to return to his meditation when he detected the ever-so-soft thuds of footfalls on the wooden walkway that connected the courtyard with the main house. The short strides meant that it could only be one person. One little person.

"Chance," Everett said without looking over his shoulder, "What are you doing out of bed so early?"

"Aww, daddy! I was trying to sneak up on you," Chance said with a voice befitting a cartoon character, adding a staccato chuckle that was infections. Her small feet made barely audible crunches on the grass as she waltzed over to her father and draped her arms around his neck giving him a kiss on his cheek. Usually, Everett would be perturbed at his meditation being interrupted. Chance was the only exception to that. He smiled and engulfed her small hands in his.

"You were tryin' to sneak up on me, huh?"

"Yep! Like a zee lot."

Her pronunciation of the title made him laugh.

"Like a zealot? Well, you gotta long way to go. I knew you were coming from a mile away," Everett said.

"Nuh uh!"

"Yes huh. You know your mom will be very worried if she checks your room and you not there baby girl."

Chance let out an exasperated sigh, "I knooow."

"So you know you have to go get back in the bed before she checks, right? Cuz she'll be yellin at me, not you."

"I said I know, jeeez," Chance snapped in an aggravated tone.

"Whoa, whoa, check that attitude young lady."

"Sorry, daddy. It's just…"

"It's just what?" Everett asked.

"It's just I made a fake me outta my stuffed aminals, heh. It's under the blanket," Chance whispered with a sneaky grin.

Everett laughed and kissed both of her tiny brown hands before he unclasped them from around his neck and stood up. He took another deep breath accompanied by a long stretch towards the sky.

"Maybe one day I'll bring you out here and show you some things, Chance. Can never start learning techniques too early. My dad started teaching me when I was around your age, even though I know your mom would never-", Evertt stopped mid-sentence as he realized he was talking to himself. His young daughter was nowhere in sight. He let out a hardy laugh.

"Just like a zee lot."

Everett walked back into the doors of his house where he was immediately greeted by Simone. It looked like she was on her way outside to retrieve him.

"Mornin' baby," She whispered before kissing his lips, "I was comin' to getcha. You're communicator has been buzzing like crazy. Woke me up."

"Wonder who could be hittin' me up this early? The shift change for the operators at the Mecca should be happening right now, so."

"Dunno, figure you'd want to check it out though."

"I will."

They both walked down the hallway towards their room and passed Chance's room on the way. Her door was open. She was snuggled in her bed seemingly sleeping comfortably. They both paused in the threshold of the door.

"She's been knocked out," Simone said with a smile.

Everett returned her smile with different reason, "Yeah, it looks that way."

"Her birthday's comin' up soon. Any thoughts about what you might wanna get her?"

"Can't believe she's about to be seven already, shit's crazy," Everett lamented.

"I know," Simone sighed as she stared lovingly at the daughter the two of them made.

Simone continued down the hall. Everett followed behind her, but not before taking one final peek into the room to catch Chance closing her eyes with a smirk.

"Well played young lady. Well played."

He picked up his communicator and placed it on his ear. Everett rolled off commands to the disembodied computerized voice of the comm.

"Everett Santeax, callsign Myth."

Analyzing...Voice recognition analysis complete.

"Return latest communicaiton attempt."

Last communication attempt from: Dane Archibald

Attempting to establish connection, please wait...

A periodic chime sounded in his ear as he waited for the connection. The familiar voice of Police Chief Archibald was the next through the communicator.

"Myth. Got somethin' for ya."

"Good morning to you, too Arch, damn. What's so pressing that it couldn't wait till I got a bowl of Commander Crunchies or somethin'?"

"You don't really eat that shit do you?"

"Archibald, I honestly don't like your tone in addressing the Commander."

"Hey, whatever floats your boat, Santeaux. Can we talk business?"

"Isn't that the only thing we ever talk about?"

"Not a couple hours ago there was a robbery attempt on an armored truck."

"Are you fucking kidding me Arch, man bye," Everett said, reaching to end the call.

"No, no, wait Myth. There's more to it than that. My guys were able to neutralize them."

"So lemme get the facts straight: you interrupt my lovely morning to disparage my cereal choice and tell me about a crime that you guys already stopped? You got twenty seconds."

Archibald, let out a sigh before continuing, "My guys were able to take the three of them down, but they were ruthless. And unarmed. No weapons of any type, they fought off eight of my cops."

"Ten."

"It looked like they were trained, at least in some capacity," Archibald explained.

"Nine."

"Anyway, we end up subduing two and taking them in, but the third, musta been the leader of the little crew, he didn't make it. He went berserk, beat the hell outta a couple guys before we took him down. We hit him with so many stun rounds he went into cardiac arrest."

Everett grunted with obvious disdain for the subject matter, "Eight, seven, six ,five..."

Archibald, noticing Everett's growing frustration, began to rattle off facts, "We found something on him, a vile, looks like, and don't laugh or say some sarcastic bullshit, but looks like blue sand. His eyes, were bloodshot, but, they were blue."

"So they were...blueshot?" Everett asked, seemingly a bit more interested.

"Yeah, yeah I guess you could say that. It's like he ingested whatever was in that vile and that's when he really went apeshit. We're waitin' on the toxicology report to come back, but I wanted to take it over to Shef and get his take on it. Can you meet me there?"

"Blue sand? You know it's taking every fiber of my being to not say something right now, right?"

"I know."

"Like how ya' moms is pumpin' Mountain Berry flavored cocaine on the block?"

"You just couldn't pass it up, could you?"

"Nope."

"Can you do it or no?"

"That's what ya' moms left on my voicemail."

"Santeaux."

"I'm firin' on all cylinders this morning," Everett said laughing, "but I somehow doubt that you bothered the other members of the tribunal with this bullshit?"

Arhicbald was silent for a moment, "C'mon Myth, it's a simple yes or no."

Everett let out a disgusted sigh, "Yeah, I'll be there."

"Thank you."

Transmission ended.

Everett took off his communicator. Simone was busy moving about the house, but she caught Everett out of the corner of her eye in quiet contemplation. He indeed was in deep thought. Though he was just giving Archibald a hard time, this new information had piqued his interest in something as mundane as an armed robbery.

"Everything okay, E?"

"Yeah, yeah. Just Arch wants me to meet up with him, discuss some things. It's probably nothin'."

"Let's hope so. I'm about to make some breakfast, you stayin'?"

Everett was hesitant to commit to the offer until he saw his daughter walk in and latch herself to her mother's leg.

"Stay daddy, pleeeease."

"Yeah, I think I will."

CHAPTER THREE

July 1995

I've been in Thailand for almost two months now. It's taken the entirety of that time to get adjusted to the heat out here, my God. I hadn't realized my stay would be this long, intended to only extend it by a week or two at best. But the things I've seen here are amazing. Revolutionary might be a more apt description. Frighteningly revolutionary is probably even better.

Tozen. He's a unique individual to say the least. He keeps ungodly hours. In the entire time that I've been around him, and I've shadowed him fairly heavily in recent weeks, I have yet to see any of his skin exposed, save for his face. The fact that he's wearing long sleeves in the middle of July in Thailand has to speak to some form of mild insanity. Our interactions remind me of a quote that Professor Dell used to have on his wall back during ARU that said something to the effect of, "There is no great genius without a touch of madness."

Wish I remembered who said it, but it fits Tozen's demeanor perfectly. I have no idea how he came to control such a compound as this. Through our discussions he's never alluded to any type of science background, which is odd for the head of a facility experimenting with the amazing scientific advances as I have seen here. I've come to realize that seeing that kid's finger grow back right before my eyes was the tip of the iceberg. I'm accompanying Tozen on a trip to one of the research facilities in hopes to speak with some of the scientists and engineers he has on staff. Should be interesting.

Cyrus and Tozen rode in silence chauffeured by an elderly gentleman. The road they were on had long since eroded, probably due to flooding or possibly from years of travel. Whatever the case, it didn't make for a comfortable trip. The car they were in didn't do them any favors, either. Cyrus was staring out of the window watching trees vibrate past the window, catching the eye of the occasional local staring at what was probably the only car within miles. Cyrus lost track of time before Tozen finally spoke.

"Mr. Santeaux, have you given any consideration to staying on a permanent basis?"

"Permanent?" Cyrus replied shocked at the adjective.

"Permanent. I'm sure you're familiar with the definition. I am not unlike you, Mr. Santeaux. I, too, have been on a recruiting mission of sorts akin to your home visits to potential enrollees at Mount Z."

"Recruiting who?" Cyrus asked.

"Are you always this naïve?" Tozen snapped, displaying an unsettling, restrained agitation, "Talent. Exceptional research requires exceptional talent. I need these people here in order to get my," Tozen paused before continuing, "pardon me, *our* ideas realized. You know as well as I that technological advancements continue to move at an alarming pace. Each generation brings about new inventions that make people more complacent in their lives. Technology is a sedative, helping to keep them asleep from what is truly happening. I don't know if you've looked around you, but the world is becoming more and more volatile. Poverty. War. Violence. I'm sure you'd be the first to admit that the zealot program was a last resort, an act of desperation in the wave of the senseless bloodshed that was washing through your precious corridors."

"You have one of the most advanced facilities I've ever seen staffed with some of the greatest scientists and engineers from around the world," Cyrus scoffed, "Yet, you make technology seem like some dark force, some kind of evil. Doesn't that strike you as a bit…hypocritical?"

Tozen laughed, "I can see I still have a ways to go before you can truly empathize with my position. Hypocritical? To a degree, I confess. But as the cliché states: sometimes it's best to fight fire with fire. Or perhaps even fight evil with evil."

Cyrus shifted in his seat uncomfortably.

"I plan on leaving an indelible mark. I hope that, in time, you will help me achieve that."

"I gather that mark will leave the world a better place?" Cyrus cautiously inquired as the car slowed to a stop. Tozen looked at him and offered up a smile that did the complete opposite of what a smile is intended to do.

"Of course."

Cyrus found no solace in this statement, nor in Tozen's grin. In his mind, he imagined that if a snake could smile, it would look something like that; the wicked smirk of a serpent coaxing Eve to partake in the forbidden fruit. Despite these growing feelings of uneasiness, he continued. He convinced himself that there was good to be found here that could benefit future zealots, which would subsequently benefit his country. After all, Tozen was right about at least one thing. The world was getting more volatile.

They both approached an industrial building guarded by two large men dressed in military uniforms. Both men stood with arms folded in front of their chests, their muscles bulging under the sleeves of their shirts, both armed with large combat knives attached to their belts. Neither man blinked as Cyrus and Tozen passed them and entered a huge set of sliding doors. They went down a gradually narrowing hallway and through yet another door. They stepped into a research facility with an open floor plan.

A large glass window lined the entire opposite wall of the room. Through the window, there was an enclosure similar to what a gorilla would be in at the zoo. Scientists of various ethnicities were milling about, shuffling between equipment and computer screens.

Cyrus made out at least three different languages being spoken as the crew moved about their business without even acknowledging the two men.

"The individuals that you see in here have been experimenting and developing different methods of genetic enhancement," Tozen began.

Cyrus continued to look around, out of the corner of his eye he caught a doctor quickly bring the curtain closed behind a grisly scene of a child hooked to all manners of contraptions as a swarm of doctors prodded, poked, and injected him with a multi-flavored assortment of needles. For a brief moment the child's eyes met with Cyrus. Silent, solemn tears fell as he disappeared out of sight.

At this point in his life, Cyrus was used to shaking off the deeply disturbing sights he'd seen, most of which were enough to haunt any other man.

He motioned towards the window, "This enclosure houses the results?"

"Why, yes. Hopefully, he'll make an appearance today. He gets a bit shy around company, I'm afraid," Tozen noted.

"The genetic research you mentioned, what does it entail exactly?" Cyrus asked with a noticeable hint of skepticism.

"Well, there's literally hundreds of years worth of genetic research across all types of disciplines. We began trying to find a cure for disease."

"Really? Which one?" Cyrus asked.

Tozen slowed to a stop and before turning to him, "Why, all of them."

Cyrus looked confused while Tozen continued.

"As such, we've taken a particular interest in gene splicing."

"Splicing?" Cyrus asked genuinely shocked, "Has that ever even been successfully achieved?"

"As I mentioned earlier Mr. Santeaux, exceptional research," Tozen said with a grin.

"You aren't exactly forthcoming with what you're doing here Mr. Tozen, is this your way of persuading me to stay because I-"

"You've already made the decision," Tozen interrupted, "You are exactly where you want to be. Your threats are falling on deaf ears."

"Sir?" A voice prodded from behind them.

"What is it?" Tozen answered, though his eyes were fixated on Cyrus.

"He's moving, it looks like he's coming out."

"Well," Tozen motioned, "would you like to introduce yourself?'

Cyrus hesitated before nodding in confirmation. The two men walked over to the window as scientists stole glimpses over their shoulders before going back to work. Presumably, all of them had contributed in some way to what was about to come out of the dark, jungle-like interior of the enclosure. Cyrus noticed the split of the sliding doors as they got closer to the window.

I do not like where this is headed.

And despite that thought, his curiosity prevailed.

One of the scientists, a demure man, shuffled over to Cyrus and Tozen.

"He's out there, within ten square meters even though we can't see him," he whispered.

"Open the door," Tozen frigidly ordered.

"Now's the part you ask *me* to go in that motherfucker?" Cyrus sternly asked. The look in his eyes made Tozen recognize the man's strength. He hadn't heard about him for nothing.

Tozen smiled, genuinely this time it seemed, "You'll go in without my coaxing. The choice is yours however, Mr. Santeaux."

With nothing and no one standing in his way, Cyrus stepped over the threshold and entered the enclosure. He immediately recognized the ceiling. Though it seemed like it from the outside, the surroundings were crafted to precisely mimic that of a real jungle, with a couple of rather comically obvious technological bits of scenery. Cyrus turned around and saw Tozen standing with one arm folded, his other hand was stroking his chin. He was watching intensely, as were all of the scientists and researchers. Cyrus looked at the crowd a bit closer and realized that his spectators extended beyond just the people in lab coats, everyone in the facility, including the conscious patients, were watching Cyrus.

Cyrus took a deep breath and exhaled only to be interrupted by a subtle sound; the crunch of a branch. Anyone else in the room, save for Tozen perhaps, probably wouldn't have noticed. But then again, Cyrus rationalized, that's probably the reason Tozen knew Cyrus would go in. He knew he wouldn't be afraid.

"Come out. I know you're there," Cyrus declared.

There was silence for a few minutes, then the crunching of footfalls on the artificially created ground. Eventually, the same boy that had his pinky sawed off emerged from the man-made jungle. His clothes were dirty and slightly tattered. Blood stains streaked across his shirt and his khaki pants that had since eroded into shorts. He didn't have any shoes on and he kept his eyes on the ground.

"Don't be afraid. Come closer," Cyrus encouraged the boy.

The boy obliged without looking up or saying a word. He just took slow plodding steps towards Cyrus. As he walked, Cyrus observed the child in more detail. The nails on his toes were sharp, pointed. The nails on his hands were the same. Cyrus thought it was a belt holding up his shorts, but upon closer inspection saw it was a tail coiled around his waist. The boy finally was standing in front of Cyrus. He slowly raised his head and looked at him with catlike eyes. The two stared at each other, both in shock for different reasons.

"You're not afraid," The boy said confidently.

"What gives you that impression?" Cyrus inquired.

"I can smell it on the others. Everyone that's come in here."

"What's your name?"

"I can't remember. Specimen 415 is all anybody ever calls me."

"And how long have you been in here?"

"I dunno. As long as they've been trying to make me better," the boy said solemnly.

"Better," Cyrus asked, "were you sick?"

"No, I wasn't sick. Mr. Tozen told me that I'm going to be better than regular people. Because of the new medicines him and all the scientists are making."

"Is that so?" Cyrus turned his head back for a brief moment and peered through the glass. Everyone on the opposite side was watching with baited breath. All of their faces conveyed the same sense of nervous anticipation, probably in the same manner that a crowd watches a plane crash to the ground. All except for Tozen, who remained stoic throughout it all.

"Your heart's beating faster."

Cyrus quickly whipped around, the child had a mischievious grin on his face made more menacing by the pronounced fangs that extended from his gums, something Cyrus hadn't noticed until now.

Cyrus, unfazed, came closer to the boy.

"Neko."

"Huh?"

"How about we call you that? If you can't remember your name, anyway. It sounds better than Specimen 415, don't you think?"

The boy smiled. The smile spoke volumes about the frequency at which anyone treated him with compassion.

"I like it."

"Good. Well, Neko. I'll be going now. It was nice to meet you. I believe we will probably be seeing each other soon."

The boy smirked, nodded, then turned and bolted into the shadowy refuge of the faux jungle with the speed and agility that only an animal could achieve. An animal or a zealot. A brief shot of excitement surged through Cyrus's mind.

Imagine what he would be like if he got some proper training.

Cyrus turned and walked towards the sliding doors. As he stepped back in, he heard the entire room breathe a sigh of relief that he could have sworn caused a small zephyr. Tozen was the first to speak upon his exit.

"Congratulations."

Cyrus looked puzzled, "For what?"

"You're the first person he didn't rip to shreds upon entering."

Cyrus raised a dismissive eyebrow, "Let's save the high fives for later. I would like to speak with him again."

"That doesn't surprise me," Tozen chuckled, "We most certainly can arrange that."

A female voice chimed in unexpectedly. It was barely audible.

"I have some additional documentation Mr. Santeaux, for your consideration. It details the extent of the gene splicing program that is currently in development as well as graphs reflecting the progress of Specimen 415. I believe you will find the information very fascinating."

She stepped towards him and handed him a dossier. Upon closer inspection, the woman seemed like she hadn't slept in days, maybe weeks. Her eyes were sunken into her face with dark circles forming around them. Her fingers were bony. She had been working tirelessly and it showed. Still, there was an underlying beauty to her that Cyrus recognized.

"Thank you, I will definitely be reviewing this."

The two men left the facility back to where their chauffeur awaited. As they embarked on their return trip, Cyrus flipped open the dossier saw a hand written note clipped to the first page.

Help us.

He swiftly closed it before Tozen could notice.

CHAPTER FOUR

Later That Morning

Myth arrived at Shef's new facility, a joint venture with the Mecca of the Metropolitan Corridor and the Metro Police Department. A sprawling, high-tech loft located on the top floor of an old remodeled high rise. Both organizations owed Shef a lot since the fiasco with the Ark, and his technological expertise had become indispensable for both. He was responsible for most of the new tech used by zealots and aided Archibald with surveillance if his cops ever needed it, amongst other things.

These days he worked as a consultant to cops and zealots alike, usually whenever something strange or immediately inexplicable happened to arise. And the events of the early morning, as reported by Archibald, definitely fit under both categories. Myth made his way to the familiar double doors of the building. He pressed a button to buzz up to Shef.

"Yo, I'm supposed to be meeting Arch here."

Shef's voice came bubbling through the speaker, "Gotcha. Come on up."

The doors opened and Myth slipped down an all-white hallway lined with security cameras to another elevator. Lasers criss-crossed patterns across his body as he moved, scanning him. He boarded the elevator and proceeded to the top floor. Six stories later, he was exiting into Shef's lab. It was such a stark contrast to the dark, musty, subterranean abode with make-shift tools where the two had their first real confrontation. The new lab was filled with light from a multitude of windows with electronic blinds. The improvised nature of his equipment was replaced with state-of-the-art devices all purchased by the Mecca, easily worth millions of dollars.

"Well, look what the wind blew in!" Shef exclaimed with genuine excitement, he pivoted in his chair and rose slowly. Having been forced to retire from the vigilante street justice game, his old age was starting to settle on him. His face had become rounder, the gray hairs more noticeable. The name Beam had been retired as well (along with his drinking), as he was strictly going by his given name these days. The forearm he lost in the fight with Orion during the siege of the Ark was replaced by a cybernetic arm of his own creation. It moved and functioned as a normal arm would sans the skin, which allowed for one to see the intricacies of its design, truly a work of genius.

"What's up Shef?" Everett said as a smile crept across his face.

"Not in uniform, either eh? Not expecting to be long I gather?" Shef deduced before continuing, "Hate to rain on your parade, but you may end up stickin' around for a bit." They both made their way back to his console, an array of interconnected touch screen interfaces, where Archibald was waiting for them. Shef returned to his comfortable looking chair and directly plugged his mechanical arm into the main CPU of the console.

"Whoa, what's that?" Everett asked gesturing to the newly formed connection.

"Oh, this?" Shef asked nodding towards the thick wire connecting his arm to the console, "Makes multitasking a little bit easier."

With graceful keystrokes and coordinated swipes of his mechanical hand, Shef brought up a detailed image of the vial that Archibald mentioned earlier. It was accompanied by bullet points of information presumably from Shef's initial analysis. A series of photos of the body that Archibald described to Myth was also onscreen, with a close up of his eyes displaying the odd blueshot condition.

"That dude looks way creepier in person than how you described Arch, damn. What's goin' on?" Myth asked.

"That's what we're here to find out," Archibald interjected, "We should be getting some information soon from my guys examining the body. Hopefully help us find out what's the deal with this blue shit."

"Word," Myth uttered introspectively, "So what's up Shef, what d' you think about this?"

"Well, it might take a while before I come to a final conclusion, but I've run some initial diagnostics trying to get a fix on the composition of this stuff. Even though there are some additives derived from natural elements mixed in, it's predominately synthetic."

"What type of stuff is it mixed with?" Archibald asked.

"Like cocaine for one."

"See?" Myth said towards Archibald "Mountain Berry."

Shef continued, "It seems like the cocaine was still in powder form when it was added to whatever the other components are. I recognized stuff like testosterone, adrenaline, different vitamins. Initially at least, aside from the coke in it, the stuff seems like some type of health supplement. Even with that, all the known ingredients only make up roughly 30-35% of the total. "

"So, like a mutant baseball player type health supplement?" Myth wondered aloud.

"Lemme tell you, these guys were doin' a lot more than breakin' homerun records. One of my officers has three cracked ribs and a fractured eye socket to attest to that," Archibald stated matter of factly.

"Make sure they put an asterisk on the police report to note the performance enhancing." Myth added.

"I'll need some more time," Shef whispered as his eyes were glazed over with the images on his many screens, "I gotta do a more detailed analysis of the composition, I have some different chemical tests I can run. Probably have to reverse engineer what the synthetic portion is and *that* will be a bitch, my friends."

"How long?" Archibald asked as he rose to his feet scooping a manila folder off of a nearby table.

"Dunno," Shef exhaled, "Tell Dunbar to speed things up down there and I can get with the gettin' up here. The faster he kicks out that toxicology report, the faster I can use that info to further my research."

"Call me when something cool happens, nerd," Myth said over his shoulder as he strolled out of the lab chucking a deuce. The sliding doors closed behind him.

Archibald let out a grunt of frustration.

"He's not taking this seriously."

"Well, Arch, that's because you have yet to show him anything significant. You can't use your relationship with Everett to try to invoke zealot intervention in mundane cases. He won't bite, and he shouldn't. He's part of the tribunal now for Christ sakes. I'm sure they have bigger fish to fry. Light the fire under Dunbar's ass. Get me his report. I have an inkling that there's more to this but I need proof. The faster the better if you don't want him to blow this off."

"You sound like you're the one in charge," Archibald snorted as he made his way towards the exit.

"The smart ones usually are," Shef said.

CHAPTER FIVE

March 10th 2004, 5:56 PM

Shef stared at the computer like he had been for countless hours. He just had a feeling there was more information he could extract out of it, with "it" being the nearly indecipherable amount of information displayed across his numerous screens and monitors. The toxicology report that Arch supplied contained some interesting variables in it. For example, the blue sand mixture also contained titanium metal shavings.

Who...Why the hell would anyone do that?

The images parsed and separated with a few keystrokes from Shef. He was directly plugged into his super computer, so the information being manipulated on-screen was largely because of thought and gesture as opposed to anything tactile. The movements were reminiscent of a symphony conductor, sound and melodies replaced with digital images and text. He stared at the screens, going over the detailed chemical breakdowns from the report. The substance, when ingested, rapidly spread throughout the subject's body. An autopsy revealed that his eyes weren't the only part of the body that had been stained with a strange blueish color.

The man's brainstem also displayed the color, as well as some of his major muscle groups and organs, including his heart and lungs. With a quick thought, Shef brought up a detailed, three dimensional replica of the man's body. He hadn't spoken to anyone since yesterday morning, though when he was tethered in, the hours felt like days, sometimes weeks. Shef tended to lose himself in situations like these. The idea of a problem going unsolved was something that never sat well with him, even back to his days programming robots back at M-CIT. He would toil over code for days until the logic made sense, sleep and food being necessary sacrifices to attain that goal. Those old tendencies remained, for better or worse. He imagined the glass vial on one of the adjacent screens rotating to get a better view of it from various angles, and so it did. Shef observed the underside of the vial before pushing out another thought command to zoom in closer to the bottom.

"Topographical analysis initiate."

The computer obliged the vocal command and scanned the object's surface. The results showed that Shef's intuition was correct. On the bottom of the vial, there was an elevated design of what appeared to be half of a rising sun with a katana blade as the horizon line.

"Hmm. A logo? They're branding it, are they? Well, this makes things a bit more interesting."

The discovery ensured that Shef wouldn't be sleeping or eating anytime soon. Not until he had a solid something, anything. He was determined to have a concrete lead by the morning and already resigned himself to work as long as it took to achieve that.

"Suicide by inquisition," Shef sighed aloud to a room full of inanimate objects.

CHAPTER SIX

March 14th 2004, 1:03 AM

Can you hear me?

Everett sat meditating in his usual position at his home. The sky was dark. Not just dark like a thunderstorm, but intensely dark. Otherworldly dark. In the sky was a solar eclipse. Hypnotizing blue flames leapt from the outer ridge, ripping at the darkness. The more he stared at it, the more he felt nauseous.

Can you hear me?

He blinked hard, squeezing his eyes together to try to shake the feeling. The air seemed heavier than normal. It was difficult to draw breath. Oddly, he could also see his breath, though it wasn't cold at all. Everett looked around. Everything was still. Literally still. No leaves rustled in the trees, clouds were seemingly paused in the night sky. The only motion was the growing flicker of the bluish light from the solar eclipse hanging in the sky. The voice was penetrating his mind, ever growing like the glow up above.

If you can hear me...

Everett was suddenly filled with uneasiness, the deep baritone voice echoed in his mind. The words sounded like they were being forced through grimacing teeth. Paranoia began to grip him. He could feel his heart racing as his intuition warned him of impending danger. He quickly whipped his head around to see a man with a sharp blade held to his daughter's throat. She was sobbing and he could see the moist tracks streaking down her face to her chin where tears had since flowed to a stop. He wanted to run to her, but despite what his mind was telling his body to do, he just walked.

"I AM COMING FOR YOU," The man said coldly, his voice echoed all around Everett like it was coming from every direction, suffocating him.

With a flick of the wrist, the man opened Chance's throat with his blade.

Everett jolted himself out of sleep with a gasp. He sat upright, breathing heavily. He swung his feet over the side of his bed and cupped his head with his hands, drenched with sweat. Simone was sleeping soundly next to him. He rubbed his face with both hands trying to shake the voice in his dream that seemed to follow him even after he awoke. The words, the chilling image of his daughter's blood being spilled by some guy he'd never seen before, all of it was frighteningly strange. Everett had weird dreams before, but nothing like this. The fear that he felt while dreaming was paralyzing, he hadn't felt fear like that maybe ever. Dreams have a way of eliciting real terror, even if the situation is utterly unbelievable. This was different, though. It was hard for Everett to rationalize, but it was like being caught between a dream and reality; the plasticity of a world created entirely within his own mind juxtaposed against the very real emotions and anxiety that he felt. The nausea that he experienced in the dream followed him back into his bedroom. Even now, wide awake, Everett could feel the words reverberating in the back of his mind.

I AM COMING FOR YOU.

The feeling that something terrible had just happened to his daughter would not relent from his conscious thought. No dream has ever affected real life, but Everett was thoroughly convinced that this was not just a dream. He jumped out of bed, with each step, a growing amount of fear. He rounded the corner into the hallway to a shocking sight. His daughter Chance, sleepily walking towards him.

"Chance, what, why are you up?"

Chance drowsily rubbed her face with one hand, "I was scared."

Everett slowly crouched down next to her, "Did you have a bad dream?"

Chance looked into Everett's eyes, "No. You did."

"How do you know that?"

"I dunno," Chance whispered as she shrugged, "I just felt like something was wrong."

Everett picked her up and they both made their way back into Chance's room. He gently placed her back in the bed and tucked her in.

"And what did you plan to do, hmm?" Everett asked as he kissed her forehead.

"Save you of course," Chance responded nonchalantly.

They both smiled at each other.

"Thanks, baby. Go back to bed."

Everett rose to his feet and walked out of the door. All the while wondering how Chance knew about his nightmare. He returned to his room to find another surprising sight. This time, it was Simone sitting upright in the bed.

"This God damn communicator has been going crazy, ugh," She groaned as she tossed it to him and ferociously turned over in the bed.

"Damn, sorry, I'll try to," Everett stopped mid-sentence as he noticed the light on his comm. It was a rapidly pulsating amber glow. Someone sent him a text, an urgent one. He picked up his comm with his index and thumb and pressed a button that projected an image onto his open palm.

"Display recent text." Everett said with a low voice as to not disturb his already perturbed wife.

The words popped into view seconds later.

I know it's late but come to the lab. -Shef

With a sigh, Everett quickly prepared himself to go to Shef's lab. Besides, returning to sleep and the possibility of continuing the dream that shook him out of his slumber in the first place was far less favorable an option. He kissed his wife, followed by his daughter, ensuring that they were both sleeping comfortably.

Then he left.

<u>CHAPTER SEVEN</u>

March 14th 2004, 1:03 AM

Adam was half asleep when his communicator started to buzz violently. He slowly opened his eyes and remembered that he wasn't at his house. The charm he laid on the bartender worked like, well, a charm. She was lying next to him naked, snoring in a way that Adam thought was cute rather than annoying. For the life of him he couldn't remember her name. She wouldn't be the first. He ignored the call and attempted to go back to sleep. No more than five minutes later, his comm started to buzz again. Adam let out a groan of aggravation before reaching down to the floor and retrieving his comm out of his pants pocket. With the flip of a small switch he altered the capabilities of his comm from phone to police scanner so he could hear any MCPD bulletins and placed it over his ear. They started to stream through no sooner than he changed modes.

"We got reports of three robberies with assault around the vicinity of 42nd Street in Queens within the last hour. Victims all describe a similar perp. He could still be in the area. Approach with caution as suspect is assumed to be dangerous. Any available units, report to the aforementioned area as quickly as possible."

Adam sat up in the bed that was not his and swung his feet around to the floor. He let out a disgusted sigh. His chasing after ass had landed him right in the general area of the robberies. If he had just gone home, it'd be someone else's problem. His comm was MCPD property, so if they needed to they could track his location and see where he was, best to just go before he heard any shit from his higher-ups.

"This is Officer Heller, I'm close by, I'll check it out."

Adam carefully clothed himself in the dark because he didn't know where any light switches were. He left his latest conquest mumbling incoherent nonsense from a dream. No cute kisses on the forehead, just disposing a used condom. That was Adam's idea of being a gentleman. Quietly, he slipped out of the door. Zealot-esque he thought to himself with a laugh. Less than thirty minutes later, Adam was patrolling the area in question.

"Where the hell are the lightposts? Just let base pop go to shit I guess," Adam said to himself as he parked his car on a block saturated with blight. He checked the stun rounds in his sidearm, made sure it was locked and loaded, and stepped out of his vehicle.

"This is Officer Heller," Adam announced via his comm, his voice transmitted to all units and back to headquarters, "I just arrived at 42nd I'm out on foot, gonna walk the blocks see if the perp is still hangin' around here somewhere."

"Copy that Officer Heller. Download the relevant info to your ADA, I'll message you a link. Don't spend too much time down there, base pop is on fire tonight. We may need you somewhere else more pertinent."

"Ten-four."

Adam strolled down the street. It was uncomfortably quiet like walking through a forest of abandoned buildings. He could swear he heard them whisper out to him. Adam had patrolled down here before, but this night felt more disconcerting than usual. Twisted shadow figures covered the ground as light radiated from the city up above shining through decrepit drywall and broken windows. Adam jerked his head around at the sound of a thud in the distance. Like a body hitting a floor. It echoed through the empty streets. He noticed a cat looking in the same direction.

Yeah, he heard it, too.

Adam pulled out the small ADA from his breast pocket. Once powered on, it allowed him to speak commands via his comm.

"Download newest case info, then show composite sketch of the assailant."

A detailed drawing of a skinny-faced white male in his mid-twenties faded into view. He was drawn with a hoodie and rectangular frame glasses that displayed damage from either being dropped too many times or being punched in the face too many times, likely a combination of both.

This fuckin' geek can't be the guy.

He turned his head up quickly at glass shattering, closer this time. Seemed like it came from maybe a floor above him judging by the way the sound carried. Adam lowered his body and began to creep now, staying in the abundant shadows, his side arm drawn and at the ready, eyes wide. He focused on isolating the noises: the slow drip of water, the soft hum of solar trains in the distance, the occasional meow of a stray cat, the sound of feet…running?

And getting closer.

Adam whipped around and checked his rear with his gun raised, the energy clip glowed slightly in the darkness of the alley. He wandered around out of the sight of his car, up and down alleyways until he wasn't sure which way he had come. The fact that most of the street signs had since been knocked down or eroded beyond being legible helped to confound him. Still, the footsteps got closer, faster. The sound of heavy breathing was added to the noises of the night. He could feel his heart rattling in his chest. Just as his nerves began to surge, everything became calmer. No longer could Adam hear any footsteps. He questioned if he ever had in the first place. Adam took a deep breath and holstered his weapon.

Pssshh…base pop drivin' me crazy.

He pulled out his ADA.

"GPS directions to my car."

A map faded into view with an illuminated green path of arrows that led back to where he parked. After a twenty minute walk twisting through alleys and dimly lit side streets, he emerged to a corner and saw his car parked a couple blocks up. Adam slid into the driver seat and quickly used his comm to contact MCPD headquarters.

"Ay HQ, this is Officer Heller."

"Go ahead Officer."

Adam continued as he stared out of his driver's side window off into the distance, "I'm down in the area of those robberies but there's nothing going on down here, not that I see. Maybe send a couple more patrols before—OH GOD!"

As Adam turned his head towards his passenger side window, a body came smashing into the door, hitting with such force the body folded through the window shooting shards of glass and bits of metal towards Adam's face, he held up his forearm to block the shrapnel. The mangled, twisted body was curled up next to him. Between all the blood and debris, he couldn't even tell if it was a male or a female.

Adam hopped out of his car and looked down the alley. He could see a lanky, shadowy figure in the distance. Two beady blue orbs floated in the distance where a person's eyes should be. Adam stared, stunned, but quickly snapped out of it and called HQ.

"HQ this is Officer Heller! I have a visual on the suspect, he's just...looks like he's killed someone, he threw them through my damn car!"

"Officer slow down! We-"

"Send back up, I'm going after him!"

"Officer Heller don't pursue, I repeat do NOT pursue."

By then it was too late. Adam was running in a full sprint towards the man with his gun raised.

"FREEEEZE! MCPD PUT YOUR HANDS UP NOW!"

The man just stood there. As Adam got closer and closer he could tell that it was the same one from the composite sketches and descriptions, without a doubt. He was within a couple of feet now. The man stood, blank faced, not even acknowledging Adam's presence or the fact that he had presumably just murdered someone in front of a police officer. The sketches didn't do the face justice, it was droopy and blemished. He stood a few inches taller than Adam but was nowhere near as physically imposing. Blue colored veins extended from his neck up to his face and lips like blue tapeworms squirming under his skin. Then there were his eyes, glowing azure like dying nightlights beneath the glasses that were in worse shape than the earlier pictures had suggested.

"Turn around and get on the ground. Now," Adam yelled to no avail. Talking to the brick walls would have elicited the same response. Adam raised his gun to within inches of the suspect's face.

"A stun round to the face is not the most comfortable way to go in. If you cooperate, we can avoid it."

No response.

Adam cocked his gun, "Turn AROUND, and get on the GROUND. This is the last time I will tell you."

No response.

"Alright, you wanna play dumb, let's go," Adam reached for the man's arm to force it behind his back, grabbing his bony wrist. In a flash the man wretched his hand away, grabbed Adam by the forearm, and slung him across the alley. Adam flew into a brick wall and immediately felt his ribs crack from the impact. He let out an uncontrollable yelp of pain and looked up from the ground to see the suspect walking towards him with a large dumpster. He used both hands to lift it with the ease that a father lifts a child. With the dumpster raised over his head, he pivoted back towards Adam. He threw it with all of his might and the flying mass of metal came hurdling at him. A front row seat to his own demise. Death by dumpster, not the most honorable way for a cop to go out. Rather cartoony, like a piano falling on him, he thought. Adam closed his eyes and braced for the impact that would surely crush him. He wondered what death would feel like. He felt a hard pull on his body as he heard the dumpster smash into the building that he had propped himself up against. The sound echoed through the mostly empty streets of base pop like a wrecking ball smashing into a concrete wall.

How…am I not dead?

Adam blinked his eyes opened and thanked any God in heaven that would hear him. His heart was beating out of his chest. A zealot stood in front of him.

"Don't move, you have broken ribs and your pelvis is fractured."

"How…how do you know that?" Adam asked, short of breath.

The zealot tapped a visor over his eyes.

"You…you guys get…all of the cool shit."

Adam could feel himself fading into unconsciousness. He struggled to stay awake because he wanted to see. He wanted to witness the difference. Each time he blinked, the darkness lasted for a bit longer. Whenever he snapped his eyes open, the landscape of the fight happening in front of him was different. The suspect, despite his freakish strength, was clearly not a trained fighter. He threw flimsy punches that Adam would have normally laughed at had he not known the power behind them. The zealot however, evaded every paltry blow with ease. He hadn't even taken out his katana as he began his counter offensive with strikes that Adam could barely count.

He nodded off and snapped awake again to see the suspect swing a wild punch that smashed into an adjacent brick wall. The zealot dodged, leaping into the air while snatching out his blade. He severed the man's hand at the wrist as he cleared his now shorter outstretched arm. The sword was back in the sheath before his feet hit the ground. Adam stared in disbelief as if it were out of a dream. Even with eyes wide open, he couldn't follow the action. He was drifting away.

No. Not yet…

He shot his eyelids open one more time to see the zealot land a fierce kick that sent the man tumbling past where Adam was slumped on the ground. The man landed, handless, and immobile. His blood looked more purple than red as it pooled around his wound. The voice of the zealot came through his mask.

"I called MCPD and told them to mark this area as a crime scene. I'll notify the Mecca. EMS is on the way for you."

"Th…thanks," Adam mustered through the pain.

And just as fast as he arrived to save Adam's ass, he was gone. Adam couldn't even tell which way he went. He lied back down on the concrete and his head fell to the side. He could hear sirens approaching now, gaining on his position. His eyes were barely open. The lights from squad cars began to illuminate down the alleyway. Then, Adam's eyes caught a glimmer from the ground within arm's reach. The light bounced off of a glass vial, half filled with blue sand. Adam eyed it and with his last bit of strength reached out and cupped it in his palm. He brought it towards his body and put it in his inner breast pocket.

As the EMS arrived, Adam faded off to sleep. The physical pain matched the psychological pain of coming face-to-face with his own inadequacy.

CHAPTER EIGHT

November 1995

Cyrus sat at a round table in a beautifully landscaped outdoor courtyard. It was early morning, but the compound was already quite lively.   Workers of all manners: doctors, scientists, nurses, geneticists, janitors, and chefs were meandering about either just arriving for their respective shifts or just leaving. All had the same exasperated look weighing on their faces. Cyrus sat calmly, sipping his morning cup of tea. He was never a big tea drinker, but it helped to relax him amidst all the commotion of the morning. Besides, Tozen said that Thailand was home to some of the finest teas in the world. Who was he to argue? He didn't know shit about tea or Thailand, and Tozen, despite his many oddities, had helped to make Cyrus's prolonged stay at his compound a comfortable one. Cyrus was given clearance to any restricted research area, though he spent most of his time with the test subject Neko. Who happened to be, as it were, the subject of this early morning meeting.

Cyrus sipped his tea once more, and watched as Tozen made his way slowly towards the table, eventually pulling out a chair and taking a seat.

"Mr. Santeaux," Tozen said as he poured himself a cup of tea from a kettle in the middle of the circular table.

"Good morning," Cyrus nodded.

"Shall we get to the heart of the matter? As much as I appreciate your company, I do have other meetings with various staff members throughout the day. The research never sleeps, as you well know."

"Yeah, that's quite obvious," Cyrus said as his eyes watched people in lab coats darting back and forth between buildings, "I've finally finished the reports on Neko, including the most recent set of data."

"Ah, Specimen 415. He is certainly one of our most prized accomplishments."

"That is an understatement, Tozen. I've never seen anything like him."

"Think to yourself, Mr. Santeaux, of the technological advances within the last fifty years that have become common place in society, especially in your American Corridors, and how they would have seemed like science fiction in a previous era."

"That fact is not lost on me Tozen, but it's still incredible, in any era, to be on the precipice of a science revolution. The applications for this gene splicing could be-"

Tozen interrupted, "World changing."

Cyrus looked up from his now empty cup of tea, "Yes. Take for instance the fact that Neko has shown a healing factor that is nearly ten times that of his regular human counterparts. That could re-define the future of medicine if we found out a way to apply it without the other consequences."

"Consequences?" Tozen asked, seemingly genuinely perplexed.

"Hell yeah, consequences. I'm sure you're familiar with them. You know, the fact that he was tearing into people with his bare hands before you introduced us? The splicing of the animal DNA with his own of course was going to make him more violent, more feral. It's hard to predict when, or if, that will ever subside."

Tozen laughed before tossing the rest of his tea back, "Where you see detrimental consequences, I see unharnessed potential. That is the reason why I wanted you to see him. I've monitored your work. I've seen what you've done, what you've achieved, and how you've pushed the boundary of human ability."

"Yes, the emphasis on *human* ability," Cyrus countered, "Neko is not entirely human, he's," Cyrus hesitated and gathered his thoughts, "he's...new."

"Exactly," Tozen said as he placed a hand on Cyrus's shoulder while rising to his feet, "Could you have imagined the caliber of men your zealot program would turn out?"

Cyrus was silent. The question caused him to be introspective for a moment.

"Let me train him," Cyrus finally uttered.

Tozen grinned slyly, "What took you so long? You should have asked when you had the initial inclination all those months ago. You'll begin next week. Select your staff and report to me the details."

Cyrus nodded in agreement and watched as Tozen walked away and gradually disappeared.

CHAPTER NINE

March 30th 2004, 7:42 PM

Myth plodded into Shef's lab, the rush of cold air from inside accompanied by the bright lights helped to knock the residual fatigue off his face. It had been weeks since the initial encounter with the weird blue drug, with little to no new info. Myth was trying his best to look interested as he arrived. It was bad enough he didn't want to be there, but at least he wouldn't walk in looking totally disengaged. All of that quickly disintegrated when an uncontrollable yawn was the first sound to greet Shef. Shef didn't even turn around, he was tethered to his mainframe with all types of documents and photos spread across his numerous screens. On one particular screen, photos were scrolling too fast for Myth to comprehend them. He wondered how *anyone* could.

"Wakey, wakey. I think I got something that will get your antennas up," Shef said as he typed furiously. His voice sounded slightly different somehow, gruff and raspy like he hadn't used it in a long time.

"Is it breakfast?" Myth replied propping himself on a table behind Shef.

"Um…no."

"So, you can't get this super computer to print out an omelet or something?"

"Not quite. And I don't have any Frankenberry Blast or whatever the hell you kids are eatin' these days."

"You sound so old. Like the type of old bastard that would keep my football if it fell in his yard."

"You damn right! Someone's gotta teach these youngins some respect. Listenin' to all that damn rap hop."

"Wow. Rap Hop?"

"No respect for their elders," Shef continued unprovoked, "Armed robberies have gone up, fuckin' hooligans just beat an old lady near to death. Could talk about it all night-."

"Don't," Myth interrupted.

Shef cleared his throat, "Well, let's get down to it then."

A couple of swipes of Shef's hand and the three dimensional model of a vile appeared on screen. Myth immediately recognized it as the one in question from the crime scene, the one that contained the mysterious blue substance that the perpetrator ingested shortly before going ballistic on Arch's squad.

"So, I was just doing some preliminary work analyzing the structure and whatnot, and I stumbled upon this."

The model rotated so that the bottom was in view. A digital overlay helped to make the design much clearer to the naked eye. Myth hopped down from the table and took a few steps towards the screen, squinting his eyes and tilting his head. Shef smirked. He knew that Myth's interest was officially piqued.

"This symbol. I've seen walls tagged with something similar on buildings in base pop," Myth said his eyes still fixated on the image.

"Yeah, well, after a bit of diggin', I found this weird rising sun over sword type thing, or at least facsimiles of the same thing, in various places."

Shef's swift hands brought up numerous pictures of the same symbol across the Metro Corridor. The advanced software analyzed each image for similarities, like a fingerprint, to verify that they were indeed the same.

"Yeah, I've passed some of these, for real. I just assumed someone else was trying to get up in as many places as possible. Typical graf shit. But for it to be related to this?" Myth asked.

"We haven't even looked behind door number two yet."

Shef went back to a dizzying array of typed and hand gestured commands. A gallery of photos appeared on screen.

"It's more than just the Metro. These pics are from the Midwest, Gulf, and Pacific Corridors respectively. Multiple places where the same emblem shows up."

"Goddamn. There has to be hundreds of pics. Son, how long did it take you to compile all this shit?" Myth asked perplexed.

"You know I'm a bit of a night owl. Did it over the last couple of days."

"Couple of days?! You would have had to look at all types of surveillance cameras, satellite pics. How did you sleep at all?"

Shef nodded towards his mechanical arm that was tethered to his computer rig, "I told you, this arm does a lot more than it looks. Even if I do doze off, I can still get tons of shit done."

"Wait…what?"

"I can still work while I'm sleeping. It's like…lucid dreaming. Lucid working, I guess. It certainly helps with productivity, but it is a bit harder to concentrate on the tasks at hand when a flying t-rex can pass by the window at any moment."

Myth just stared at Shef in silence, trying to wrap his head around the concept.

"Are you on drugs?"

"Define drugs. I mean, I get high on my new ideas and inventions, bro!" Shef yelped enthusiastically.

"So, yes. Got it."

"The question you should be asking is how all this jibes together. Luckily for you, I've more where that came from so whenever you go back to sittin' on your throne…"

"C'mon son," Myth said, recognizing Shef's now sarcastic tone. Shef continued.

"Nah nah, when you go back to your throne to make sure everything is in order."

"Shef, you know it don't even go down like that. The Tribunal is put in the best possible position to help negate and coordinate-"

Shef interrupted, "It sounds like you're reading off of a fucking cue card."

Myth hung his head in a mix of agreement and shame. So many times that he wanted to go out and complete a mission that he himself had assigned, thinking it would probably get done a lot faster with less notice and certainly less collateral damage. Shef's comments only exacerbated the guilt Myth already felt. Though he was made a member of the tribunal because it was widely recognized that he would excel as such, he couldn't help but wonder if his skills were better suited for being on the streets, especially in light of these recent developments. Myth paused to determine what the options were, he was interrupted by the blaring of multiple alarms going off throughout the lab, along with many of Shef's monitors powering on. The sudden noise startled both men.

"What the hell is going on," Myth asked, "You need this many alarms to wake yo' ass up out of your sleep?"

Shef looked around the lab, "Only a few are alarms, like alarms, the others are alarms...like *alarms*."

"Because that made perfect sense." Myth said with a furrowed brow that demanded further explanation.

"Ok. Some of these are alarm clocks. When I'm sleep and tethered in, if I'm not careful, I could have a difficult time waking up. The others, though. They send me notifications about anything worth knowing about. Whether it's some big news story related to crime in the corridors or communications between zealots and MCPD with usable info, whatever. It helps when you boys in the tribunal need some surveillance video from God knows where."

Both men walked over to Shef's main console, where he plopped down in his chair and swiftly connected his arm to the CPU. Both men stared mouths agape at the images that began to populate the multiple screens. Breaking news stories from around the world.

"Oh my God. This...can't be real."

Myth's communicator began to buzz. He promptly answered. The familiar voice on the other side was Zetsuka.

"Get to the Mecca now."

"I'm on my way."

CHAPTER TEN

November 1996

Tozen casually walked down a dirt path lined with trees on either side. It gradually opened up to a clearing where a make-shift platform had been constructed no more than two months prior. His eyes widened with excitement at the sight of Cyrus and Neko, intensely sparring at the center of the ring. It was rare that such an emotion as excitement, or any emotion for that matter, was evident on Tozen's face, but the implications of what was taking place before him made his mind race thinking of the possibilities. The applications of his scientific research coupled with Cyrus's knowledge from creating the zealot training program. Tozen smiled to himself at the thought. His goals were coming to fruition in a manner that he couldn't have dreamed.

Some issues to iron out. Yet, near perfect.

"Again," Cyrus barked at his new protégé as he rested a Kendo stick on his shoulder.

Cyrus couldn't move around like he used to, but the Kendo stick balanced that out nicely. Over the last month or so he felt better physically that he had in a long time. He just attributed that to the vitamins he took along with the consistent exercise, a luxury he missed because of his always hectic travel schedule. It bugged Cyrus out that he could still remember the young men they were at the ARU like it was yesterday. Still remember being in the forest watching the lift come up for the first time with Jerry. Cyrus often poked fun at his own age in a self-deprecating manner. It helped him remember Jerry. If he were still alive, he would waste no time with the jokes. Cyrus briefly laughed at the thought. Meanwhile, Neko panted for breath as he gathered himself into fighting position. Tiger Style. A perfect technique to take advantage of Neko's unique skill set, Tozen thought. Neko pounced. He covered ground alarmingly fast, advancing on all fours. Cyrus waited until he was in striking distance before whipping the Kendo stick across Neko's face with a graceful side step. Cyrus's sense of anticipation had been honed to an amazing degree over the years. Neko flipped backwards and regrouped.

"Owwwww," he groaned.

"You're attacking, but not thinking. Physical power isn't enough to win against a skilled opponent. You don't know what they're capable of."

His memory flashed fondly to the initiation match between himself and his old friend Gerald. The words he spoke were from personal experience indeed.

"Again."

Neko gathered himself and returned to his stance. This time, more calm, more focused. He advanced with cautions steps. Then he exploded towards Cyrus. Cyrus struck with the Kendo stick, this time Neko gracefully dodged. Cyrus spun the stick in his hand, blocking each of Neko's strikes with precision. He delivered his own series of counter attacks. Neko eloquently evaded the strikes with a series of flips and rolls, floating between moving on his feet and scurrying about on all fours. Tozen stood off to the side, unbeknowest to both, gleaming with pride. Neko leapt skyward. With his jumping ability enhanced by the experimentation, he seemed to hang in the air. A perfectly executed triple jump kick snapped the Kendo stick into splinters. Cyrus immediately dropped the remaining portion and engaged Neko in hand-to-hand combat. The two exchanged blows with increasing speed. Cyrus delivered a fierce elbow smash to Neko's shoulder, followed by a roundhouse kick to his torso that sent Neko sliding backwards. He popped back upright and zoomed towards Cyrus on all fours.

He's adjusted. Fast at that.

Neko slashed at Cyrus legs and stomach, his low center of gravity made it difficult for Cyrus to counter attack. He quickly found himself on the defensive. Neko launched a devastating head butt into Cyrus chin, causing him to stumble backwards. Neko was already waiting to deliver a kick to Cyrus's back. His young pupil's mouth pealed back into a smirk, showing his fangs. Cyrus swiftly caught Neko's foot around his ankle, and twisted it with enough force to spin Neko to the ground.

"Glorious!" Tozen's voice boomed as Cyrus helped Neko to his feet. Cyrus turned in surprise to see Tozen walking closer.

"You've been watching the whole time?" Cyrus said, gasping for breath.

"No. I've seen enough to recognize the advancement is far beyond what I could have conceived."

Cyrus turned and smiled towards Neko, "That is putting it lightly, I'd say."

Neko grunted. He didn't like being bested, an admirable quality in a warrior. He reminded Cyrus of Everett in that way.

"I think it's safe to say that Specimen 415 is a resounding success."

"My name is Neko," Neko said with a sneer.

Tozen's eyes turned fiery as his brow furrowed. He stared at Neko for a moment. Cyrus could feel the situation becoming tense. Tozen broke into a small chuckle accompanied by a fraudulent smile.

"So it is...Neko. Cyrus, I believe that it is safe to say we can move forward with the proliferation of The Dawn. I have another subject who has volunteered for similar treatments."

"The Dawn?" Cyrus asked as he wiped the blood from the corner of his mouth.

"That is the serum's codename," Tozen noted.

"I see. I guess the more pressing question is: Who would be crazy enough to volunteer for this shit?"

"I will assume you are attempting to be humorous and not slight the advances that you've seen and been a part of," Tozen said matter of factly.

"I think he's allergic to laughing," Neko said lightly as he approached Cyrus from behind. Cyrus smiled in acknowledgement. Tozen remained stonefaced, lending credibility to Neko's theory.

"It so happens that he is here. I would like you to accompany me to a meeting."

"That's fine. Neko, go back to the main compound. Practice your katas. You did well today."

"Thanks, sensei," Neko replied with a gracious bow. He turned and darted back up the path like a feline, but not before giving Tozen the gasface behind his back. Cyrus held his laughter.

"Shall we? I believe it would be wise if we all sat down for a chat," Tozen said motioning back towards the path. With that, the two began the trek back up to the compound.

"So, you really think this…The Dawn is ready for use?"

"Certainly. Don't you? You've worked with Specimen 415 more than anyone here at this point," Tozen responded.

"I have," Cyrus muttered, ignoring the face Tozen called Neko out of his name yet again.

"And you don't see how far he has come?" Tozen inquired, slowing his pace to wait for an answer.

"No doubt. His agility is off the charts. Hell, we had to create a super advanced training regiment in conjunction with Dr. Aldridge's intravenous therapy to push our zealots to the point where we felt like they could function in the corridors. For Neko, it's second nature. His movement, his strength, the way he can adapt. It required little training and more…"

"Guidance," Tozen replied completing the sentence.

"Yeah, guidance. In the brief time I've worked with him, I'd put him at about a sixth or seventh year zealot right now. I mean, that in itself is just insane."

"I can hear the exuberance in your tone," Tozen noted, "I've noticed that the rapport between you two has grown significantly. He's gaining more of his humanity back, bit by bit. He was such a savage case when we first began."

"What would you expect, especially under these circumstances? This is a far cry from normal development for a child," Cyrus noted.

Tozen cut his eyes towards Cyrus, "The hint of self-rightousness in that statement is ironic, is it not? Considering what you have subjected hundreds of children to in the corridors. Including your own."

Cyrus didn't respond, but Tozen's assessment definitely rang painfully true. They arrived at the main compound to the familiar site of workers hustling about carrying on with their duties. Cyrus had become comfortable within the commotion. Tozen nodded in the direction of a man walking towards them. The crowd moved out of his way and stared as he made his way towards Tozen and Cyrus.

"That's him."

Cyrus noticed his uniform immediately and recognized his unmasked face shortly thereafter.

"I believe you two may know each other," Tozen pointed out.

"Yes, we do," Cyrus said as he reached out his hand, "Orion."

"Mr. Santeaux."

<u>CHAPTER ELEVEN</u>

March 30th 2004, 8:40 PM

Everett stared out the window as they drove through Five Pointz, an old factory building that had become a graffiti monument. Basepop's angst-filled creatives couldn't be confined to just one building, Five Pointz turned into sprawling city in its own right. Block after block of abandoned buildings, emptied by the more upwardly mobile folks, were transformed into giant murals tens of stories high. Even the solar rail tracks weren't safe.

One of Everett's favorite pieces was painted on either side of a stretch of the solar rail tracks. On one side, a huge portrait of Medusa's face was painted onto the side of a building, her eyes created using shards of glass to reflect light. On the other side, there were large buildings with Greek soldiers painted on them, their bodies made to look like the bricks, frozen in Medusa's stare. It was truly ill. At the right time you could catch a team out bombing a building; rappelling down the side, moving with the coordination of a stunt team, creating something beautiful where there was once decay.

He used to get around everywhere mostly on foot, especially while he was on duty. Either that or he would hitch a ride on the solar rails, attaching to a passing train with his grapple gun if he needed to cover a large distance. It felt more organic that way, moving about the city using only his body. Things were different now and, not unlike his house, being able to summon a chauffeur out of the ether was one of the perks of a Triad Sensei, the title bestowed upon members of a tribunal. The cars that acted as personal transports were custom made sleek, black SUVs with dark tint on all the windows and a larger than average sun roof (to easily get in and out of). A long, rectangular siren was right above the windshield. When activated, the sirens blared an elongated whine while flashing crimson light. The aerodynamic design made the four-door truck resemble a muscular concept sports car.

The unique look also introduced unique problems, however. If anyone wanted to harm a high ranking zealot, all you would have to do is find one of the transports and blow it to hell. Wisely enough, roughly fourty transports were always circulating the Metro Corridor, like the Tribunal's own personal taxi service. You'd have to take out every one you saw if you wanted any chance of getting who was inside (if anyone) and the consensus assumption was that criminals just didn't have the patience to do so.

The backseat had all the amenities of a mobile office. A high-powered computer station was embedded into the design. A monitor was suspended from the roof and could be flipped up if it was not in use. As Myth found out early on into his tribunal tenure, these monitors were always in use. If you were one of the three, you always had something to look at, some document to review, some debriefing to hear, a new mission to assign, lives to save, and a corridor to keep safe.

In comparison, life as a Premier Zealot wasn't nearly as stressful. Ascending to the tribunal was the desire of most zealots, if not all, but how many could handle the pressure that was associated with it? Heavy is the head that wears one-third of the crown. Everett didn't know who he felt worse for: the next bright-eyed zealot that would be in for a rude awakening once anointed as part of a tribunal, or the guys who had to drive around empty cars as decoys. Myth exited the vehicle in full uniform, adjusting his sword.

The main mode of transportation was still riding the rails, though there were more and more hybrids on the streets every day. A few zipped down the street behind him with a low hum. Even the fully electric cars were gaining popularity. If you really wanted to flaunt your paper, you could get one with a hydrogen drive. Thanks to Shef, the SUV was just another example of the cutting edge technology that zealots had at their disposal. It'd be years before the general populace saw anything resembling it. It always amazed Myth to think about the scope of Shef's research.

When he started officially working with the Mecca, word traveled that his databases were vast digital storehouses, terabytes of information involving advanced computation and robotics, quantum mechanics and cybernetics, advanced data structures and programming, networking and biotechnology, particle physics and nanotechnology. He had schematics for devices that couldn't theoretically be created because the supporting technology did not exist yet. More often than not, the blueprints for the supporting technology were not far away. It wasn't in Shef to sit on his ass waiting for someone else to invent it.

Everett arrived at the Mecca after watching numerous screens display global calamity on the breaking news updates in Shef's lab. He was still trying to wrap his head around it all. It seemed like a joke, so over-the-top like a pivotal scene in an action movie. The one where the main character slowly turns his head as the camera pans to show the shock on his face.

"Oh. My. God."

Cut to an alien attack or a zombie attack or an alien zombie attack. But this was real life. It had been confirmed by all of the corridors already, not to mention international intel corroborated what the reports were saying. The other two members of the Tribunal were awaiting his arrival. Myth was familiar enough with the protocols to know that any official tribunal business would not commence until all were present. Still, he didn't want to keep them waiting and he was just as eager to obtain more information, any information, about what was going on as they were. Myth reached up to his communicator.

"Everett Santeaux, call sign: Myth, Metropolitan Corridor Tribunal. Operator, open the access to the private lifts."

"Yes sir."

Myth approached what appeared to be a wall as his body was scanned dozens of times by security cameras and cross referenced with the biometric data being sent from the tech embedded in his suit. A set of hidden doors parted and granted him swift entry. The doors assuredly only opened for those with the appropriate permissions, you wouldn't want to approach otherwise. The idea of zealots approved to use deadly force on unauthorized personnel was disquieting for most. Through the doors he glided as they closed off the world behind him. Down a well-lit, industrial hallway lined with the familiar black orbs that were part of the security system. Each one automatically rotating as he strolled down the hall to where the lift was open and waiting.

He stepped on and pressed the button to go to the floor designated for the meeting hall. He always felt anxious when making the ascent to his seat next to Vega and Zetsuka. Many times he had come to the same place as a premier, kneeling in front of the three as they glared down upon him. He could remember the condescending tone of Orion that he hated so much. In an instant, he could see Orion's mutated countenance snarling in front of him.

After all this time...I can still remember that bastard's face like yesterday. Gross ass.

The slow murmur of the elevator being pulled upward was the only sound. Oddly calming given the mental stress caused by the unknown threats at hand, coupled with the added pressures of being a high ranking official that the entirety of the Metro Corridor zealot force looked up to. He was the youngest zealot ever to ascend to a tribunal seat after all, and his peers were inspired by that fact. It made him reminisce about being the child prodigy at Mount Z, so focused on the tasks he was near oblivious to the adulation. Going even further into the recesses of his mind, he could see himself training in the backyard with his father.

Dad…where are you right now?

The elevator pulled to a stop and the doors slowly parted. Myth stepped off and proceeded down a dimly lit passage and under a steel archway into the Tribunal Hall, a large circular room with metal plates lining the floor and high ceilings. A ring of tiny ice-blue lights formed two circles, one where the walls met the floor and one where the walls touched the ceiling. A walkway to the middle of the room was lined with the same types of lights. Emerging from under the archway placed Myth directly behind the pillars that acted as the seats for the members of the Metropolitan Corridor Tribunal. On the opposite side was the general entrance that lower ranking personnel used. The three pillars formed a small arc opposite the common entrance. Myth noticed Zetsuka and Vega both flipping furiously through touch screen images on their respective interactive tables in front of them. He walked over to his seat at the far right pillar.

The pillar itself was a crescent moon shape, with the crescent being a touch sceen interface, slightly angled towards whoever was seated. He stepped into the pillar and took a seat in front of the table. Early into his tenure, he jokingly asked what button opened up the snake pit to no laughter. Like you had to sacrifice your humor once you ascended. Slowly, the pillar's mechanical components began to whir and hum. Steadily, Myth was raised into the air until his chair was ten feet off the ground. The seat locked itself into place and the touchscreen interface in front of him illuminated to life, prompting him for a retina scan. After the verification process was complete, his tabletop was instantly populated with the same images that Zetsuka and Vega were thumbing through Myth took a deep breath as one last endearing thought of his family at home evaporated in his mind. He swiped through numerous photos from around the world and began to recognize landmarks.

He saw angry looking mobs by the Berlin Wall, protesters outside of the Kremlin, huge crowds in downtown Tokyo, along with some other places he couldn't immediately identify. No matter where in the world the pictures were from, they all displayed a similar image. Intense rioting had broken out in the streets. Scenes showed the UK Parliament in near chaos. Italian diplomats were ready to declare all-out war. It was worldwide panic overnight. Zetsuka's voice was the first to cut through the silence. It came spilling out of the embedded speakers in the pillar's tabletop.

"I hereby declare this session of the Metropolitan Corridor Tribunal underway. And none too soon, I'm afraid," Zetsuka lamented.

"What's the situation here?" Myth asked as he thumbed through more photos, noticing that the picture count was still increasing from the stream being downloaded.

"To cut to the chase," Vega chimed in, "One of the most daring, coordinated terrorist related kidnappings ever pulled off in the history of the United Corridors…or the world for that matter."

Myth glanced across to Vega's seat on the far left pillar, his fingers were folded with the tips of his pointer fingers and thumbs touching. Vega's face was also shown on Myth's monitor, right under Zetsuka's. In the close-up, Myth noticed his eyes darting back and forth between photos and intelligence documents, what little they had amassed at this point. They also displayed a rare emotion.

He's worried.

No…No, that's fear.

Zetsuka cleared his throat then sat up in his seat at the middle pillar. He glanced at Vega, then turned to Myth, "At approximately 8:00 a.m. Eastern Standard Time, every leader from a country in the Group of Eight was kidnapped."

"The G-8," Myth said, "Kinda brazen to engage the world's most economically powerful countries."

"Exactly." replied Vega, snapping out of his trance.

That explains the locations in the pics. Japan, Russia, Italy, Germany, Canada, France, UK, and…the U.S.

"If that's the case then, the President? He must have been…"

Zetsuka interjected before Myth could finish his theory, "The President is safe. He was moved to a secure location less than half an hour after the news broke, accompanied by the Prime and a few of his personal guard."

"The Prime is with him? That's…reassuring," Myth said sarcastically, "When's the last time the Prime even seen a decent sparring match let alone something as intense as this bullshit?"

"You are well aware that Zealot Prime acts as the political representation of all Zealots, Premiers, and Master Sensei," Zetsuka said with the slightest hint of annoyance, "But he is obviously not without skill and I mentioned his personal guard is with them. The President is in capable hands."

"So he is," Myth said as he compiled all the digital media spread across the interactive table into a large folder with a few eloquent hand gestures. With a few more he parsed the media by type, country of origin, and chronology. Working with Shef so long had started to rub off on him. He was pretty swift at adapting to new tech and it showed with the deftness that he manipulated the interface in front of him. There was silence as he prodded through more photos and video clips, the stream had started to slow, but the number was still well in the thousands. He heard Zetsuka through the speakers after a few moments.

"As you can see, the stability of some of the world's foremost powers has been thrown into a state of turmoil. Some of the populations of these countries aren't even aware of the full extent of these crimes. Their respective governments won't be able to conceal the entire truth for long. The United Nations has called for emergency sessions, but other leaders are hesitant; worried that it could act as a beacon for the organization that committed these abductions. They fear it would call attention to them and some in attendance could be subsequently targeted."

"A worthy concern," Vega noted, "I am apprehensive about any meetings right now. Not until we know more. The G-8 countries, as well as many other countries affiliated with the U.N., have been pointing fingers, and the brunt of that accusation is reserved for the United Corridors. We pioneered the zealot program, more specifically, your father did, and, seeing as that these abductions were the work of highly skilled individuals to say the least, the assumption is that we must have something to do with it. The eye-witness accounts corroborate these concerns. I've read at least seven from different regions describing assailants moving too fast to fully comprehend. Any surveillance cameras that weren't hacked or dismantled in some way only produce blurred images."

"Add that to the fact the President is safe and sound and no wonder they're looking at us with the shady eyes. Shit ain't adding up," Myth said introspectively. Zetsuka remained still, eyes plastered to his screen. Vega nodded in acknowledgment before finishing his thought, "Since we still don't know what they want, or why they've chosen this type of assault to bring notoriety to their cause, it's difficult to quell the paranoia that many are feeling about this incident."

"The money question is: who would *they* be exactly?" Myth inquired.

"Clearly *they* have the wherewithal to execute a plan of this magnitude, across country lines. Such a massive coordinated effort. And the fact that it was simultaneous? They were planning this for a long time," Vega said, "and executed it flawlessly."

"What is their end-game?" Zetsuka added, "As we sit here, we have yet to hear any demands. For all we know at this point, every captive could be a cadaver."

"They have to be alive," Myth said plainly, "If an assassination was the mission, they would've killed their targets where they stood. Seems to me like this organization casts a wide net and they clearly have their shit together. They wouldn't waste the time or the resources to transport dead bodies. And besides, this bunch is worth a lot more alive than not. Killing them would be like burning the winning lottery ticket."

"I concur with Myth's assessment," Vega chimed in.

Zetsuka continued, "Yes, for that reason, this seems no more than a diversionary tactic, a cleverly orchestrated ruse. While we wade out of the chaotic waters, the entity responsible for this is waiting, watching us scramble to pick up the pieces," Zetsuka's voice trailed off as he sat back in his seat contemplating. Vega mumbled something in Spanish, but Myth wasn't paying enough attention to understand it. He continued to scroll through a litany of pictures, the hand motion was idiosyncratic at this point. After all this time sitting up high, the mighty tribunal was no closer to knowing who was behind the mass kidnapping than when they started. And then he saw it.

Spray painted on an unsuspecting wall near France's Élysée Palace. It was almost too far to make out. Myth zoomed in as close as possible and was able to gather a couple of different angles. It looked fresh, certainly fresh enough to fall within the time window.

Eight in the mornin' here…that's like, what two, three in the afternoon in France?   No regular dude would just bomb in the middle of the afternoon that close to the palace. It has to be a sign. No…a signal.

After running the initial pictures through image purification it was obvious. He cross referenced it with their now swollen database of pictures quickly after. It returned a handful of hits, under a hundred in total, sprinkled in different countries. But still, there was no mistaking it. A rising sun over a katana. The same emblem he saw in Shef's lab.

CHAPTER TWELVE

December 1995

Orion, Cyrus, and Tozen all sat at a glass table in elegantly crafted wicker chairs. The setting was another outdoor section of the sprawling compound. There was a man-made stream that squirmed through the yard, with small wooden bridges to cross. A large tiger roamed freely as if it were normal. It was impossible not to notice that first. Cyrus caught himself on a few occasions just staring at it off in the distance, watching it pace slowly in the shade of trees that lined the far side of the courtyard. It was almost hypnotic to watch his huge body lumber under the trees, slashes of sunlight blasted through the canopy and flittered against him, making his stripes appear to shimmer like they were aflame. He looked majestic, and at the same time, that did nothing to quell the anxiety that Cyrus felt when their eyes happened to meet. He cleared his throat and turned towards Orion.

"What brings you this far away from your pillar?"

Orion snickered, "Ah yes, the duties of a Triad Sensei. I have left those tasks in the capable hands of my colleagues. I've filed this excursion under…research and development."

"Orion is interested in what we've been working on here," Tozen said, almost giddy, "He's volunteered to go through clinical trials,"

"Did he," Cyrus asked clearly not shocked.

Orion's smile shrunk, but did not completely disappear. He sipped a glass of water and turned to Cyrus, "Mr. Santeaux, I respect you to the utmost. Heading up the development of the zealot training program is a work of genius. Truly."

"Well, thank you."

"Even after the slaughter of the Appalachian Incident, you still found it in yourself to contribute to the cause in whatever way you could."

Cyrus knew that Orion was bringing up the failed mission that resulted in the death of his best friend to provoke him. He wouldn't give him the pleasure. The veiled insult appeared to wash over him as if he'd heard it a thousand times before. Showing little emotion, Cyrus replied dryly, "You're called a zealot, but you never went through the training at Mount Z. I'd say perhaps other people should contribute *more*."

Orion leaned back in his chair.

"Perhaps."

Tozen seemed to sense the tension creeping into the conversation like a fog.

"Now, it is a time to be excited. This is a culmination of all of our hard work."

"You say *our* like we are working together," Cyrus reminded.

"Aren't we? We are all working towards a common goal. The program that you created has been largely successful in what it was intended to do, correct?"

"Yeah, that's right. Arms in the streets have been steadily decreasing across the corridors ever since zealots were deployed."

"The numbers don't tell the whole story," Orion spat, "You are only taking into account the amount of guns that are taken, you are not taking into account the violence that sprouts in its place. A deviant is the same with or without a gun at his disposal. Also, if you consider that ever since the first class of zealots the government has been chomping at the bit to use them for various international operations, it can be assumed that numbers will be decreasing in the corridors to accommodate this. There are various foreign interests that need to be preserved, after all. A reduced force at home could only lead to more problems."

Cyrus had heard rumblings about that, but nothing confirmed, at least not to him. Why would they keep him in the dark? Taking zealot operations worldwide was a risky maneuver. Each one was a walking biological weapon, capable of taking large numbers of enemy soldiers down with relative ease, guns or no. The amount of collateral damage that could happen in a place unfamiliar with zealots would be substantial.

Again, Cyrus was calm, cool. Too drastic a reaction would give away the fact that information was being passed around above his head. That would appear weak. He was careful how he proceeded. It didn't take Cyrus long to realize that both Orion and Tozen were hyper analytical, and any seemingly negligible word, look, or movement could be enough to betray his thoughts.

"I do agree, especially considering the expanding role in high-level military operations as well as the standard operations throughout the corridors. Maybe thinking about improvements to the program is what we need," Cyrus finally replied.

"That's what brought you here initially, isn't it?" Tozen asked.

Cyrus couldn't argue with that at all, "Yeah. Yes, that's true."

"Orion is just confirming what you already know. You've been a witness to incredible things, a front row seat to accelerated evolution," Tozen said regally, the statement dripping with self-congratulation.

"That is certainly one of the reasons I am willingly subjecting myself to these tests. I am honored to give my body in the name of advancement, not just for me, but for every mecca in the corridors. I want to be a template to build upon," Orion chimed in.

"How gracious of you," Cyrus said, almost too candidly. He felt the tone of the room shift ever so slightly, and Orion recoiled back into his seat like a cobra when a snake charmer takes a respite from playing his melody. He wondered if his subtle sarcasm had been just enough to draw the suspicions of their ever-scanning eyes. Cyrus swiftly followed up the statement as to not let the awkwardness saturate the discussion.

"Nah, Tozen's right. I have seen some rather interesting things he-"

"Like Neko?" Tozen interrupted, smiling.

"Yes…like Neko," Cyrus answered glancing at him nervously. *Did he notice that, too?*

Cyrus took the hint and continued to speak about Neko, "He is like nothing I've ever seen. His speed, agility, dexterity, stamina are all off the charts. The regeneration is…it's awesome to behold."

Orion's eyes lit up, two dark ovals in pale, clammy skin. He sat more attentively now.

No wonder he keeps his mask on most of the time, Sweet Jesus.

Cyrus continued, "It's like they've found a way to drop characteristics into someone's skill set with a tweak of the genetics. The resulting combination is the best of both worlds. Neko's are taken from a Bengal tiger, not too different from your buddy who," Cyrus stopped abruptly as he noticed that the tiger had slowly, discretely, made his way to within 15 feet of the table. He prowled around the perimeter as if there were an invisible wall stopping him, but there was nothing but the words of men dissolving in the air between them. Cyrus knew that. The tiger definitely knew that.

Eaaasy.

As he expected, Tozen seized on the moment immediately. He nodded back over his shoulder where the tiger was strutting, huge paws padding softly on freshly cut emerald lawn. Each one of his clawed feet left indentations in the grass that slowly sprung back in his wake. His body was massive, much bigger up close.

"Don't fear him," Tozen said endearingly, "His name is Aureus Rex."

"First and last name? Clearly, he's a tiger amongst tigers," Cyrus said. He followed that up with a chuckle until he realized the other two men weren't laughing along with him.

Tozen ignored the jibe and kept speaking, "It's Latin. At least, that's what I was told when I purchased him as a cub. It means

Golden King. Though you'll have to forgive me if my translation is off, it's been forever since I've *seen* Latin, much less spoke it."

The tiger's ears perked up when he heard his name. He slowly plodded over to Tozen. With each step, he grew larger and larger, so close now that you could hear his breathing. Tozen had to reach up from his seated position to pat the beast on his enormous head. Aureus stretched out on the ground next to the table. He was easily ten feet from his tail to the tip of his nose, probably more.

"He is the source of the genetic information used in Neko's treatments," Tozen said as he gently rubbed the tiger's head between his ears. The tiger tilted his head back and yawned. His tongue flapped out of his mouth past gold-plated teeth.

"He has gold teeth," Cyrus asked perplexed, "I know drug dealers with similar fashion sense."

Orion chuckled unexpectedly.

Tozen smiled that disingenuous smile of his, "The teeth are more for vanity, I'll grant you. But we cannot thank Aureus enough for what he has provided. The gifts he usually gets are gone within the hour."

Tozen and Orion both laughed hardily. It was an annoying duet that made it obvious they were reveling in an inside joke. Cyrus didn't smile. Aureus settled himself on the ground and continued his pursuit of a nap. Tozen retracted his hand and resumed talking.

"I've agreed to let Orion take some treatments with him back to the corridors. This is after we do some initial, on-site tests and whatnot. Treatment time may be up to ten months. It'd be wise to begin now, or run the risk of ill preparation when we need to act the most. " Orion nodded silently in agreement.

"Act on what?" Cyrus wouldn't quell his suspicions any longer. He had grown tired of being talked around because he wasn't privy to their previous discussions or whatever the fuck.

Orion picked up the conversation, "Mr. Santeaux, the situation on the home front has been in a state of flux, to put it mildly. I will say, the Metro Corridor continues to lead by example, with your son very much a part of that. Other places just aren't seeing the gains that the Metro has. Furthermore, violent crimes in some places have actually seen an increase, even *with* considerable arms reduction."

Cyrus quickly responded, "I've been in touch with the Prime and some other tribunals across the corridors, their reports haven't been enough to cause for any alarm. Nothing to get too hype over. And that still didn't answer my question."

"I assure you," Orion said, more forceful this time, "If we are not proactive in our approach, the situation can and will get worse. You think the problems just end there? The military back home is starting to wonder if your little science experiment is proving to be *too* effective."

"What are you talking about?" Cyrus inquired.

"The zealot program was created, and government funded I might add, to reduce arms within the *civilian* population. Eyes have taken notice. If a zealot infantry was to attack, no one in the Corridors, or anywhere, could stop them. Enough to make some very powerful people nervous, I'd say."

Cyrus sat silently pondering Orion's words.

"What Orion has taken so long to say is that the time for action is now. Starting with the Ark," Tozen said.

Cyrus' face scrunched up, giving way to brief laughter, "The Ark? The corridor gangster's fable? Even back in the ARU guys knew about it from someone or another. Barely anyone thought it was real."

Tozen laughed, "It's real. We've found it."

"Bullshit," Cyrus returned.

"No. Not at all. With Orion's help, we've been able to narrow its location down to within a few square miles. Once he returns to the Metro Corridor, he'll be able to do a thorough search."

Cyrus turned his head to Orion, "He says he has *your* help, but what about the rest of the tribunal?"

Orion leaned forward, "Do you think there are any tribunals that would scoff at the chance to say they've uncovered the Ark? They would be hailed as heroes!"

"I would hope the entirety of the Metropolitan Corridor Tribunal would want to find the Ark, if there actually is one, for a strategic reason that goes beyond patting each other on the back." Cyrus rebuffed, the venom in the statement was palpable.

Orion looked at him for a moment before providing his rationale, "It would kill the moral of the organized crime community who have held the Ark to the same esteem as the Holy Grail. Conversely, it would embolden the lower levels of law enforcement because they wouldn't have the specter of the Ark looming over them, the threat of a huge influx of guns rushing into the streets ever present. The Ark would be a trump card that we could use to force the government's hand to aid us in whatever we needed. Zealots are the first and best tool to be used in crime prevention and arms recollection."

"I don't need you to explain what their purpose is. I'm the one who created the program," Cyrus reminded Orion just as forcefully.

"All members of the tribunal work together to further the goals of the organization and the country."

"I'm getting pretty fucking sick of you not answering my questions," Cyurs shot back with fire.

Orion's eyes twitched and his brow furrowed. Cyrus took notice.

"You won't do shit," Cyrus warned, leaning forward. Saying the words made his chest warm like he'd just taken a shot of vodka. Orion leaned back into his seat, smirking.

Tozen put both hands in the air with his palms facing the ground and made a lowering motion. The same motion a teacher might make to a room full of unruly children.

"Come now gentleman, only a few more items to discuss and we'll all be on our respective ways." Tozen could only do his best to slightly reduce the tension in the air, though everyone was aware of it at this point. Even Aureus Rex had picked his head up and was casually surveying the ruckus that had ended his nap prematurely.

"So, let's wrap this up. I want to return to the research compound and work with Neko a bit more. What do you need from me?"

"Just a confirmation to move forward with Orion. He has a schedule to keep."

"We all do," Cyrus replied.

"True," Orion added. Cyrus took a deep breath, "You have my blessing to move forward, but you should be aware that, since the research is ongoing with these genetic treatments, the side effects aren't fully known yet."

"I am aware of the risks," Orion said cooly.

"Well," Cyrus said standing up, slowly as to not rouse Aureus too much, "I'll take my leave. Orion. Tozen. If you need me, you know how I can be reached."

Tozen nodded and Cyrus turned to walk towards the villa that had served as their meeting's backdrop. He disappeared into the house shortly thereafter.

"Are you totally certain he knows which side he's on?" Orion asked exasperated.

Tozen sipped some tea, "I think Mr. Santeaux is a man of virtue in a world in which it's hard to discern who possesses the same quality. He still has work to do yet."

"I think we should kill him. His attitude…seems like he could waver. Complicate things," Orion coldly noted.

Tozen took another long drink of tea until only a brown semi-circle in the bottom of the cup remained. He peered through a back window and saw Cyrus standing inside, engaging in small talk with one of the doctors. The talented, nervous woman. They both walked out of sight.

"Maybe. But we still need him."

"And his son?"

"Keep watching him. You have the perfect vantage point from your perch."

<u>CHAPTER THIRTEEN</u>

March 30th 2004, 8:40 PM

"We have to bring Crewshef in on this," Myth stated as he looked over the images, further confirming his theory, "Call Chief Archibald, too."

There was no mistaking it, the emblem was the same.

"Myth, what have you seen that warrants such action?" Zetsuka inquired.

"It looks like whoever is behind these abductions is already operating within our borders," Myth answered.

"How," Vega interjected, "It's safe to say that, if they already established a presence in our country, they would have taken the President before we had a chance to move him."

Before Myth could respond, there was a soft bell sound followed by digital text warning of an incoming video call. Shef's face pixelated into view on Myth's desk. Chief Archibald's was the next to appear.

"Shef, Archibald, you guys patched in?"

"Yeah, I'm here. Zetsuka, Vega."

"Ten-four Santeaux. Good evening to the tribunal."

Vega nodded to acknowledge the greetings. Zetsuka followed suit, then he began to speak.

"Mr. Bales. I understand you have some additional information that can help us?"

"Help you or scare you shitless, not sure which," Shef said lacking the tact usually associated with tribunal meetings, "I'm sending some stuff over now."

A progress bar appeared on Myth's screen, shortly thereafter, a cascade of documents, graphs, and pictures populated his virtual desk.

"If you would Mr. Bales, could you expound on what we are looking at right now?" Vega asked as he began analyzing the information.

"Sure. Long story short, the documents detail the composition of the blue substance-"

Zetsuka interrupted, "What is this substance you speak of?"

Arch, sensing the confusion, picked up from there, "Not too long ago an armored truck was hijacked in base pop. The assailants were all under the influence of some type of narcotic that made them all stronger. And a lot more crazy. I've never seen anything like it."

"Myth, what is the connection here?" Zetsuka prodded.

"If you both would consider this image file that Shef, pardon me Mr. Bales, sent over," Myth dragged and dropped the file into the boxes containing Zetsuka and Vega's video image. Moments later a three-dimensional rendering of the vial appeared floating above their desks.

"If we rotate the vial that was found at the crime scene by Archibald's team, we can see the shape of an emblem or logo on the bottom. I've cross referenced it with the images that we have from every country where a leader was abducted. I got hits, over a hundred of them."

"That is clearly not a coincidence." Zetsuka said solemnly, to himself more than to anyone else.

Vega mumbled something under his breath. It sounded like, "Mi padre en el cielo."

"No, you're right 'bout that Zetsuka," Shef added, "Moreover, this emblem also pops up in the Midwest, Gulf, and Pacific Corridors. Whoever did this is in, and they are in deep. If you want to find out who's behind the abductions, find out who's behind the drugs."

"Seems like a reasonable assessment. Myth, what do you say to this?"

Myth sat back for a moment while everyone eagerly awaited his response.

"I'm with it."

"Vega, what say you?"

"I agree. The benefit would be two fold. I believe it would point us towards the ones who are orchestrating these offenses, and also we could prevent the spread of this...garbage. As of right now, the Metropolitan, Gulf, Midwest, and Pacific Corridors are the only ones that have confirmed instances of this emblem. We can still stop it before it spreads to the others."

"That is a valid point," Zetsuka agreed, "Then the matter is settled. We will organize a cell. Send it to follow this trail. It will require going to the aforementioned corridors, so we should contact the respective tribunals to notify them of our operations. Keep in mind, time is not on our side. The G-8 countries are still in an uproar. The President is safe with the Prime, but if these terrorists have infiltrated our borders already, they could be pursuing him even now. Every day that passes, it will become harder and harder to keep him out of harm's way."

"This is true. We should grant this mission the highest level security clearance. We also should choose the team wisely."

"And *fastly*," Shef interrupted with contempt, "I'm still going to keep looking into this blue stuff. I want to conduct some more thorough tests on how it affects the body and performance. See what all the fuss is about. As always, mi casa es your casa. Any support tech the tribunal needs, it is at your disposal."

"Noted Mr. Bales." Zestuka nodded.

"Archibald, you still there," Shef hollered.

"Yeah, Shef. I'm here"

"The kid that did the toxicology report. It's a nice piece of work. Send him up to the lab. I think he can help. Two hands are better than one, especially considering we're behind the 8-ball a bit here."

"Ten-four on that."

"Now to the matter of the team," Zetsuka pondered aloud.

"If I may interject, here," Shef said boastfully.

"Ah shit, cmon Shef." Myth said under his breath before he had a chance to reconsider saying it. The fact that he said it under his breath was irrelevant, as his voice was being broadcast to everyone anyway.

"The answer should be pretty clear that Myth should head this mission." Shef continued without prompt, "We absolutely need to get answers fast."

That fact was very true. There was an awkward silence as everyone cautiously eyed each other.

Shef continued, "There's no one better to lead this. Everyone in here knows the shit."

"Mr. Bales, I command you to show some respe--" Zetsuka said as he leaned forward in his seat.

"Command?! First off!" Shef yelled.

"Oh boy," Myth mumbled again. Everyone heard it again.

"First off, I'm the reason all you zealots have any of these toys! The Metro Corridor is on the cutting edge and that's because of me. M. E. If I pull the plug on my tech, your lil' force goes back to the Stone Age. Good luck tracking, scanning, running any kind of-"

"Crewshef Bales!" Myth snapped so suddenly that everyone straightened up in their seats, "This is officially sanctioned tribunal work here, fam. You're gettin' all hyped up and you start getting' loud and spit starts flyin' outta your mouth. We need your experience not fucking Macho Man Randy Savage."

Everyone seemed to calm down once Shef slunk back into his seat in silence, folding his arms. The robotic one sporadically reflected light back into the web cam.

Vega cleared his throat, "Everyone needs to quell their anxiety. Our reason need not be clouded by such things," Shef shook his head dismissively, which everyone saw on their respective video feeds. He didn't say a word as Vega continued, "There is no doubt that Mr. Bales is an indispensable part of zealot operataions."

"Tuh!" Shef spat. Everyone ignored his tone.

"And Myth. My reservations about making you lead on this are not an indictment on your talents."

"I   don't   take   them   as   such."
"Still, I believe your place is here. You can oversee numerous operations and coordinate strategy on a large scale. I have a feeling that the situation will get a lot worse before it gets better, and the Metropolitan Corridor Tribunal will be at full strength to meet these challenges."

"Bravo. How inspirational," Shef said sarcastically accompanied by a condescending slow applause.

"I agree with Vega," Zetsuka said, "Your seat is here. We can't risk losing a third of the tribunal. Not now. I will propose that you take the lead on the selection of the team. I have faith that you will choose suitable personnel."

Myth looked at all of the images across his table top. Shef, Arch, Vega, Zetsuka, all staring at him waiting with baited breath, along with photos from across the world and documents from Shef's report crowding them. The thoughts in his head reflected what he saw before him: clutter. With a gesture of his hand, he wiped the table clean, save for the faces of his meeting party. He sat quietly for longer than he thought.

"Triad Myth? What say you to this?" Zetsuka inquired, with the slight sting of impatience.

"I agree. I would be best suited here," Vega and Zetsuka seemed to physically exhale.

"But we have to get answers as soon as possible. I already have connections in places across the corridors. I can select the personnel. But I will act as their Premier."

"Damn right!" Shef yelped uncontrollably with a robotic fist pump.

Vega shook his head, "How? How do you even propose to do this?"

"I'll select a member from each of the corridors where we have a documented occurrence of that logo. That's Midwest, Gulf, and Pacific. If they're worth shit, they should be able to provide additional intel about the product being circulated within their own corridors. With that, we hustle to find who is running the import and distribution. The final boss. It's obvious the same people that are behind the G-8 abductions are behind this. It should lead us straight to them. The issue is that, once this is set in motion, there's no reversing course. We gotta go all in."

Zetsuka's voice was stern and steady, "I see. They've already caught us off guard once and look at the worldwide damage they caused. This is our counterstrike. You will have to assemble a cell and be prepared to rendezvous with the Prime."

"Zetsuka, don't tell me that you are actually *considering* this," Vega asked, "If need be we can put it to a vote. The two-thirds majority would keep Myth in the Metro Corridor for the duration of this operation."

"This is true," Zetsuka replied, "But you are also aware that the only way to supersede the two-thirds vote is for an individual to step down of their own accord."

Vega let out an exasperated sigh.

"I will step down from my position as one-third of the Metropolitan Corridor Tribunal to head this mission," Myth said confidently.

"You are aware that by going back into the field, you relinquish your voting and decision making power, and that power will remain with the remaining two?"

"Yes."

Vega continued, "You are aware that the title of Master Sensei is bestowed for life and that the only way one is relieved is by following the replacement process and choosing a successor or," Vega paused, "Perishing in the line of duty or otherwise?"

Myth was silent for a moment. He looked at the digital image of Vega as if he were actually staring the man in the face, "I am."

"Then I suggest you move out," Vega commanded.

Zetsuka picked up where Vega left off, "I agree. You should head out immediately. This situation is fluid, and could change at any moment. Best you leave within 48 hour's time. Sooner if you can help it."

Myth was already lowering his seat back down to ground level.

"I'll contact the police departments in the corridors you mentioned," Arch said as he rubbed his brow with his fingers, "We got some long God damn nights ahead."

"Thank you Chief Archibald," Zetsuka said, as he watched Myth get up silently and proceed out of the room.

"I hearby call this meeting adjourned. Everything discussed has been logged," Vega said. There were nods in agreement from both Shef and Arch. Their digital faces faded away shortly thereafter. Myth was walking down the hall from whence he came, silently plotting his next move. He got into the private elevator and turned around, watching the door slowly close in front of his face. His hand went up to his communicator immediately.

"Call Shef."

Connecting…Connecting…Connection established.

"Whoo! That's what I'm talkin' about!" Shef's voiced screeched.

"You sure shoved me in the shit, Shef."

"Hold on, my computer's alliteration scanners are going off the charts!"

"No jokin'! That was some bullshit that you pulled back there! I brought you in to help us."

"I am helpin'!"

"By making yourself look like an ass in front of the tribunal?"

"Fuck the tribunal. I'd say no offense, but technically *you're* not part of the tribunal anymore," Shef responded casually.

"I'm a Master Sensei as long as I'm alive. And I intend to sit my ass right back up on the high chair as soon as this is done. And when I do, and I have to bring you in on something, don't fucking embarrass yourself, me, or the Hall of the Tribunal like that again."

"I *said* I was trying to help! Look, shit is getting bad, that part is clear as day. This is probably even a lot worse than we know. There's probably no probably about it."

"Um…What?"

"Look, what I'm sayin' is if we have any chance. Any chance. It's going to be because you did something," Shef stated sincerely.

"I'm sorry for snappin' but, you gotta be a bit more mindful of how you conduct yourself in there. For me, please."

"Will do," Shef, sensing something was wrong, prodded further, "What's your deal?"

Myth took a deep breath and exhaled slowly.

"So, you can just up and take the leaders of seven countries, at the same time, with little resistance, and the President is just fine? You don't even attempt to grab him?"

"Yeah…I knew you'd say something about that. But you have to think, we're the only ones who have zealots. Hell, I'd take the odds that *you* coulda pulled this job. Maybe wouldn't been able to do it all at the same damn time, but still."

Myth silently agreed.

"A couple of zealots could keep the President safe, easy. And he's with the Prime and his guard so you know they're pulling out all the stops."

"Whatever force they have at their disposal, they're at least on par with zealots. There's no way they could've done this otherwise, Shef," Myth reasoned.

"I have some theories about that. We can discuss those later. So, I think there's someone else you should probably see before we-"

"Fuck no."

"C'mon Everett! At least talk to him. If anyone knows about some new drug being sold around here, it's him. Shit, he's probably selling it!"

"You are going way too hard right now, Shef."

"It makes sense. He's familiar with the underworld in a way that you aren't. He's probably got some good info. Good connects. We can use him. For one, taking him out of the Metro Corridor will disrupt his operations. You know this. Between me and you, we'll be able to keep an eye on him. He'll be under our control. We have to move fast, right? That means pullin' all types of shit out the box. Once this is done, you can do what you want with him. Or to him."

Approximately two and a half minutes of awkward silence ensued before Myth spoke again.

"Are you done?"

Shef let out a sigh of defeat, "You gotta make decisions fast, bro. There's a lot riding on this, I just," another more forceful sigh erupted from Shef, Myth interpreted it perfectly. He knew Shef was searching for words and didn't have them. Rare.

"Check out those files. Narrow it down, and we can try to identify who we're goin' to get. Or recruit, I think recruit sounds better. I figure you've some time before we head out. We'll be flying out in something special?"

"Yeah?"

"Ohhhh yeah," Shef said in anticipation, "But seriously, Myth read 'em. I'll know. I can see you through your TV."

Shef broke out into genuine belly laughter that gradually tapered off into an elongated sigh.

"Funny. Wait, you were just jokin', right?" Myth asked.

"Nope. Can totally do that."

"Now on to the fun stuff," Shef continued sounding more energetic, "I have some candidates for you, the top performers in their respective corridors. All have received glowing praise for their service."

"Send them," Myth said as he approached the tribunal transport to take him back to his home. Ironic that he was just waxing poetic about the luxury of traveling in such a manner not knowing this would be his last day using one. At least for now. He should be gone in less than 48 hours and the only thing that came to mind right now was his family, Simone and Chance. He didn't want to leave them, especially now that things could get particularly crazy. Myth slumped into the back seat. He rubbed eyes tired from being glued to digital screens for the last hour and a half only to have them follow him on the ride home. The monitor in the back seat illuminated. He spoke one, simple vocal command.

"Show new documents from Shef."

Meanwhile, a meeting of two continued.

"How confident are you in Myth?"

"Again, I don't question his talent. But we are dealing with a threat that we have *never* faced before."

"Zetsuka, should we begin searching for a possible successor?"

"I don't think we have any other course of action. We know how this will end."

CHAPTER FOURTEEN

March 30th 2004 10:38 PM

Dunbar sat at the bar sipping the drink that he ordered when he first took a seat. The melted ice watered down the potency of the alcohol, the negligible amount that was present, anyway. He took another small sip and sat it back down, rubbing his finger around the rim of the glass. A hard slap to his back pushed him forward. He adjusted his glasses back up on the bridge of his nose and whipped his head around to see his friend taking a seat on the adjacent stool.

"The Souse House? Of all the places in base pop you had to pick this shit hole?" Adam said before motioning to the waitress, "Lemme get a whiskey straight. Put it on his tab."

The young woman smiled and nodded.

"Paul, you really need to get out more," Adam said cooly as he glanced at the waitress' huge breasts, "And what is that you're drinking? A Capri Sun on the rocks?"

Dunbar dismissively shook his head, "I just needed to get away from the lab. It gets a bit claustrophobic."

Adam took a large swill of his whiskey and sucked his teeth as it burned its way down his esophagus, "You spend more time in the lab than you do at your own place. I would imagine it'd feel like the walls are closing in when you're consistently the only motherfucker in the building."

"It's just…this stuff going on with these drug busts, and now everything going on with these kidnappings. I mean, you go to sleep one night and you wake up the next and the world is in a panic."

"I think you think too much, Dunbar."

"How so?"

"We are part of the Metropolitan Corridor Police Department," Adam said, "We protect the basement population. That's what cops do now. Anything else gets left to the Zs."

"So, what's your point?" Dunbar asked genuinely disgusted.

"The *point* is you can't get carried away worrying about shit that is out of your scope? Focus on what's in front of you. There's no way in hell you can help the Mecca or the Zs track down some worldwide terrorist cell."

"I...I'm not so sure about that," Dunbar replied lightly.

Adam threw back the remaining bit of whiskey in his glass and signaled for another before he even swallowed down the contents, "Have you ever even *seen* one?"

"What? Me? Of course I've seen one. I work closely with Chief Archibald and he works closely with Myth and-"

"No, I mean have you seen one, in action?"

Dunbar hung his head before silently shaking it.

"Myth? You don't even know his real name! Well, lemme tell you. I was in that ware house a couple years back. The one they tried to apprehend Myth in."

"I remember that," Dunbar said as he listened intently.

"Yeah, well, I've seen some crazy shit patrolling base pop, but I'll never forget seeing a zealot for the first time. I swear to God, I would blink or turn my head and he'd be ten, twenty feet away. There was a room full of cops and three zealots and he *still* got out. Our entire squad was no match for him."

"He's one of the best for a reason."

"I thought I was hot shit coming out of the academy," Adam sighed, "I was cocky, a little arrogant."

"Was?" Dunbar shot back with a smile.

"Pure hilarity. But seriously, I've never felt more humbled in my life. Before I was always wondering what makes the Zs so much better than cops? That day I saw it with my own eyes."

"Sounds…crazy," Dunbar said

"Is. Is crazy."

Just then, Dunbar felt the slight vibration that signaled an incoming call to his comm.

Incoming call from Chief Archibald

He reached up to take the call. Adam was too busy flirting with the big boobed waitress to notice. The waitress was too busy peering into Adam's open wallet and noticing that he had more than enough for a sizeable tip to hear any of his advances. She leaned closer.

"Chief? Yes? Understood."

Dunbar abruptly stood and gathered himself.

"I gotta go."

"What? I thought your shift just ended?"

"I guess I just got called up to the big leagues," Dunbar said moving towards the door.

"S'that so? Bet that means you'll be leaving the force for a while. That's a shame Paul, I had my fingers crossed that we could be a team, ya know? Like Riggs and Murtaugh."

Dunbar looked absolutely perplexed, "Who?"

"You've never seen *Lethal Weapon*?"

"No."

"Any of them?"

"Can't say that I have."

"What kinda cop are you?"

"I could never get into movies like that, showing cops blasting away with real bullets. It always seemed so…far fetched."

"Cmon," Adam exclaimed, making it evident that the whiskeys he'd slammed earlier were beginning to make their presence felt, "That's every cop's dream! Smoking a room full of tough guys. No stun rounds, baby! You ain't wakin' up!"

"And on that note. Good night, Becca," Dunbar said as he walked out,"You can close it out."

"Okay, thanks. G'night Paul."

Dunbar strolled out of the cigarette smoke fog and back into the night. Adam looked back at the door with stunned confusion. He turned back to the waitress.

"Well, I think I'm about to get out of here. Maybe, you know, if you're about to get off we can leave together."

"Hmm, I'll think about it," she said playfully, "But first you have to settle the tab."

"I said put it on *his* tab."

"Well, he opened a tab in your name before you got here. Soooo."

Adam just chuckled, as he took out a fifty dollar bill to pay, "He is a smart guy. I'll give him that."

CHAPTER FIFTEEN

March 30th 2004, 10:38 PM

Everett walked into and the sounds of tiny, fat feet slapping against the wood floors like pellet gun shots.

"Daaaaadddy!"

"Hello there my baby," Everett said as he lifted his daughter high into the air and brought her back down to his face with a tight hug. Chance wrapped her small arms around his neck, then kissed him on the cheek.

"Smell me," Chance said lifting up her arm. Everett rubbed his face in her armpit and took a deep smell, Chance was laughing hysterically.

"MMM! You smell like...Nachos!"

"Noooo, I don't. I smell good. Like candy. Mommy gave me some smell good lotion, huh Mom?"

"That's right baby," Simone said as she ushered Chance's feet to the ground, "Go wash your hands and get ready to eat."

Chance dashed away. Simone took Everett's hand in hers and rubbed it gently with the other. It was obvious she had seen the news online and on TV. How could she not? It was the most prominent political disaster ever in the era of instant information. It was all anyone with an opinion could talk about. Still, she didn't say anything, just rubbed his hands and silently drew him closer into an embrace. She placed her head against his chest and held him tight. Like he was slipping away from her.

"I know you're going to have to leave," she whispered without moving.

Everett sighed and gripped Simone tighter, "To know me is to love me."

Simone chuckled lightly, "That's true. When?"

Everett pulled her away and looked into her eyes. Before, it used to hurt because Simone always looked heartbroken every time he had to leave on a mission. This time, though, there was something about it that was more disturbing. A calm demeanor grown from experiencing this brand of heartbreak to the point of numbness. This was an example of the quiet preparation that she had done in the anticipation that Everett would leave and not come back one day. It made Everett feel very uneasy.

"I have two days," Everett finally said.

"E…What??"

"And I don't know when I'll come back."

Simone backed away from him with a hand on her scrunched up brow.

"And you don' know when you're going to *fucking* come back, are you kidding me?!"

"Yo, yooo. Chill, I know you see everything that's going on, right?"

"But, you're on the tribunal, you don't have to go anywhere?" Simone rightfully reasoned.

Everett's eyes darted to the floor for a split second. And that was more than enough.

"What?" Simone yelled, her eyes drilling holes into Everett's.

"What?" Everett said feigning confusion.

"What did you do?" Simone yelled, louder this time. Everett walked and sat down on a stool in the kitchen, dropping his bags on the way. He rolled his head on his neck like he was warming up for a fight.

"I stepped down from the tribunal. I'm going to create another cell for a new, classified mission."

"Your 'classified' mission is plastered all over the FUCKING INTERNET," Simone spat with heavy emphasis, the aggression in her tone was starting to get on Everett's fucking nerves.

"Who else would they send? At this point, the military could only do so much compared to you guys? I've read the military has even started usin' them," Simone argued.

"Is that what you read? On some conspiracy theory site?"

"Whatever, E, I know this shit is gettin' real. But do you even know how real? YOU made the decision to step down so you have to have some idea of what you're getting into."

"I know I'll be heading out to some different corridors. And that I don't have a lot of time. You're doing such a good job uncovering info," Everett said sarcastically, "what else do you really need to know that you don't already?"

"I know that your daughter's birthday is coming up and-"

"And what!?" Everett exploded, "You think you need to remind me of my own daughter's birthday!?"

The rest deteriorated into a yelling match between the two. Growing in intensity until they both noticed Chance off to the side, tearfully watching from down the hall. Her small face twitched as she tried to conceal her emotions. Both of her parents were at a loss for words, searching for a way to console Chance while slowly drowning in the pool of guilt brought upon from being seen by her.

"Chance," Everett whispered, it was the first time he noticed how hoarse his voice had become, oblivious to how loud he must have been. Chances face convulsed in conjunction with her hyperventilation. Her small chest jerked up and down, rhythmic like a wide-up toy powered by tears. She forced most of it back as she walked towards them, by the time she was standing at Everett's feet with her arms raised to be picked up, there were only tear streaked cheeks and a tired hint of a smile. Everett held her and she rested her head on his shoulder. Simone walked over and gently rubbed Chance's back.

"Don't be mad guys. Daddy, you have to leave, huh?"

"Yes my baby, I do. I have to leave in two days?"

"That's like in two mornings?"

"Yes it is."

Chance dropped her head, "You gotta stupid job."

Everett began walking Chance to her room. Simone walked closely next to the father of her child.

"I do not! I have an awesome job. I get to help people and make sure that the bad guys go to mega-jail."

"There's no such thing as mega- jail! Mommy is there a mega-jail?"

Simone laughed, "I don't know. You're daddy might be right."

"And you get to fight people?" Chance asked Everett as he placed her in the bed softly. Simone tucked the blanket up around her.

"Yes, baby, I get to fight people."

Chance's eyes lit up, "Do you...get to kill people?"

Everett's and Simone's eyes quickly met each other's with simultaneous surprise. Everett always joked what it'd be like when Chance asked where babies came from. But this?

"Well," Everett started before cautiously glancing at Simone one last time, "Killing people is...not ...um...nice."

"What if it's bad people, like the ones on the news?"

"Yes. Sometimes mean people do bad things to other people and people like me have to go...deal with them. I...yeah."

"Wait, when did she start watching the news?" Simone asked aloud to no one in particular.

Everett leaned down and kissed Chance on the forehead.

"I promise when I'm gone, we'll video chat."

"Okay, I love you daddy. G'night."

Everett rose to his feet and Simone took his place, "Good night my princess. Sweet dreams."

"G'night mommy."

Simone and Everett left towards the door. Chance could see their silhouette joined at the hands outlined in the threshold. Everett slowly slid the door closed. Chance listened to the sounds of their feet walk down the hallway providing a rhythm that was helping lull her to sleep. She blinked for a long few seconds and jerked herself back awake with one last thrust, to say a prayer.

"Dear God Jeevus, please let my daddy come back home safe and not hurt. Make sure my mommy doesn't cry. And most importantly, help my daddy kill all the bad people. Amen."

Chance rolled over onto her side and closed her eyes. She felt the hilt of the kunai that she had hidden under her pillow and went to sleep, content and comforted.

CHAPTER SIXTEEN

March 30th 2004, 11:50 PM

Son...It's all bad...

Olufemi rose to his feet. Of all the moving around to different houses that he had done over the last couple of years, he made sure to always, always, have a dojo installed. Keepin' the skills razor sharp, he would boast. Intense training fueled by equally intense paranoia. His bald head glistened in the low light from the sweat while cool air lapped against his naked scalp. That still took some getting used to.

His fingers touched slim gashes on his face, cutting into his beard. He retracted them and rubbed the blood between his fingers before wiping it on his shirt. As he walked out to a huge open floor plan home tucked away beneath the towering buildings of the Metropolitan Corridor, four hulking men on his security team were removing the incapacitated bodies of three more of the men paid to protect him. Times like these only seemed to highlight their inadequacies.

Smoke all my weed up and don't do shit.

Olu was escorted to his room by more men. The conundrum of never wanting them around and always wanting them around, he was surrounded in isolation. Wrestling to find an answer wore on his mind and it started to creep into his physical state as well. He had gotten noticeably thinner, though he was still strong. He insisted on constantly training, even if it meant just beating the hell out of three or four of his security team. *Security team.* It almost made him laugh to think he referred to them as such. A bunch of clingers-on and kiss assess.

"Leave. Go...search the perimeter or whatever," Olu muttered as he snatched a towel out of one of his maid's hands and laughed quietly to himself. The others around him tried not to look uncomfortable.

A maid. A nigga like me with...a maid.

He held the towel to his face despite the stinging sensation that was growing with each minute and entered into his room, where he had to tell another three men to leave him. They resigned themselves to standing outside of his door. Olu's master bedroom was spacious, fitting a large, gaudy, bed as well as a sitting area, a door to a landscaped backyard, and countless video screens with feeds from the many cameras that were placed around the compound. He sat on his bed in this huge, lavishly furnished and designed room, alone. His eyes darted around. Paintings he paid thousands of dollars for from artists he never heard of adorned the walls. Next to his bed on an oak nightstand there was a jewelry case filled with diamond watches, chains, bracelets, rings, and earrings.

One of his favorite things, an onyx bust of the Egyptian god of the underworld, Anubis, sat on a white podium. The ruby inset eyes hauntingly flickered when any light hit them. Olu had all the trappings of success, what everyone desires in this life, and still it did nothing to soothe him. He walked into a closet lined with boxes of sneakers, boots, and expensive loafers from ceiling to floor. Racks of suits from the finest labels hung in plastic, hardly ever worn. As he moved up the ranks of drug dealing and organized crime, he felt it necessary to buy suits. Olu could give a fuck less about Armani or Gucci, but he had to project that authority. He had to look the part of the boss, his standard uniform of white t-shirts and Jordans didn't seem to command enough respect. He was on a bigger stage now and he had to act accordingly. Slanging to white kids coming down to base pop looking to score some green seemed like an eternity ago.

He snatched a shirt off of a hanger and changed into it, tossing his bloodied one to the closet floor. From there he moved to a mini bar in another corner and poured himself a glass of potent vodka. He took a large gulp and exhaled through clinched teeth. Olu poured the rest of the alcohol on the towel and shoved it back onto his face before he could think otherwise. The intense and sudden burn took his breath away for a brief moment. His pain turned into a guttural grunt as he glanced at the wall of monitors. For a moment he thought he saw something flicker past on one of the outdoor cameras. The vodka had started to work its magic, so he just attributed it to that. But still, something made him uneasy.

Seems like everything made Olu uneasy these days. Heavy is the head that wears the crown, they say, and Olu was the undisputed king. He moved more work than everybody combined. If you snorted, inhaled, popped, or injected, chances are you contributed to Olu's profit. Ever since he stumbled upon the new blue shit everyone was raving about, his empire exploded. The reward he got from helping catch Myth was more than enough to come in the game heavy. His connect was more excited than he was at first. Olu's plan to cut it up and sell it for a ridiculous gain on the initial buy was pure money. Once people started using and the word of mouth spread, it went crazy.

Since flipping that, all the other stuff he used to push seemed like small change. He was shipping out to the Atlantic and Midwest Corridors. His clientele consisted of people from across the Metro Corridor. Doctors, athletes, attorneys, judges, soccer moms, base heads, white, black, it didn't matter. If they came once, Olu knew they'd come again. And again. And again. And call until he had to switch phones, show up at his doorstep until he had to switch houses. Some nights he would be tempted to try it, see what the fuss was about. But he had listened to the *Ten Crack Commandments* so many times he knew better than that.

Besides, he made too much money off of it to waste any product. He walked over to a nightstand by his bed and retrieved a small stash box filled with pre-rolled joints. That was one of the awesome things about having maids, he always felt. He sparked the L and inhaled deeply. A cloud of smoke stampeded out of his lungs and perfumed the room. An ever-so-slight breeze sliced its way through, dissipating the cloud. By this time Olu was standing back in front of his monitor wall, cautiously looking over them. This position was becoming as familiar to him as going to sleep in his bed. He always said it would probably make him feel a little more comfortable after watching the grounds for a few minutes. It never did. And, "a few minutes" assuredly turned to a few hours every time.

His eyes darted from room to room, to hallway to garage to the courtyard to the driveway and back to his room. To a figure standing in the corner next to his Anubis bust. He quickly turned around and squinted to make a more precise image, though he already knew in his mind who was there. The only one who could make it past all of the cameras and men *and* slip in unnoticed. For the first time in a very long time, Olu felt something different at the sight.

He felt comforted.

"Ink. They still calling you that?" Myth said as he continued to appraise the Anubis sculpture.

"They call me what I tell them to. The ones who ever even seen my face," Olu muttered without turning around.

"Well be careful, people can look at you through your TV now."

"Wait, they can't really do that shit, can they?"

"That's what I hear. Either way you should probably watch your shit. No more smashing maids in here," Myth suggested.

Olu turned around, "How do you even know about that?"

"I didn't, but *of course* you're smashing the maids. Obviously, you have the bread to spend extra for super model maids, most people only pay for functionality. You get to have a fucking Miss Universe pageant for who cleans your toilet."

"They're all functioning just fine," Olu said as he creepily stared at a camera in the maid's quarters.

"Well, you get what you pay for," Myth reasoned.

"Son, did you come here to play muthafuckin' word games? Riddles and shit? What do you want?" Olu snapped with tinge of impatience.

Myth's eyes became increasingly serious. Olu recognized the look well. Myth seemed more imposing as a part of the tribunal, imbued with certain powers that were intimidating in themselves. Myth was also one of a handful of tribunal members that were actually zealots, not ARU holdovers, which made his rank even more impressive. Olu was aware of all of these things. The people he had on the police force would report back if they happened to cross paths with Myth, which was rare. When it did happen the stories were recited with the zeal of a freshly fucked groupy. Olu would stop listening within seconds.

"It's been a minute," Olu noted.

"Yeah," Myth laughed, "You thought that if you cut off your dreads and grew a nappy ass lumberjack beard you'd just fade into the background, huh?"

Olu took another long pull of his lit joint. He spoke through holding the smoke in his lungs.

"Why you worried bout it? Thought you wouldn't be fuckin' with us anymore. Too busy on your tribunal shit to be bothered."

"Well, clearly business is doing good enough for you to afford this. Which is one of the reasons I stopped by," Myth paused and turned his head to the side. Olu could tell that he was smiling under his mask and he hated it.

"What happened? Baby cut himself shaving?"

Olu had forgotten about the scratches across his face, "Sparring."

"Ahh, keepin' the skills sharp! Ain't that your catch phrase or something?"

"Whatever nigga. Again, what the fuck do you want?"

"Like I said," Myth said decidedly more aggressive in tone, "Business is doing well. Ballin' much harder than you've ever been, clearly. So just cut the bullshit and tell me who your connect is."

"Man, please. Get the fuck outta my house," Olu replied laughing.

"Nah son, I don't think you understand how this is going to go. You *will* answer all of my questions. Or else I'll make it really unpleasant in this bitch. Do you know the types of things I could authorize as a member of the tribunal," Myth was very much aware of the fact that he had renounced his place on the tribunal before making this largely empty threat, but fuck it. What Olu didn't know wouldn't hurt him and time was of the essence, couldn't waste any of it on unnecessary negotiations.

"Threats. You gotten good at givin' em, I will say that. Reminds me of the first one."

Myth knew exactly what Olu was referring to.

"You're whole pretend high life can come collapsing down on you in a *blink*. You think anybody on your weak ass security detail has a chance against one zealot? Let alone the twelve I could have here with one command? Do you *really* feel protected?"

Olu absolutely knew the answer to that question, but he wasn't going to say those words in front of his former friend and rival. Pride has a strange way of showing itself at the most inopportune of times.

"I know you've seen the news," Myth continued.

Olu ashed his joint, "I haven't but my people have. I know what's going on."

"You have people that watch the news *for* you? Son, where is your financial advisor that seems like a waste."

"Ay, I been out here a minute. I'm startin' to learn that information costs more than muscle, on the real. Pay em' what they want so they tell me what I need. Keep it one hunnit. Everybody moves cool," Olu said, reeling back a bit when he caught himself confiding a bit too much, "I know shit's fucked up."

"That's quite the understatement, "Myth replied in a calmer manner which took some of the tension out of the room, "There's no other reason a member of the tribunal would be standing here. You think we just…make housecalls?"

Olu took a deep drag of his lit joint and left it burning closer to his fingers. After a few seconds he released a steady stream of smoke from his ice grill. His eyes were locked on Myth as smoke billowed in front of their faces. His eyes remained steadfastly on Myth's even as the smoke gradually dissipated. At that moment, they both shared the same thought.

He's hiding something.

Myth broke the glare and looked down as if at a wrist watch. He proceeded to speedily type a few commands on a touchscreen interface that became backlit as his fingers got closer. A three-dimensional representation of the vial with the blue sand in it appeared seemingly floating above his outstretched forearm.

"You know what this is. That isn't a question."

"…I do," Olu confessed.

"It gotta name?"

Olu snorted out a short burst of laughter, "Indigo, blue dream, smurf—"

"Smurf?"

"Smurf. Most of the people I get down with call it The Dawn."

Myth used a hand gesture to rotate and zoom in on the bottom of the vial.

"You seen this before?"

Olu took a final pull from his joint, quickly putting it out in an ashtray when it singed the tips of his fingers. He cautiously observed the emblem on the bottom of the vial, "I've seen it around, tagged on walls and shit, no different than anybody else."

Myth cancelled the image, "We've found this across the world in areas where the abductions took place. The tribunal has determined that the two are connected, and finding out who's behind the supply will lead us to who's behind the kidnappings. And that needs to happen ASAP."

"What does this shit have to do with me?" Olu asked.

"I'm tasked with connecting the dots, getting to the bottom of it. And you sir, are a huge black ass dot."

"Surprise surprise, another job for the golden boy," Olu chided sarcastically.Myth ignored the jibe, "You're coming with me."

Olu let out a guffaw, "Yeah? A free trip on the Mecca? Nah son, I got business to handle here."

Myth's brow wrinkled, "See, that's part of the problem: the business you got here. I'm not just gonna leave you here to keep peddling the shit I'm trying to stop. It could be worse. I got enough on you to take you in tonight. Right now. So again, you *are* coming. Be ready in two days."

"Man hol' the fuck up!" Olu bellowed, "Whatchu think this is?!"

"I think this is me telling you exactly what you're going to do," Myth snarled through an icy glare.

A loud knock on the door interrupted their heated discussion. A voice came from the other side of the door.

"Yo Ink, everything good in there? Is there a problem?"

"Yeah, everything's straight," Olu replied quickly.

"Bet. Just holla if you need us."

Myth shook his head and chuckled condescendingly, Olu was infuriated by it.

"Don't gas your team up too much. The minute one of them runs in here trying to act tough, I'll make sure he knows the difference between our skill levels," Myth sternly warned. Olu couldn't argue with that fact.

"What if I say no to this bullshit."

"There is no *no*. Either you come with me, or I put the call in and your empire falls in a week. Watch how fast all your homies turn on you. You think when you're in the bing any of these niggas will miss you? These same dudes on your team are starving for your spot. Just like you when X was running shit in the Metro."

Olu shook his head solemnly, "Who's to say that whenever this fuckin' field trip is over, that shit isn't going to happen anyway?"

"Good question. Irrelevant, but good. You don't have any options. You can actually…help? Shocking, I know. For once, do the smart thing."

Myth turned away, and headed towards the doors to Olu's patio.

"I'll do it," Olu said.

Myth turned his head around, the shock was evident in his eyes.

"A bit easier than I thought, but I'll take it. I'll send you a message when we're about to move out. You should get one of your maids to pack your shit. You won't need much."

Olu rubbed his eyes with his hands. When he opened them, Myth was nowhere to be found. The cool night breeze swirling in through the open door to the courtyard was the only thing that remained. Olu sat on the edge of his bed. A knock at the door made him nervously jump, something that even he realized was uncharacteristic. One of his maids peaked in shortly thereafter. A gorgeous Columbian woman with long dark hair tied in a bun entered his room.

"Sir, would you like something to eat?"

"Nah, I'm not hungry."

As she turned to leave Olu called out, "Wait…hol up. Stay. And close the door."

CHAPTER SEVENTEEN

March 30th 2004, 10:44 PM

"Ca-"

He was dead before the warning was out. The entirety of his throat was splattered next to his collapsed body, fast enough for him to see it before fading to black. Inaudible steps through tree limbs evaded others walking on the ground. One smelled scared. Both did when they found the condition of the comrade they had been trying to reach. Silent footfalls above them hastily moved in the opposite direction, towards the mansion. He leapt from a branch and down to the ground gracefully, without breaking stride or making a sound, and raced towards the main compound. He caught a whiff of a new scent on the breeze. There was a salty, metallic taste lightly coating the back of his throat, familiar from his training.

They have guns.

He picked up his pace, on all fours now, a low blur that no one would see until he was too close and it was too late. He wasn't here to kill, just to deliver a message. A growing urge inside slowly coaxed him into killing the first guy. Although it wasn't entirely necessary, it felt good. Fun. The bonus, as it turned out, was that freshly spilled blood smelled like sausages. Who knew? Olu was at his kitchen table in front of a steaming pile of pasta prepared by his chef. He literally just sat down to eat when Big Ax burst into the dining room accompanied by two others.

"Ink. They found Joe-Joe out on the perimeter dead. Ripped up, like a fuckin' bear got him or somethin'."

Olu slammed his hand on the table, causing the plates and glasses to rattle.

"So, you sayin' a bear killed him son?! A bear, son?! A bear is *eluuuding* our security, cuh?!" Olu yelled, livid.

"Sir, My-my bad son. But I just thought that—"

Another one of Olu's security team came bursting through, looking more disheveled and out of breath. Olu threw up both of his hands in disgust.

"For real?!"

"Sir, there's something out there. Moving around in the shadows, down in the grass like a wolf or a dog or some shit!"

"Ax, *get* this dumb ass nigga the fuck outta my-"

A scream pierced through the air, gradually fading off into a gurgling last whelp. It came from outside but it rang throughout the house like it happened in the adjacent room. Olu quickly stood up.

"Go. I'll check the cameras."

His team nodded in acknowledgement, and hastily left their boss. Olu walked casually to his room thinking it was probably nothing, a rival crew trying foolishly to make a move. Besides, there was a budget that covered how many men he lost, a few more could bite the dust before it started to really affect his pockets. He entered his room and approached the console for the monitors. With a wave of his hand, they all glowed to life. His eyes moved back and forth between screens as he quietly observed. A blur on one of the outdoor cameras caught his eye. Then another. And another. All on different monitors.

A zealot? Fuck...Everett? Why?

His attention was brought to the upper left quadrant, a cluster of cameras from outside. Two brolic guys dragging a third body, leaving a blood trail on freshly cut grass. Another shorter dude was leading them, with his gun out no less. Olu was perturbed by that, to say the least. There was a vetting process before someone was even in the running to get a gun. They were expensive and just brought extra heat if you ever used one. More trouble than they were worth at this point due to zealots. Still, flashing one proved to go a long way in settling disputes. This dispute, though, seemed to be beyond the rules of street diplomacy.

He watched as the leader of the group crept low with his weapon drawn, like he was on the underground railroad. He held up his hand to the others who stopped in their tracks. The guy in the back's face showed contempt and it looked like he was complaining about having to stop. Olu couldn't blame him, getting stuck with body disposal duty always sucked. Suddenly all of their eyes got wide and they stood still. Olu could make out one of the guys mouthing, "What was that?" as he continued to intensely watch. The two men dropped the arms of the dead man they were dragging, his limbs falling comically to the ground. They clumsily reached for the machetes they were both armed with. Now, the three of them were looking around frantically in the darkness. Olu changed his gaze and fixed to another monitor showing a tree-lined walkway leading up to where his three goons were cowering in a circle.

Two beady, glowing lights hidden in the leaves of trees were seemingly floating, unmoving. Olu squinted at the screen, it looked like they were pointed directly at the camera. The tiny lights flicked on and off. That's when Olu realized they were a pair of eyes. Immediately after, a rustle of leaves and the lights zoomed away. The three men from the other camera looked up in unison towards the same direction. The one with the gun stepped forward, cocked, and raised his gun.

Ah shit...

Before he could fire, a dark flash zipped into view, he retracted his arm as chunks of hand and metal from his gun tumbled to the ground in unison. The flash came to a stop. He stood with his back to the camera. Olu could make out a short sword attached to the stranger's back horizontally. His left hand was covered with a metallic gauntlet with sharp points at each fingertip, it was spattered and dripping with blood. The two men with machetes gradually gathered themselves into some semblance of a fighting stance.

Weak. Fucking weak.

They crept forward slowly, cautiously, as the unknown assailant stood lackadaisically. His hands quickly shot up, everyone including Olu tensed up at the sight. The intruder just stretched his hands above his head, like a cat stretching in the sun. Foolishly, one of the guards thought this was an opening and took a few awkward steps forward with a thrust. It was easily sidestepped, and with a swift flick of his arm upward, the machete blade was cut into gradually smaller pieces before falling to the grass. Another blade came swinging at the intruder's neck. He jumped, at least eight feet straight up from standing and landed behind his attacker, this time his hand fondled the hilt of his short sword, but he still didn't remove it. Olu recognized the restraint, commended it even. It seemed like the intruder was talking to the guards now, possibly trying to get them to reconsider their assault. The guards looked at each other, then at the intruder, then back at each other. The remaining armed guard dropped his weapon and both held up their arms in surrender.

"Bitches," Olu muttered to himself.

The two guards began tending to the handless hotshot that started the confrontation in the first place. Everyone totally forgot about the initial body they were dragging with them. The intruder looked directly into the camera, his eyes glowed inhumanly. He was wearing a scarf that wrapped around his neck that concealed the lower half of his face, but it clearly wasn't a zealot uniform. He stared in the direction of the camera, then coyly flipped his middle finger at it. Both stepped to the side as the man bolted passed them on all fours like an animal. Olu watched as the blur scattered across multiple screens then he quickly ran out of his room. He knew Big Ax would still be out there.

"Hey this muthafucka is making a move. From the cameras it looks like he's on the far gate, that's gotta be like, a quarter mile or so from—"

He was interrupted by a thunderous crash through the front door. A body, one of his own security guards, hideously slashed across the chest and kicked like a soccer ball. A dark mass came rolling in afterwards, springing out and dashing along walls with freakish leaps and bounds. A giant ax smashed through an adjacent wall to deflect a slash at Olu's face. Dust from the drywall clouded the air and the intruder's arm recoiled from the move. He gracefully turned his momentum into a one handed backflip. It looked like he was showing off. Two of his guard came in from behind, Olu screamed out to them.

"WAAAIT!"

The intruder stood unflinching while the guards slowed to an uneasy stop behind him, both with machetes raised. Eyes darted around nervously. Beads of sweat collected on foreheads. Chests were heaving up and down in a cocktail of confusion and fear, everyone except the new visitor. He stared at Olu calmly, the vertical slits in his eyes never veering away. Olu swallowed hard. For the first time in a very long time, maybe ever, he was afraid.

"Who are you?"

He blew air quickly out through his nose, an animalistic sound that was filled with condescension. Olu didn't have to speak animal to feel offended.

"I said who the fuck are you?" Olu snapped.

"I'm Neko the messenger. That's all that needs to be said about who I am. Tell the guards behind me to retread those steps or I will kill them."

Quietly, Olu's guards had been advancing with careful footsteps towards the intruder. Everyone was surprised when he commented on that fact without turning around. The guards quickly took heed, laughably retreading their exact steps, intimidated into following the order literally.

"Also, one peed on himself. The smell is making my stomach hurt," Neko mumbled, disgusted.

Olu noticed the guilty party's eyes quickly dart to the ground in embarrassment. Big Ax stood to the side as Olu stepped around his massive frame.

"Ink, I dunno about this dude, maybe-"

Olu raised his right hand and silenced his right hand man.

"You're the messenger, huh? So, what's the message?"

The messenger crossed his arms, "Everett Santeaux. You know him?"

Olu hesitated. He was becoming increasingly annoyed by this dude in his house talking mad shit.

"What kinda fuckin' freak are you anyway? Cosplay type bitch?"

"Cosplay?"

"Yo, where you from?" Olu was the one in control of the conversation at this point, taking his turn interrogating.

"You ask too many questions," Neko responded.

Olu wanted to rip him apart right then and there, but he showed restraint. Even he had matured with age, albeit moderately.

"You smell like you're about to do something stupid. I suggest you don't."

Olu's hand twitched. He felt a tight grip around his wrist the moment he raised it, jerking him backwards like a mother does a bad ass kid out in public.

"DON'T."

Much to the messenger's surprise, a spinning elbow broke them apart. Much to the messenger's shock, it was immediately followed by a flurry of punches and elbows directed at his stomach and groin. He fought to parry each attack, saw an opening to escape, and parried Olu's flying knee. The impact sent him sailing backwards, sliding to a stop. The messenger backflipped and landed perfectly standing, looking just as lazy as he had when he walked in. It seemingly took no effort at all. The two guards behind still hadn't moved a step. Now the other guard looked just as shook as his counterpart.

"You bout to piss on yourself, too?!" Olu barked at his subordinate. The messenger sneered with arrogance. He flashed sharp fangs in his mouth.

"Hmph. Well, then. Maybe you should tell your children to leave so I don't murder them."

The guards made for the door before he could start his next sentence.

"Worthless muthafuckas!" Olu spat at their backs over the clang of their machetes hitting the floor, loosed from their cowardly grips.

"You use such bad words. It's…ironic. I'm the one who's part animal, but you *act* like one. He was right about you," Neko commented, his tone was oddly friendly.

Olu rolled his head on his neck and his arms in their sockets. He extended his fingers and balled them into rapid fist, like an exercise.

"Ink, this guy bruh, shit, he ain't human no more," the deep voice of Big Ax reasoned, all the while clutching his namesake. It was dirty but razor sharp. When he swung, a deathly groan sang with it. A battle with him was accompanied by the guttural chant his weapon made as it cut through air.

"Your big friend can watch me take you apart. He's scared too, though. You all are."

Olu and Big Ax both went quiet and looked at each other. Ax looked into Olu's eyes and slowly nodded. He stepped backward, still holding his ax at the ready. Olu didn't wait. He swiftly skipped towards Neko. Neko somersaulted over Olu easily, landing between him and Big Ax, who tensed up to a double-handed grip of his large weapon. Neko ducked the huge ax as it floated above his head. He scurried on all fours to get from underneath the full radius of the swing. He pounced up towards Olu's face. His fists were there in an instant, three quick punches shot out like a cat playing with a yarn ball. Olu noticed his hands as he narrowly avoided the blows.

A feint, followed by a fierce jumping punch. Neko's speed was gradually increasing to zealot levels and he was barely breaking a sweat. Olu resolved to make him break *something*. He weaved out of attacks and timed his actions with Neko's. When he saw the opening, he swiftly threw a punch into the side of Neko's knee, it sent him stumbling. That was enough time for Olu to follow with a counterattack of his own using odd punches and kicks with no particular structure, but a noticeable rhythm. Neko saw this lack of structure in Olu's fists immediately. He placed a kick into Olu's chest and pushed himself into a series of defensive flips and cartwheels. He landed, breathing heavier.

"How you're holding your hands," Olu cried out gesturing at his opponent's. Now that he was closer, he could see the gauntlet on Neko's right hand in better detail. It was robotic in design and appeared to enclose his arm from the elbow down with a smooth, metallic gold. There were different hinge points for his joints lead up to his fingers. It looked like he was wearing thick rings on each one of them, "I know your techinique."

"I'm surprised since you so obviously have none. I've fought jungle animals with more, more...I dunno the word for it, yet. Showing you would be better."

"Son is Forrest Garfied," Olu muttered with disdain. Ax laughed.

Neko flicked his wrist and the rings on each finger unfurled like metallic snakes, gradually elongating into claws. They extended from his fingertips like pointed pyramids. The razor edges and golden metal of Neko's hand combined to shimmer light almost unnaturally. Every edge looked sharp. And thirsty.

"I'm starting to wonder why I'm even here delivering this message to *you*. Seems like such a waste. Obviously Santeaux is the important one," He held out a long, shiny golden finger and invited Olu to come at him, "I hope I don't kill you by mistake."

Big Ax watched nervously as Olu slowly stepped towards the messenger. One step turned to a dash with fists raised. Neko laughed to himself.

Predictable to rush in.

Olu's fists moved back and forth like pistons, jabs and crosses all aimed at Neko's face. This close, Olu could make out the slight discolorations in his skin, like tiger stripe birthmarks. He could also make out the sneer on Neko's face as he easily avoided his string of attacks. Olu hopped backwards, tossed a small stand, lamp included, into the air at Neko. He ran in quickly after it. Neko cut the décor into pieces. Even the glass in the lamp was sliced perfectly. He was wielding one finger like a symphony conductor wields his baton.

For a brief moment, Olu was angered, the next moment he was on the defensive. Neko advanced quickly, he attacked by slashing like he was finger painting in the air. Olu dodged slashes at his face and throat, along major arteries. His opponent's intent was definitely to kill, despite the smile that was smeared on his face. Olu blocked and parried, used an adjacent wall as leverage to launch a knee. It caught Neko in the ribs. He spun out of it. They exchanged expressions once more. Olu was the one smiling.

"And you're stupid as fuck, too?" Olu wondered, "You are actually tryin' to kill me when you have a message to deliver? Pshh, you don't know the value of info, witcho' dumb ass."

He put up his hands like a boxer and waited. Neko opened his clawed hand wide. Flexing all his fingers.

"I don't give a fuck how many fingers you use. I'm gonna rip you in half."

The two clashed again. The brawl took them all around the first floor of the house as Big Ax pursued like a biased guest referee. Neko's gauntlet glimmered as it ripped through furniture and slashed walls. Olu rolled and flipped to avoid his attacker. He was growing increasingly winded, as opposed to Neko, whose stamina looked like it was still going strong.

I'm not gonna outlast him. Gotta inflict some pain.

Olu became the aggressor, rushing back into battle, ducking a series of swipes at his head and deflecting a kick with one of his own. He landed blows to Neko's mid-section, who grunted at the impact of each one. Neko kicked him back down the hall, Olu stumbled over the debris of their battle and toppled backwards. He looked up to see Neko was airborne with every intention of crushing Olu's chest in with both feet. Olu rolled backwards, into a handspring as Neko smashed into the hardwood floor. Olu landed upright and found himself quickly on the defensive again. He noticed Neko's face. The smarmy smirk had dissolved into fierce focus and resolve.

Olu dodged the attacks as Neko's advances became more ferocious. He leaned backwards as his opponent's outstretched fingers tore the flesh from his face, leaving crimson streaks across his skin. The blood ran into his beard causing one side of it to appear as though it was died red. "Shit!" Olu exclaimed as he clutched at his stinging new wounds. Neko moved in to finish the job when a huge ax slammed into the ground, altering his path. He leapt high into the air and landed out of harm's way.

"Your big friend maybe shouldn't have done that. The message is for you, not him. If I kill him, it won't matter."

"That's a big dude, so I guess that's a big *if*," Olu returned unfazed, nodding with his head in Neko's direction, speaking with his eyes for him to take a peak. Neko snorted a rebuttal and glanced behind him. Big Ax stood towering, readying his weapon.

"The Santeaux, he's your friend?"

"You talkin' about Myth?"

Neko just continued to look at him, waiting for an answer. His catlike eyes were unsettling, like the moments when you unexpectedly see a black cat and it looks like he's been staring at you the whole time.

"I don't know where you're gettin' your info from, but we had a couple," Olu hesitated, carefully choosing his word, "disagreements. I ain't seen him in a minute fam."

"Are you always this stupid? I already know he's going to come here. He's going to ask something of you and you're going to say yes. And if you do not, I will kill you right now. It's really easy, actually."

He's going to come here?

"You are to keep an eye on your friend."

"He's not my friend."

"Who cares?" Neko said with a surprising amount of force, "You are very *annoying,* I think is the right word."

"Fuckin' Heathcliff Scissorhands over here, is getting annoyed with me?!" Olu bellowed back.

Big Ax laughed stroking the hilt of his ax as he spun it in his hands. The blades flashed in the light like propellars on an airplane whose engine was sputtering to life.

Neko darted at Olu, swiping his clawed hand at major organs and arteries, trying to rip them from their host. Just as Olu felt that he couldn't keep up with the onslaught of attacks any longer, he saw the giant ax blade lift abruptly into the air and come crashing down. Neko sprung away just in time. Or so he thought. He could fill a stinging gash along his back shoulder. A voice inside chastised his hubris. His conscious began to cast guilt on whether he would die doing the one thing he was tasked with. Maybe he had bitten off a bit more than he could chew. "I clipped 'em," Big Ax said as he looked at the purple colored blood dripping from the edge of his weapon.

"I tol' you not to take him lightly son," Olu chided.

Neko sniffed and turned around so that his wound was visible to his opponents. Slowly, the nasty gash across his shoulder began to bubble and ooze a thick, dark purple mixture of blood and pus. Then, the blood turned blue, and the wound began to seal itself before their eyes.

"It's going to take more than that to hurt me, I think."

Big Ax and Olu looked on with a combination of amazement and disgust.

"I tol' you, Ink. Dude's not human," Ax reiterated.

Neko interrupted before Olu could answer, "You are right big man. I am much more."

He sprung forward on all fours with increased tenacity. Big Ax stomped forward to engage. He held his weapon with one hand, swinging in a giant circle around his head before slamming it into a wall where Neko had been seconds earlier. He yanked his weapon back for another go when Neko slashed at Ax's wrist, hoping to sever his hold. He retracted his arm with a surprising amount of agility. Still, the difference in speed was very much apparent as Big Ax was on guard almost immediately, blocking advancing attacks that were taking their toll, even on his massive frame. A flipping kick to his chin sat him on his rear with a thud. Neko lunging at him figured to be the last thing he saw before crossing over into the next life. Olu tackled Neko out of the air just in time, both rolled through the door of his home dojo. Neko sprung to his feet out of the roll with cat-like quickness.

"I was warned about you. The styleless man who is unpredictable in battle. I am not…interested? No, impressed. I am not impressed. Not much of a fighter."

Olu returned with a smug grin to counter Neko's. Upon seeing it, Neko's face twisted up.

"That's what you heard, huh? Turns out I'm a much better thief," Olu replied as he held out a short sword. Neko paused before realizing it was the one that he had strapped to his lower back. He laughed. Not a condescending laugh but one that was born from genuine amusement.

"As I said, do what Santeaux asks of you. When the time comes, we will let you know what to do next. And you should probably make sure he doesn't die."

"And what if I say fuck this and you? What then?"

"Then I go pay your family a visit. From what I understand, they have...*disowned* you, I think is the right word. That makes sense. They seem like nice people, but you...you? You do not."

Olu tried not to let the fear inside of him show on his face, he had become increasingly good at that over the years. Not knowing who to trust will mold the meanest poker face on anyone.

"Bullshit."

Neko's quick recital of Olu's parent's address, as well as some of his brothers and sisters, put that notion to bed.

Damn...he gon' play that card on me? Alright, shit, let's put it all out then. I mean, would he really do it? Like Ax said, son not human. What IS he? Nigga straight outta Thundercats. Don't look like he care 'bout dyin' neither. He'd prolly kill 'em if he had to. No doubt. Would it be sad an shit if he does? Yeah. But the funerals would be laced. Nothin'. I can't afford for them to be killed, some of my fam my biggest customers. And I love 'em and shit, too. So much that I pay for everything now. Nigga just built a park! A whole park! Waterslides and basketball courts and all that shit. Everybody wanna turn they head but spend the money. And this muhfucker here. Pshh. All I gotta do is whatever E say do. Keep an eye on 'em. Bring my ass back home.

But I dunno...E could ask me to do some wild shit...

Somethin' jus tells me...

"Ink," Big Ax's voice snapped Olu out of his trance.

He charged at Neko, flipping the short sword into a reverse grip hold. His movements were even more erratic than they were before and fueled by a maniacal ferocity that emboldened every blow. Neko couldn't make out any type of technique or style, just a sporadic, spastic whirlwind of punches and kicks, elbows and knees. The occasional boosted short sword made an appearance, but Neko could tell Olu wasn't trained well with a blade.

Olu flipped the short sword in his hand. He swung the blade out towards Neko's face and throat, deft slashes that betrayed Neko's initial assertion. Olu raised the sword up over his head to bring it down like a serial killer, resistance stopped his arm from going forward. It was Neko's tail wrapped around his wrist. Olu dropped the sword and caught it with his other hand, swinging to cut the tail then to cut Neko's throat. *How…is he doing this?!*

Olu offered a quick feint, followed by a punch to Neko's stomach. The impact sent him sliding backwards, quickly somersaulting to avoid his short sword that was thrown at him. As soon as Neko landed, he felt the impact of Olu's knee into his thigh. His femur cracked underneath with his body moving quickly to repair it. Neko threw a panic driven counter punch that Olu nullified with a jumping arm bar. Both men fell to the floor of the dojo.

"Grappling…too?!" A shocked Neko grunted squirming.

He cursed himself for not realizing that Olu was baiting him the entire time. Not only did he wait for him to counter, he waited for him to counter with his gauntlet-covered hand so that he could get a hold of it, which he most assuredly had now. Neko tried not to let his face show the pain, but underneath the gauntlet, he could feel his tendons stretching unnaturally. Even with his advanced being, and his crafted weaponry, he could still feel the tightening strain through it all. He marveled at Olu's new found strength. Or had it always been there all along and he was so inebriated by confidence he hadn't noticed before? Either way, with each passing moment, it felt like his arm was about to be ripped out of its socket.

"Whatever I gotta do to win is what I do. No such thing as a fair one in a fight," Olu violently leaned backwards, causing the pressure on Neko's arm to build. His elbow was on the verge of snapping in the opposite direction. Neko let out an animalistic yelp. Olu's eyes flashed sadistically, something that became a part of his reputation from years of moving up the organized crime ladder in the Metro.

"You're fast as a muthafucka, I'll give you that. I'll do what you're askin'. Not because of you and not because of who you work for. Leave my fam alone," Olu ordered.

A large shadow cast down upon the twisted pile of limbs, it was Big Ax entering the threshold of the dojo. He stood like a guard with his weapon, visibly relieved that his boss had the situation under control, finally. Neko noticed him, too. The thought of his face being smashed by the huge ax's blade seeped into his brain. There was nothing he could do to stop it.

"I'm good Ax," Olu said wrestling Neko back into submission after a sudden fit of defiance, "I'm about to let 'em up. He gets crazy, murk him."

"No doubt."

Neko felt the pressure ease. When he was able, he snatched his arm and rolled back onto his feet. His golden hand hung limp and lifeless. Using his healthy arm, he grabbed his other wrist. With a sudden yank accompanied by a disgusting pop, he reset his limp arm in its socket. He rolled it around a couple times like a pitcher warming up prior to throwing a fast ball and looked down at Olu, who was still lying on the ground.

"The message has been delivered. I hope to never have to see you again" Neko said.

"Ax, make sure he makes it to the door."

Before Ax could respond to the command, Neko flipped over him and bolted towards the door. They both watched him charge into the darkness on all fours with the odd grace of an animal never before seen by men.

CHAPTER EIGHTEEN

December 1996

Neko's face twisted with frustration. This bit of training was just as taxing as any other, maybe even more so. His teacher wasn't letting up, either.

"Do it again," Cyrus commanded.

"But…"

"AGAIN."

Neko sucked his teeth and sighed loudly. He squinted his eyes. The word on the flashcard seemed to be squirming ever so slightly. "Ecks-croo-she-a-ting."

"Boom," Cyrus nodded with a smile, "See, just calm down and break the word into pieces. You're getting better."

"Thanks," Neko responded sheepishly, but happy to be recognized.

"Sensei, do you have kids?"

Cyrus paused for a moment, taken aback by the sudden change in subject.

"Yes. Well, one. A son."

Neko nodded silently.

"What made you ask that?" Cyrus inquired.

"It was a word that I had remembered from before. Remembered? I don't think that's the right thing to say…"

"I think the word you're looking for is *memorized,*" Cyrus corrected with a warm smile.

"Yeah. One that I memorized."

"Well, what do we have here now?"

A voice came from behind them, by the path leading back up to the compound. They both immediately recognized it as Tozen. He slowly made his way towards them, but his icey gaze was fixed on Cyrus. He didn't look particularly pleased.

"His training should be ending by now so that he can continue with his treatments, it looks like you two have yet to begin?" Tozen forcefully inquired. He looked down on both of them seated cross-legged in the center of the sparring ring. Cyrus held a stack of note cards with words written on them and definitions on the back. Neko had a smaller stack of his own.

"We still had about five minutes left until you interrupted," Cyrus lamented rising to his feet. Neko sat quietly, nervous.

Tozen stepped closer. He looked directly into Cyrus' eyes.

I do not care if he can *read*," Tozen spat with disdain.

"Such a narrow minded view," Cyrus returned, "You actually want to make a weapon of him and not give him basic skills? And then what? Send him on a mission with a picture book for intel?

Tozen turned his head. The anger was starting to encroach into his face more and more by the second.

"He needs a book just as much as a bullet does. Their function is the same!" he yelled.

"So what the fuck, is that you're idea? Making mindless killers?," Cyrus responded without flinching, "You brought me in so that I can impart my knowledge and help you in whatever way I can, correct?"

"How exactly are you doing that by letting the focus of all of this research waste time. You have NO idea what's at stake here or else I doubt you would be acting so blissfully casual, Mr. Santeaux."

Cyrus stepped forward, visibly perturbed at being scolded, "I know that I created a successful program at home with an equal focus on cultivating the mind as well as the body. I also know that applying my curriculum to Neko will yield the results that we both want and are excited to see."

The reasonable assessment quelled Tozen's anger.

"Besides, you shouldn't be so quick to condemn my practices," Cyrus said as he fumbled around for something in the pocket of his slacks. He removed his hand and opened it. Tozen eyed the object, then looked back at Cyrus awaiting some sort of explanation.

"Neko, what do I have in my hand. Use only your olfactory senses."

Neko looked up with a scrunched face, "Olafu-who what?"

"Your sense of smell."

"Ohhh. Oh, ok."

Tozen watched Neko over Cyrus's shoulder tilt as he tilted his head. His eyes gazed upwards as if he was in deep thought. He took a couple violent sniffs of the air. Then a few more followed by one last long one.

"That's a .45 caliber."

"And in my pocket?"

"Two .38 caliber bullets, I think."

Tozen nodded seemingly to acknowledge that he approved of that trick at least.

"Neko, go back to your quarters," Cyrus ordered over his shoulder. Neko wasted no time gathering up his note cards and placing them in a satchel. He bounded off quickly without saying a word. Though at this point, Cyrus could tell when he was afraid.

"Neko is such a special case I've had to adjust my approach to his training. He displays many of the characteristics of a zealot, but there are other aspects that are unique due to his genetic modification. We can't rush him. You have to let me do what I do."

"I...apologize. I've just become slightly stressed over the last few weeks. Things have become a bit complicated concerning our project in the Metropolitan Corridors."

"Is that why you're pushing the issue? Neko is nowhere near ready for that type of action, at all."

"The sooner the better, I admit," Tozen said as he turned around and made his way towards the path.

"What's this newfound urgency?"

Tozen partially turned to look at Cyrus once more, "I assure you, the urgency has always been there. You'll feel it soon enough."

He watched in silence as Tozen made his way back to the compound. When he was out of sight, Cyrus began his own return trek. He had a meeting to attend and he didn't want Tozen's prying eyes following him. Though, to be true, everyone that worked at the facility was essentially another pair of Tozen's eyes. Save for a few.

After a brief stroll, he was at his quarters. He unlocked his door with a swipe of a keycard, entered, and headed directly to the desk in his room that was littered with documents about Neko's training and treatment regiments, as well as some letters that he was meaning to send back to Master Xi at the zealot training facility in the Rockies.

It was funny to think that they had fallen back on such an old school method of communication in this day and age, but often times Cyrus's trips took him to remote locations where internet access was slim to none. Besides, with tech advancing in the manner that it was, Cyrus trusted his messages with a zealot courier rather an easily hacked email.

There were also reports from the Metropolitan Corridor. Cyrus had his hand on the pulse of zealot operations in every corridor for that matter. He was technically the Special Advisor to Zealot Prime in DC, but the behind-the-scenes rumors all said the same: Cyrus was the one actually in control. That probably could actually be the case if he wanted, but Cyrus didn't desire that weight on his shoulders. Zealot Prime dealt with a lot of the bureaucracy that came with being in the political arena, even more so now that the value of zealots was so readily apparent.

Cyrus didn't miss any of that bullshit. Traveling the world and learning new ways to help his program back home was infinitely more fulfilling. He flipped through some documents, just looking at words and not really reading anything to kill a few moments. Before he knew it, he was lifting his head groggily from an unexpected nap by the smooth chime that echoed in his room to signify someone at his door. He stood up slowly, smoothing his clothes off before he let his guest in.

"Mr. Santeaux."

"Please, come in."

She walked in and reached under her tank top. Tucked in the back of her pants was another thick folder with documents. Then she reached up to one of her earrings and pulled it from her ear.

"Here. It's a flash drive," she said handing it to him.

Over the last couple of months the doctor that slipped him the note when he first was introduced to Neko, Dr. Jasper Singh was her name he'd find out later, had become a friend. An ally was a more apt description. There was a mutual uneasiness they felt about Tozen and their surroundings. Those feelings were only exacerbated with the increased level of secrecy that Tozen was exhibiting. People seemed to be hustling harder about their work, with faint looks of fear and anxiety hidden beneath fake smiles.

"This...there's some weird stuff in here," Jasper sighed.

"Might as well be the slogan for this place. What did you find?"

Jasper sighed again, rubbing her forehead, "For starters there is extensive research into nanotechnology and cryogenics. More than even I was aware of at first. It's weird because we don't use any of this research in any of the projects I've worked on, or the ones I oversaw."

"Hmm," Cyrus mused.

"But this other stuff? I've been looking over all of the final reports from each experiment one through..."

"Lemme guess, 414?" Cyrus asked, finishing her sentence.

Jasper continued, "Yes. It's hard to nail down definitive trends because The Dawn was being refined as it was being injected into the patients, but I did notice something...odd."

They walked over to the desk. Cyrus sat down, Jasper leaned in over his shoulder. Cyrus caught some of her cleavage in his peripheral vision. Her perfume gently brushed his nose. She typically was so covered up…quickly he diverted his attention to the computer.   He inserted the flash drive into his laptop and loaded up the documents.   There were hundreds of brain scans, maybe thousands.

"Pardon my ignorance, but what am I looking for?" Cyrus asked confused.

"Oh, right, sorry.   Those images there are in sequential order. The dosage amount is the only constant so I attribute the changes to the rise in potency."

"Tozen's suggestion, I'm guessing."

"I'd say so," Jasper replied pointing, "You see these darker spots right here and here.   It represents high activity.   Higher than normal, actually."

"Seems to be affecting the brain in a pretty drastic manner," Cyrus mumbled as he stared at the screen.

"It is.   You've seen it in 415," Jasper abruptly stopped after realizing she had referred to Neko by his old patient ID.   It was natural for her, but she tried not to revert back to old habits in front of Cyrus.   She knew it bothered him.

"People are talking.   Whispering.   Saying that Tozen is planning on doing something drastic soon," Jasper whispered.   The fear in her voice was quite real.

"If people are so scared, why haven't more people tried to leave?" Cyrus asked.

"Tried to leave?" Jasper returned incredulously, "Mr. Santeaux, you really have no idea the circumstances that brought most of us here, do you?"

Jasper walked over to the bed and took a seat.

"I've been here for almost three years now.   I'm a pediatrician but I've also done extensive research on genetics.   I guess that's why I caught the eye of Tozen.   One night, I'm on my way home from work.   It was a late night, I remember, and I was just so drained.   I was working on a thesis about genetic treatments tailored to children suffering from different diseases.   I get home, get ready for bed, and go to sleep. I woke up in a van with four men in masks. And Tozen. He told me we were on the way to the airport and that I would not be harmed. If...," Jasper's voice trailed off.

"If? If what?" Cyrus asked.

"If I cooperated, I'd be treated fine. And to his credit, I haven't been abused per se, not physically anyway. But I was ripped from a life, MY life. My family, friends. To them, I've just disappeared. Gone. They don't know if I'm dead or alive. Our messages are monitored. Even the handwritten letters I've sent...I haven't gotten a single response back."

Cyrus thought about the letters that he had sent to Master Xi back in the corridors. Had they met a similar fate?

"So you see Mr. Santeaux, people are afraid to leave because of how they were brought here. There's only been a few to try, to even ask. After they were never seen again, the inquiries started to taper off."

"I bet." Cyrus said.

"But you? You came willingly. People are saying things. Wondering why *you* stay. I mean, I wonder it myself. You could just leave whenever you want to, right?"

"Yeah, I suppose I could," the self-doubt in his statement was palpable to both.

"I would...before the dreams start."

The dreams?

Cyrus quickly gathered himself, "I guess there's only one way to find out for sure, though."

Jasper returned a confused, if not frightened, look, "How?"

"By leaving. Going back to the corridors," Cyrus stated.

Jasper's silence indicated that she wasn't fully confident in his confidence.

Cyrus tried to diffuse the situation with a laugh as he rose to his feet, "A skeptic, huh? I wouldn't expect anything less from a woman of science."

Cyrus calmly walked over to an illuminated touch panel on his wall. He pressed an emerald button and the sound of a woman came through the embedded speaker.

"Mr. Santeaux, may I help you?"

"Yes, please inform Mr. Tozen that I will be taking my leave immediately. Something urgent requires my attention back home. Please, prepare a flight for me. Leaving tomorrow."

Cyrus peeked over his shoulder as if to comfort his guest.

"Not that hard."

Jasper looked like she was watching a horror movie anxiously anticipating the next scare. Cyrus turned back to the embedded wall comm.

"Thank you, can you confirm the information for me by the morning?"

There was no response.

"Hello?"

Nothing.

Cyrus' eyes glanced to the floor nervously, then back at the panel. He jerked his head towards his door when he heard the chime. He saw Jasper flinch at the sound in his peripheral vision. Slowly he walked towards the door.

"Cyrus, don't," Jasper said as she stood. Cyrus gave her a reassuring look before proceeding. The door opened to two burly guards.

"Mr. Tozen would like to see you."

"Well. Shall we?"

They made their way slowly, in silence, through the compound. The half-moon in the sky illuminated brightly, as if it were full. One guard marched in front, followed by Cyrus, followed by the other guard.

One walking behind to keep me from running, huh? Yeah…this is some ol' bullshit.

There journey by foot took them to a wooded path, one that was not instantly recognizable by Cyrus. A small oval building was ahead on a slight hill, shrouded by trees. The two guards nodded to two more guards that were standing watch at a door. One slid a key card in and the door parted. Cyrus was escorted down a long, black hallway to another door.

"He's waiting to speak with you."

Cyrus nodded and walked through. Inside was a large, circular room. Everything was black: the ceilings, the walls, the floor. It was painted as the universe. Stars and galaxies as if you were floating among them. Tozen sat in the middle cross-legged with his back to the door. His silhouette was outlined by the light from the doorway. He was seemingly in deep meditation.

It doesn't even look like he's breathing…

"Cyrus," Tozen said without moving.

It was the first time he called him by his first name.

"Tozen."

"It's been brought to my intention that you'd like to leave the premises, is this true?"

"If you heard it, it's true. Is there an issue?"

"Of course. I obviously cannot allow you to do that."

Cyrus took a hard step forward.

"I'm not like these other people that you've…abducted. I'm my own man. I decided to come here, and I'll decide when I leave."

Tozen laughed. It seemed to echo around the room in a supernatural way.

"Abducted? It seems like you've been making new friends around the compound. A particular affinity for Dr. Singh, I take it? You seem near old enough to be her father, I'd think you'd have a bit more tact."

"Tozen, cut the crap," Cyrus demanded, "I didn't come here to bed any of your captives. I came here to further my research."

"And you will do just that. Specimen 415 is too valuable. You've come too far with him for me to let it end."

"As much as I enjoy Neko, I'll say again: I'm leaving," Cyrus said sternly as he turned towards the door. Two guards walked in through the entrance armed with machetes, blocking his path.

"Fuck is this?" Cyrus asked incredulously.

Tozen's voice sounded closer but he hadn't moved an inch, "This is to insure that your work with 415 will be completed to my liking."

Cyrus eyed the soldiers and got into a fighting stance. He stood tall, one hand folded behind his back with his other outstretched in front of him, palm up. Token snickered. It sounded like he was right behind Cyrus, right over his shoulder whispering in his ear. A chill ran through him as a subtle, throbbing pain began to bubble in his temple.

"By force is it?" Cyrus asked one of the guards. His candor made the man nervous where he had once been brave. Cyrus noticed his grip slightly loosen on his machete.

"You WILL finish what you began, Mr. Santeaux. You have little choice." Tozen commanded from his seated, statuesque position. One of the guards gently grabbed at Cyrus, betrayed by his age. A quick series of straight hand jabs peppered the man's midsection, ending with a strike to the hand that launched the machete in the air. Cyrus reached up and caught it by the handle. He threw it at the other advancing guard, nailing his ankle and foot to the ground. Cyrus walked over and put him down swiftly, with a few quick strikes to the pressure points in his neck.

Tozen laughed. It rang like there were multiple versions of him in the room positioned in each corner. Cyrus stomped over to direct him face to face. He found him with his eyes and mouth shut When he spoke, it was like he was right next to Cyrus, but his face remained the same. The voice carried with no corresponding action.

"Mr. Santeaux. The members of my elite special forces, the Lightrays, will be arresting you."

"My ass!" Cyrus shouted, "I'm not waitin' till they get here!" He made a move for the door.

"They are already here," Tozen's voice said loud in Cyrus's ears. It was at that moment that three people emerged, camouflaged against the mural of infinite space. Their goggled eyes began to radiate a blue glow. They were completely covered from head-to-toe in a black uniforms, a rising sun over a katana was emblazoned on their chests. Holsters held their swords at their sides.

Cyrus eyes them cautiously, "Arresting me?! For assaulting these guards?! For trying to leave?!"

Tozen remained seated and perfectly still, his voice rang clear though he didn't shift from his position in the slightest.

"Your rights have been forfeited."

"What. What are you talking about?"

"The evidence suggests you murdered Dr. Jasper Singh when she came to visit your quarters," Tozen said calmly.

Cyrus felt his heart sink. A knot formed in the pit of his stomach. He swallowed hard in attempt to dismiss the creeping urge to vomit.

"That's bullshit and you know it!" Cyrus took a hard step towards Tozen. His speed as an old man shocked the Lightrays to attention. He had three sword tips at his throat instantly. Cyrus stared at Tozen in shock. There he was, covered from the neck down in a black, cloth robe. He sat cross legged with outstretched hands resting on his knees, palms up. Cyrus looked further. Tozen gave no indication that he was breathing, his chest didn't move at all. Not so much as a finger twitched. He was like a corpse positioned in some odd way as a funeral tribute. Cyrus continued to look on in disgusted disbelief. Tozen's voice rang loudly but his mouth never moved.

"You will be apprehended and imprisoned at a new location on the compound. There's no way that you can go back to the old one considering."

"Considering what?" Cyrus asked staring at Tozen's seemingly lifeless body, his disembodied voice piercing the back of his mind.

"Considering what you've done."

One of the Lightrays lowered his sword, the mechanical holster on his thigh locked it into place. He retrieved a small tablet computer from his belt and showed it to Cyrus.

It was a picture of his room. Jasper was slashed to death, sprawled across his bed. Her shirt was ripped, hanging off at the shoulder. Blood made the sheets glimmer with wetness.

"So, as you can see Mr. Santeaux, we are taking the needed precautions to insure the safety of the rest of our staff," Tozen mocked.

"Tozen…you mutha…what *are* you?"

"What am I? I am the true master of the Lotus Palm and evolved beyond your comprehension. And you are more important to our studies than you know, yet another reason I cannot grant your request."

"That's nonsense! There's absolutely no record of the Lotus Palm! You are *truly* insane to say you've found it, let alone *mastered* it," Cyrus yelled as the Lightrays bound his hands.

"And yet, here we are," Tozen's disembodied voice quickly said in return. The Lightrays all simultaneously nodded as if given a silent directive, then they escorted Cyrus out.

CHAPTER NINETEEN

March 31st 2004, 5:19 PM

Adam pulled up to the latest crime scene.

"Surprise, surprise, another shitty, dirty ass, unused ass, fucking apartment building," He complained to himself.

It was suspected this was a zealot's work, but that hadn't been confirmed yet. Usually, MCPD will initiate the call for a zealot cell, but it was common sense that some zealot operations were classified even to the police force. A large portion of the work done by a cop these days consisted of cleaning up so-called collateral "damage sites". Sometimes a zealot's mission would spill over into the unsuspecting lives of everyone around them, and since there's no way that a regular person could prepare themselves beforehand, they typically ended up really hurt or really dead. One second you're drinking your morning coffee on your way to work, the next minute you're accidentally hit with an errant kunai by a zealot you never saw. It's messy business. Typing up condolence letters to families was the worst part.

If this incident turned out to be collateral damage, it would be the eleventh such case in a week, an unusually high volume. Anyone with half a brain in the MCPD could tell you that. Adam realized that zealots were having a harder time out here. They were dealing with a growing number of criminals high out of their minds on The Dawn. Like the guy who had almost smashed his face in with a dumpster. He thought fondly of that night as he did the night he lost his virginity. They both were kind of the same, a step towards changing for the better.

Adam took his first hit shortly after he was discharged from the hospital. Within days, the fractured ribs that were supposed to take weeks to heal repaired themselves. He canceled all of his follow up appointments out of fear it would get back to his bosses, because it most certainly would get back. People didn't heal that fast. Shit, zealots didn't heal that fast.

The routine had become as systematic as brushing his teeth. Tap the vile with his finger gently to empty some ice on his nightstand. Then, he'd make neat lines with the key card to his apartment before inhaling them one by one with a small glass tube (you could buy one from any dealer). The high? The high was amazing. But the *dreams*? The dreams were *incredible*. The drug enhanced the lucidity of a person's dream state. It allowed them to be fully aware. His fondest one starred him in a hotel with every girl he's ever had sex with spread throughout some hotel, one in each room. Sometimes two.

Adam recalled the tingling numbness that began around his nose and gradually spread to his lips, followed by the warming sensation that spread across his skin. How his thoughts would race as the strength of all of his senses increased. How the surging feeling of invincibility felt almost like a sexual climax. Just thinking about it made him salivate. No more busting his ass trying to move up the ranks by taking down half-way crooks. He was finally moving on to greatness. Years of crawling around in the shit of the Metropolitan Corridor and now things were finally swinging in his favor.

That vial came in handy…that's for damn sure. But I'll never get as bad as these disgusting bastards. I mean, that blue tongue shit?

Adam shivered at the picture he could see in his mind, a side effect of heavy dreaming (the street term for using): the encroaching bluish hue from the back of the throat that stained the tongue and the thick indigo saliva that accompanied it. All he had to do was think of the face of some of the people he'd busted in base pop, people that would be holed up in an abandon building dreaming for days on end. It wasn't pretty.

No using on the job.

Adam rubbed his face and snapped back to the present. He hopped out of the car and made his way down the block, where several other squad cars were parked. Officers were sealing off the entrance to the blighted building with light-tape, others were on their comms giving orders or receiving them. Adam surveyed the crowd and found the chief.

"Chief Archibald, Officer Heller reporting."

"Heller," Archibald said as he turned around he flicked a cigarette onto the ground and extinguished it with his weathered leather shoe, "Glad you could join us."

"Glad you thought to ask for me personally, sir."

"Well, you're starting to develop quite the legend for yourself kid," Archibald noted, "Survive an attack by some psycho hopped up on smurf then come back to apprehend six perps in a week? That's enough to get anyone's attention."

"Well, it's not like I wasn't out there bustin' my ass *before*."

"Don't start smellin' yourself just yet, kid," Archibald reminded, "Your record is good. But it's not *that* good. Either way, glad to have you aboard now since you've had a lot of experience dealing with these freaks."

"Still got the scars to show it. What's goin' on here?"

"Looks like we got about eleven dead in the building, ran some scans and got some hits on a few. Some gang members, Ink Boys. This was probably a stash house for *his* supply."

"Olufemi 'Ink' Anyogu, the head of the Ink Boys and one of, if not the, biggest dealer of the Dawn in the Metropolitan Corridor."

"Wow, you can use the internet? Was I supposed to be impressed by that?" Archibald shot back. Adam was caught off guard by the sudden change in tone, he stumbled over his response.

"N-no, sir. I mean, you do know it, sir."

"Well then, shut up and listen. Someone was precise, knew where they were going, and knew what they were after," Archibald explained walking through digitally projected yellow tape marking the crime scene. Adam's enhanced senses did him no favors as he entered. The pungent smell of decaying flesh and everything that comes with it. It was disgusting when Adam was normal, but now? After his breakfast line? Shit made him want to projectile vomit right onto Archibald's bald spot.

"Jeeesus," Adam said covering his nose.

"You never smelled dead bodies before? I find that hard to believe, Heller."

"How long have they been in here?" Adam said quickly.

"My guess? Probably a week or two," Archibald said as he retrieved a pack of cigs from his coat pocket. He pounded it on his open palm before extracting a loose one and putting it to his lips.

"What about forensics?"

"Well, as they say, mention the devil and he appears," Archibald nodded his head in the direction behind Adam. Adam's head turned to see Paul walking up.

"Dunbar," Archibald calmly greeted.

"Sir. Heller."

Adam nodded in acknowledgement.

"Well, you guys have fun on your play date. With all this shit going on in the world, the pressure is coming from the top down. Everyone's feeling it. We can't continue to let these blue fucktards terrorize the Metro. It's going to get to the point where we won't be able to do anything to stop them…honestly."

"That's where we come in, sir," Adam chimed in with confidence. Archibald shot him a look that was equal parts shut the fuck up and get over yourself. That confidence dissolved like a sand castle at high tide.

"Bravo. Get to fucking work. Keep me posted," Archibald said as he took a drag from his cig.

"10-4."

"Yes, sir."

Archibald made his exit leaving a smoke trail, Dunbar, Adam, a few other officers, and a building littered with dead bodies in his wake. They were standing in what was presumably the lobby, but so many walls had been knocked down it was an even larger space.

"What the hell is wrong with him today? He's more of a douchebag than usual," Adam asked Dunbar with a smile.

"You know how he is. And he's not kidding. Everyone is feeling the pressure from these G-8 kidnappings, man," Paul sighed.

"Why the hell are we even worried, reports say the President is fine, right?"

"Today he is, but what about tomorrow? Or the next? You think the people that did this in one night really are having a problem finding where the President is? Even if he is with Zealot Prime's guard like they say."

"Sounds like working with your new buddy is making you more paranoid than usual. I could take you drunk off your ass talking about UFO cover-ups, but now? C'mon man, we all know that dude Bales is fucking weird," Adam dismissed.

Something caught Dunbar's eye. He walked over to a bloated corpse that had deep lacerations across his back, exposing his spine. The blood had congealed to a disgusting paste. The smell made Dunbar's face twitch. Meanwhile, Adam's artificially heightened sense of smell continued to do him no favors.

"Shef is…eccentric. But he's also a genius."

"I wouldn't know," Adam said as he surveyed the area, swearing that he just heard footsteps.

"Welp, that's why I brought this as proof. One of his creations, called a forb."

"Forb?"

"Forensic Orb."

"Not too imaginative with the names, I see," Adam chuckled.

Dunbar reached into a duffle bag and pulled out a smooth black orb that was a little bit larger than a grapefruit, "He said this is a prototype, but we're about to give it a go."

Dunbar pressed a button on the top of the forb and tossed it into the air. As gravity started to bring it back down to earth, the forb smoothly transformed and began to hover. It looked like a giant robotic eye with small pincer arms extending on each side. It immediately went about scanning the entire room with infrared beams.

"Yup. Genius it is then," Adam quipped as he sneezed into his hand. Blue specks of spittle were sprayed on his palm. He wiped it on his clothes before Dunbar could notice.

"All the info is being uploaded to my tablet computer. A couple minutes and we'll have everything from the dimensions of the building to the blood type of the victims," Dunbar said, sounding amazed.

"A couple minutes and this floating robot's going to put you out of a job, Paul."

A corner of Dunbar's mouth curled into a smile, "I think there's still a lot to be said for the human element."

"I guess," Adam spun around, his eyes went to the roof, "Wait, did you hear that?"

Dunbar was furiously scrolling through the new data on his tablet,
"Hear what," he asked without lifting his head.

Adam didn't respond, his eyes were glued to the ceiling seemingly following an invisible line or some unseen insect. He didn't notice Dunbar staring at him inquisitively. The other officers present exchanged confused glances with each other.

"You, you," Adam said pointing, "Go man the exits on this floor, don't let anything in or out. I'm going upstairs."

Adam moved hastily over to a flight of stairs. There was someone else here. And they were alive. His head jerked suddenly as he heard footsteps hitting another set of stairs

The fire escape?

Adam turned and yelled back at Dunbar, "Where's the nearest fire exit? The stairs?"

"Ah, yeah. The forb has everything you need about the building, the entrances, exits, the structural integrity, building materials, even the-"

"Paul! Muthaforb the forb! The exits to my ADA, please!"

"Geez man, sent," Dunbar said quietly turning back to his work as Adam went racing by. He kicked a rusted metal door off the hinges and saw the stairs. He started running up, taking them two or three at a time until he hit the third floor just in time to see the door gently close.

Adam took out his side arm and loaded a stun round into the chamber. He crept down the hallway, noticing subtleties in his surroundings that would have gone missed before, when he was normal. Another odor quickly invaded his nostrils. It didn't smell like the dead bodies on the first floor, but it was no less awful, an aromatic mix of unkempt homelessness and poor hygiene.

Smells like pure butt cheeks.

Adam didn't even realize that he had, in fact, used the scent to track the potential suspect. The Dawn was working on a subconscious level, altering his very nature. Adam could make out the faint traces of footsteps lightly in the dust and grime on the floor. He slowly raised his weapon and steadily crept further down the hallway, passing eerily ajar doors on either side. He stopped, faintly detecting nervous breathing from a bit further down.

Enough of this bullshit.

"MCPD! I know you're in there! Come out with your hands up!" Adam boomed, his voice reverberating throughout the building. He heard footsteps coming up the stairs behind him and knew his voice had raised the suspicion of the other officers. Adam took one moment to glance backwards. Two officers emerged from the staircase, followed by the forb floating behind them. When he turned his head around, he saw a vagabond burst out of an empty apartment a couple doors down and run in the opposite direction. He was fast. Had to be dreaming to be that fast. Without thinking twice, Adam charged after him in pursuit.

"Stop!" Adam shouted as he rounded a corner, the unknown man was a blur, he charged into another apartment, smashing through the door with his shoulder. Adam was close behind. He turned the threshold and immediately dived out of the way as an old refrigerator flew out, crashing into the apartment across the hall.

"Someone gonna drop a piano on me next?!" Adam asked aloud to no one. He rolled back up to his feet and bolted after the perp. They both rounded a corner into another long hallway. The perp reached for a door to smash through and quickly recoiled his hand as a stun round whizzed by. A few more followed, passing his face leaving wispy blue trails in the air. He felt the sting of one to his leg. The jolt of electricity would have paralyzed it, but he was so high he couldn't tell if this was real life or a dream, so he kept running.

He kept running towards the window at the end of the hallway because, in dreams, you don't get tired and jumping out of a window seems like a sound idea. Adam was close behind now. So close he could his footfalls cracking rotted wood with each step. The perp jumped through the window with no regard for himself and Adam followed suit. Officers on the ground looked up at the sound of the smashing glass, to see the two dark masses shooting through the air and into a large hole in the side of the adjacent building.

Adam hit the ground and effortlessly rolled to one knee, weapon drawn, aiming at the vagrant as he continued to run. Four shots hit him square in the back. He stumbled, then dropped. Adam was standing over him in moments.

"Don't fucking move!"

The man slowly rolled over onto his back with his hands up. His clothes were dirty and tattered, typical of the homeless crowd that infested base pop. He was a white male, probably in his mid-forties. His crusty beard was matted with dirt and grease. A dark blue color stained the hair around his mouth, a sure sign of blue tongue.

This guy's a heavey user. No doubt.

"You make one crazy move and I'll empty the clip into your face. Who are you?"

The man began to fumble over his response. The residual electric current was still surging through his body. A lesser person would've gone into a seizure by now, but The Dawn kept him conscious enough for this interrogation.

"Is…is this real?"

Adam kicked the man hard in the ribs, "Did that feel real, dumbass!? Name!"

"D-Dennis."

"Why'd you run?"

"You saw what happened to the rest 'em?! I didn't know if the guy who did it was going to come back or what…I always come here to dream, I didn't know there would be anybody else!"

"Dennis, I swear to God if you're bullshitting me."

Dennis's eyes widened. Adam could see the blue veins in them.

"No, I swear man! I swear!"

"Did you see who did it?" Adam asked sternly.

After a long pause, Adam yanked Dennis up by his shirt like a bully does a weak nerd. He held him up with one hand while he pressed the barrel of his gun up against his heart, something that he could never have done before. The adrenaline surged through him. He had to force back a smile.

"Listen you fuckin' freak. I squeeze off one more round right into your heart, you're goin' into cardiac arrest. I'm sure no one will miss you. So, TALK."

Dennis coughed and began to speak, "I…I just heard them all comin' in. There are holes everywhere so I just peeked through one to see what was goin' on."

Adam shook Dennis violently, his head snapped back causing another series of spastic coughs, "And?"

"And…and they were talking setting up a deal. A big one. I'm not gonna lie man, I was high out of my fuckin' mind! I didn't even know if I was still dreamin' or what. They're talkin', then all of a sudden blood sprays…it was already kinda dark but…but one guy man…he took *everyone* out. And quick. He was moving around like…like…"

"Like what?"

"Like an animal, bro."

Adam dropped Dennis and he crumpled to the ground coughing up dark blue spit.

"You hear him say anything?" he asked.

"I didn't hear nothin'. Only the screams. The screams will be back when I get high tonight, I guarantee you that… but fuck it, am I right man?"

Adam scowled back at Dennis as he holstered his weapon and took out his cuffs, "What're you talking about?"

"C'mon, man! A dreamer can always tell another one. We can see it on ya. We can smell it on ya," Dennis said as if he had suddenly made a new friend.

Adam snatched the man up and turned him around. He cuffed his hands tightly.

"You don't know shit about me."

Adam pressed the comm on his ear, "I got 'em. We're headed down now."

He pushed Dennis hard in the middle of his back and escorted him down and out of the building, into the sun. They both squinted hard when they emerged. The enhanced vision caused by the Dawn made a user's eyes more sensitive to light. They staggered back out into the alley between the two buildings where a throng of officers awaited. Dunbar came out of the apartment with the forb floating behind him like a mechanical pet.

"And another one," Adam said with arrogance. He noticed quickly it was a one-man celebration. Everyone else's faces were filled with a mixture of furrowed brows and stunned confusion. The same men he sent to man the exits of the building saw him leap through the air in a distinctly inhuman manner. He had to say something.

"Man, this bastard. He threw me across the alley into the other building like a rag doll. Tossed me just as easy as he threw that refrigerator."

Adam made sure to mention that since he knew some officers had witnessed it. He felt clever adding needed credence to his story. Some officers accepted this explanation and went about their business. Others looked on with reduced suspicion. Reduced, but still present. Some were glancing down at Adam's leg, which caused him to do the same. He must have cut himself during the jump. His slacks had a tear on the side, revealing a gash in his leg. The blood was an odd purple color. The cut was to the bone.

Shit…shit!

There was no amount of explaining for this particular situation. The blood discoloration was one of the easiest signs of a person under the influence. Coupled with his earlier super hero stunt, all the glares seemed justified. Cops had been kicked off the force for less. It was like finding out the MVP was juicing. He saw Dunbar's face in the crowd. The face of a friend allowed for a brief respite from the anxiety that was starting to choke him.

"Paul, make sure that guy makes it to the station. He may have some more info. Bribe him with a hot meal or somethin'," Adam said forcing laughter. Paul didn't respond in-kind. Instead he swiped furiously at his tablet computer. The forb hovering close by, its robotic eye fixated on Adam.

"Adam," Dunbar began, "Maybe…maybe you should come back to the station with us. You need to get that checked out."

Adam silently looked around and noticed some officers converging on him. Their weapons weren't drawn, but twitching fingers floated over holsters in wait.

Don't believe him.

Adam's eyes cautiously surveyed the surroundings. There were more officers present than when he arrived earlier. They couldn't have been called for one homeless dude and a bunch of dead bodies.

Dunbar stretched out a hand, sensing the tension rising.

"Adam, it's cool man. Just come back to the station," Dunbar said lightly.

"Fuck you, Paul!" Adam unexpectedly erupted, "You think I don't know what you're thinking, what all of you are thinking! I know that damn thing has already scanned my blood!"

Dunbar's eyes went to the ground subconsciously confirming Adam's theory.

That's not all…

"Get the hell outta my head!" Adam snapped. Everyone became visibly disturbed by this. To them, he was talking to himself.

"Wait. It's not from the cut in my leg."

Dunbar's eyes got big as saucers. Big ass saucers. Like a child caught doing something he had no business. Or an adult for that matter. Dunbar didn't respond.

"You scanned me after I sneezed? You knew about the shit *then*?"

"Adam…"

The forb had indeed scanned Adam's saliva and now his blood. It revealed what everyone around him had already deduced. Adam watched Dunbar's eyes go swiftly to his tablet, undoubtedly picking up some new information being streamed to him.

That fucking forb!

The ability to sniff out a hobo didn't seem like it was of much use in the present situation. Then Adam remembered that he was stronger than everyone and it emboldened him. What Dennis had said to him earlier was right. You *could* smell it. It was more like you could *sense* it. Adam knew no one else there was using.

If you run...I'll find you.

Adam's eyes widened.

What? Who was that?

Paranoia instantly gripped him. Every set of eyes that he looked into seemed evil, like all they wanted to do was hurt him. And humiliate him. He wasn't about to let anyone force him back to who he was before. Not even a friend. Not even his best friend.

Adam quickly pulled out his gun and fired a stun round into the forb. The electric overload caused it to malfunction, revert back to ball form, and fall to the ground.

"Shit! Adam don't!" Dunbar yelled as officers pulled their guns in response. Adam's remaining shots dropped as many cops. It only took one to incapacitate a normal person. They seemed so weak now. He reached to his waist and took out a retractable baton, MCPD standard issue, and turned to run back down the alley towards the street. There were five cops standing in front of him. Judging him. Their smug stupid faces were just asking to die.

Do it.

He charged at them as stun rounds sizzled past his ears. He crushed the teeth of the first with a swift swing of the baton and ducked under return fire faster than his counterparts could decipher. To Adam, everything was moving slowly and covered in a haze that resembled heat radiating from a street in the summer. Devastating blows to the knees and femur crumpled another of his once fellow officers. Before one could hit the ground, Adam scooped him up to use as a human shield. Stun rounds plugged him and he began to convulse. Adam threw him at the remaining cops in his way with a sling of his hand. The mass of bodies slammed into a nearly parked squad car denting it and shattering glass. The ferocity with which he fought frightened the rest from a direct confrontation. With no one in his way, Adam bolted down the alley. He didn't feel tired. It felt like he was floating over the ground.

It felt like he was dreaming.

He emerged into the street and eyed the platform for the solar rail. He could hear sirens wailing in the distance and laughed to himself.

I can hear that shit and none of them can. Heh, advantage me.

He took a deep breath and jumped towards a series of fire escapes. Using his new strength and agility, he made for the roof like a monkey, leaping and pulling his way up. He stood, reached to his ear, and yanked off his comm before tossing it over the edge. Adam sized the distance between where he stood and the next building. He gathered himself like a track athlete and charged in that direction. He leapt and soared high over the ground and repeated this until a mischievous grin was plastered across his face. His feet hit another roof when he noticed someone perched on an adjacent ledge. Adam came to a complete stop, cursing himself for getting so lost he didn't reload his weapon.

The perched silhouette, shadowed by the skyscrapers and solar rails, spoke deliberately.

"You heard me," The voice from the dark said.

"How do you...was that you? In my head?" Adam asked bewildered.

"Yes. I'm glad you followed my directions. It was for your own good."

Adam reflected back on what he had left behind. His high was coming down and the pain in his leg was starting to become more prominent. He took a step forward. The silhouette quickly hopped off of his perch and stood with sword drawn in the dark.

"Don't come any closer. I will kill you if you don't agree to answer my question."

Is this a...

"No. I assure you, it is not," the voice in the dark commented.

"You're responsible for those murders, aren't you?"

"Yes."

"Why did you do it?" Adam asked/

"I believe I said you would be answering *my* questions."

Adam thought for a moment.

"You don't have the luxury to weigh your options either, Mr. Heller. They will definitely remove you from the force for this. Using? Using on the job? Assaulting an officer, no offi-CERS, with deadly force *while* under the influence? What are you going back to?"

Adam's solemn silence was enough for the shadow to continue.

"Assist me and I will show you things. Show you how deep that power goes."

Adam looked up towards the voice as he emerged from the shadows and tossed a blue vial. Adam caught it and wondered at the blue liquid in the palm of his hand.

"That. Is uncut power."

CHAPTER TWENTY

Seventeen Minutes Later

"Get Archibald now," Dunbar ordered the closest officer. He immediately obliged. Dunbar's eyes were glued to his tablet computer. The information scrolling across the screen and launching into different windows would have been dizzying to anyone else, but to him they were forming a picture.

I hate that I'm right all the time. Everything says it's him.

Dunbar made an urgent call of his own. The line picked up after one ring, if that.

"Shef?"

"You sir, have some good timing," Shef said, "I have some bad news and some bad news."

"Shef, before you get to that. You need to look at the info from the forb. These murders-"

"I know about the murders," Shef coolly interrupted, "The forb looks like a big ass eye for a reason, Paul. I can see everything that happens in real time."

Way to make yourself look stupid.

"Yeah," Dunbar laughed off, "Yeah, of course."

"That guy? Officer Adam Heller is it? A friend of yours?"

Dunbar's eyes went to the ground, aware that the forb was acting as Shef's eyes.

"I've known him for a long time. Good cop."

"Doesn't seem too good right about now if you ask me."

"I didn't," Dunbar shot back.

"Well, that's funny because you're the one that called *me*. So there must be something you want to ask," Shef replied annoyed.

There was an awkward pause as Dunbar was forced to silently acknowledge Shef was right. He let him proceed.

"I got the floor now? Good," Shef said sarcastically, forcing the last word, "I reverse-engineered this product, The Dawn. I'm within 80% of the original composition, still a good number to see how it works. Man, Paul...this is worse than I thought."

"I know."

"And I think of some pretty wild shit."

"That is true."

Shef sighed, "Come to the lab so you can see it for yourself. A livestream won't do it justice. You seem like the type that needs to be scared into action."

Dunbar hesitated for a moment, not entirely certain how to take that remark. He let it roll off of his back, like he did most things.

"I'll be there momentarily," Dunbar finally said.

"I'll get some donuts for you, bro. No bullshit, not even trying to be funny because you're a cop."

"I genuinely appreciate that, sir."

"Sir?" Shef chuckled, "I told you about that, Paul. I'm not a cop or a zealot or in the military, you don't need to do that type shit."

"I think you're mistaken," Dunbar replied calmly, "I call you *sir* because you're old."

Shef burst into laughter, "Score one for the kid. I was gonna hang up on you, but now I'll give you a second to speak on the crime scene."

"I'm not sure what you know already, but..."

Shef interrupted Dunbar again, "I know the body count, caught a glimpse of the fridge tossing scene, awesome by the way, pulled the IDs, ran them against the MCPD database, pretty much every other corridor's database as well, AND international..."

It was Dunbar's turn to interrupt. "Wow, are you just going to ramble or will I have to run an algorithm to pull out anything useful in what you're saying?"

"Funny," Shef said short and humorless, "I think there's a connection. Just get to the lab, smart ass

"10-4."

CHAPTER TWENTY-ONE

348 Toothpicks

Cyrus sat across from Tarin as tears streamed down her face. They were seated at the same table in the courtyard where he met with Tozen and Orion.

"You took my only son from me."

"Tarin...it was only because I knew. I knew he could do it," Cyrus pleaded.

"Only because you pushed him so hard, Cy. You pushed him *so* hard. He was a kid who never got a chance to be a kid. I barely got a chance to be his mother. Mount Z raised him. Not me."

"Tarin, don't say that."

"It's true," Tarin responded, her voice sounded multi-layered like there were many versions of her speaking at once, "You took him away. And then you went away. Is that how you show love to your family, Cyrus?"

"No, I..."

"Is it?!" Tarin's voice boomed with anger, the tears streaming down her face started to glow like embers in a dying fire. Each tear became a flame that left a black, charred streak as it trickled down Tarin's face. When they fell they melted through the glass on the table. They fell onto Tarin's clothes, causing the cotton to erupt in flame. In moments she was engulfed, only her silhouette through the fire remained.

"Cyrus, I love you. But you caused me too much hurt. You love your work, your science, your globetrotting and the bitches that you have in all these different places more than me and Everett. You gave me no choice."

The flame flashed brightly and dissipated leaving only ash floating in the wind. Cyrus dropped his head as tears welled up in his eyes. His ex-wife accidentally overdosed on prescription meds a couple years after Everett graduated from Mount Z. Cyrus always felt that it wasn't an accident. He lifted his head and was startled to find Tozen grinning maniacally across from him. Before he could say anything more, the ground underneath the entire compound exploded like a volcanao. Cyrus sat up in his bed soaking in sweat and breathing heavily. The dreams that Jasper had warned about had become common place now. Cyrus woke from a nightmare two or three times a week. Most ended in his death. All had Tozen in them. His life was starkly different than when he first arrived and was treated like a king. Now, he was just one of the staff, no more important than the person who picks up Aureus's shit.

The weight melted off since Tozen had him arrested for Jasper's murder. That seemed so long ago, clouded in the mist of nightmares. Cyrus had no way of knowing how much time actually elapsed. All of his communication with the outside world had been severed. A rough estimate came from toothpicks. Once every week, he was brought a turkey sandwich for dinner with an olive stuck to the top with a toothpick. He used those to gauge. He had over three hundred of them. Guards were constantly monitoring his every move. He couldn't take a dump without one standing at the door. The bones in his cheeks became more visible, even under his newly grown beard. He swung his thin legs over the edge of his bed and got himself ready for the day. Training with Neko was set to begin within the hour.

The lasting damage from the sparring sessions started to leave their mark on his frame. Tozen insisted upon increasing the intensity of the physical training in particular. Sometimes he even sacrificed members of his own security detail to the ring. Neko had become ferociously adept with the Tiger Style, his proficiency approaching master level by all estimations. The surge of his repressed animal instinct often times flashed during battle, for better or worse, something that Tozen seemed to relish. His villainous laughter at the sight of one of his guards being ripped to shreds grated in Cyrus's mind. Physically, Neko was growing faster than normal, the body of a 25-year-old Olympian with the mind of an impressionable teenager. The thought of Tozen spending more time with Neko made Cyrus want to throw up. The poison of his ill intent was enough to corrupt anyone; Orion was a testament to that.

During his imprisonment, Cyrus took it upon himself to do as much research as he could about one subject in particular: The Lotus Palm Manuscript. Rumors were circulating about it since Cyrus first walked into the subterranean headquarters of the ARU. A document passed down through generations of monks and coveted as holding the secret to the ultimate hand-to-hand fighting style. The God Style or the Omnipotent Fist were also common names for it. The one style from which all were derived. Xi would always stick to the common refrain of, "It doesn't exist". Yet, every time Xi dismissed the speculation, it was accompanied by an ever-so-subtle nervousness that Cyrus was hip to. Almost like Xi didn't believe the words himself. Or more appropriately, Xi was *hoping* that it did not exist because he knew the dangers that would come to fruition if it did. Cyrus assumed he was seeing Xi's fears realized.

The internet usage was monitored almost as heavily as his movements. Finding information was much more difficult than it needed to be, but that was Tozen's command. The library on the compound became a bit of a sanctuary. Though, he was always followed by guards to and fro, they didn't stand over his shoulder as he read. He deduced it was because most couldn't read. Seemed par for the course for a bastard like Tozen. His ego would ensure that he was the smartest person in the room, in tandem with being the most vicious. Cyrus was only able to piece together bits of information from what he could find. Most of it consisted of accounts passed down over the years from different monks, masters, and kung-fu gurus.

It was increasingly difficult to discern what was the truth and what was a hyperbolic fairy tale. There hadn't been a known practitioner of the Lotus Palm in over two hundred years, if not longer. There were many reoccurring Chinese characters that Cyrus could recognize from the documents: generation, lineage, family. The style itself was said to require a near incomprehensible level of focus, and even still that was not enough. People who sought to learn the technique allegedly also consumed a serum derived from a rare lotus flower, that's how it got its namesake. Ingesting the mixture sent the user into a near comatose state of meditation.

"The master of the Lotus Palm is also the master of traversing the line between life and death. Through this, a grander enlightenment will emerge."

That excerpt stuck with Cyrus slong after he read it. It brought back memories of seeing Tozen's lifeless body somehow communicating with everyone. Had he found it? There was no way he would be able to conduct the research needed to find all the answers.

I have to contact Xi and tell him that the manuscript is real.

No...warn him...warn him that the manuscript is real.

A chime rang through the air. Cyrus threw on a clean shirt and limped towards the door. He opened it expecting a guard. It slid ajar to reveal Tozen.

"Good morning, Mr. Santeaux."

"Tozen."

"You look weary," Tozen said with a smile as he slinked past Cyrus into his quarters. Cyrus noticed that he was holding an aluminum briefcase in one hand.

"To what do I owe the pleasure of this visit," Cyrus asked with disgust.

Tozen laughed, "I have something to deliver to you, well, to your understudy since you'll be seeing him in a bit."

Tozen walked over to a counter top and dropped the aluminum case down on it with a metallic thud. He unlocked and opened the lid. Light flickered off of the contents of the case as Cyrus walked over to get a better look. He noticed a slip of paper in the case as well.

"What is this?"

"This," Tozen said stroking the gauntlet lovingly, "Is the product of years of research. Technology that is powered by the very blood in a person's veins."

Cyrus eyed the golden gauntlet in the case, "Powered by blood?"

"More accurately," Tozen said as he gazed into the case, "A person who has been injected with The Dawn. The more of it that exists in a person's body, the better the reaction. We have devised a means to create symbiotic technology."

"Hmph. I remember a time when you were decidedly anti-technology," Cyrus noted, reminiscing about one of their very first conversations.

"Well, times have changed," Tozen replied.

"I'd say they have."

There was an awkward silence as Tozen stared at Cyrus for a moment before breaking into the smile that Cyrus had grown to detest over the years.

"What's the note inside," Cyrus inquired.

"Oh, that's from you," Tozen said, his disgusting smile widening with delight, "It's important for Neko to feel comfortable enough to put the gauntlet on. A note from you should do exactly that."

"But I didn't write anything. You have me held up in here."

Tozen picked up a pen and pad that was sitting in close proximity to the aluminum case. After a few moments of scrawling on the paper, he turned it around and showed Cyrus. The shock in his face created delight in Tozen's. The signature looked exactly like Cyrus had done it himself.

Mother...he's been writing my letters...I'm sure of it.

"Nice trick."

"It does prove useful," Tozen laughed, "I wrote Orion on your behalf shortly after the Ark was lost to us. Thanks to your son, I might add. Quite the zealot, that young man."

"You wrote Orion pretending to be me? For what?"

"I was still uncertain of his dedication. I had to assure him that another man of stature from the corridors was willing to take up my cause. I don't think I have to worry about that anymore."

"He's a fiend for the Dawn. I'm assuming *that's* where his loyalty lies."

"Perhaps," Tozen conceded.

"Why are you disclosing this to me now?"

"Because you will die here."

The statement caught Cyrus off guard. He responded calmly despite that, "Sorry to disappoint, but we don't share the same vision."

Tozen sneered at the comment before breaking into light laughter, "Be that as it may, you still have a job to finish with Neko. Take this to him."

Cyrus nodded as Tozen made his way out of the door. He turned back to the case and rubbed his hand over the top. The next doorbell would be the guards to escort him to the training grounds. He took the rest of his time to finish getting dressed and grab a solid oak walking staff that he had fashioned for himself. No sooner did he finish, an electronic bell sang through the air. The doors slid open and two guards stood waiting.

"Mr. Santeaux."

"Gentlemen."

The party traveled the familiar tree-lined path to the training grounds. The eyes of the employees were glued to them as they made their way through the compound. Cyrus could understand why. When he first arrived, he was looked at as an equal to Tozen. Now, with his deteriorating physical condition, the gazes reflected pity more than respect. Every bit of his age was beginning to show coupled with the added stress of being held against his will. The restrictions didn't allow access to the many exercise facilities anymore. The complimentary vitamins regiment was stopped and the menu got considerably distasteful. Truly, the only workouts he got now was with Neko. They rounded the bend and came up upon the sight of Neko meditating in the center of the ring. He smelled them as they approached and his eyes shot open with excitement and genuine happiness.

"Sensei!"

"Neko," Cyrus warmly greeted as the guards took to standing on the edges of the square.

"Sensei, what is that? Did you bring food? You brought food!"

"No, Neko," Cyrus laughed, "this is a gift."

"A gift of food?"

"Wrong again."

Cyrus placed the case in front of Neko. He eyed it suspiciously before looking back up to Cyrus.

"It's yours Neko. You can open it."

Neko cautiously fumbled with the locks before opening the case. The sunlight reflected magnificently off of the gold finish of the gauntlet.

"Whoaaaa," Neko exclaimed with the jubilation of a kid that just got Castle Grey Skull for Christmas.

He picked up the note that was laying in the case and unfolded it. He eyed the words before slowly reciting them back to his master.

"To Neko, my prized student. I love you more than my own son. –Cyrus"

Cyrus concealed his true feelings under a warm, smiling mask. The words he knew he didn't write made Neko's eyes light up with pride. A cruel sleight of hand trick executed by Tozen. Cyrus could envision him laughing at this very moment.

He truly is evil.

"Well, are you going to try it on," Cyrus asked to break his train of thought.

Neko slowly slipped the gauntlet out of the case. A golden arm piece that extended up to the elbow with five circular rings built around each finger. He flipped it upside down where there was a small button on the side of the wrist. Neko turned the gauntlet around in his hands a few times before returning to the mystery button. His eyes moved from the button, to Cyrus, and back to the button. With a deep breath he pressed it in. The underside of the gauntlet unfolded to reveal a section to insert the arm. There were four hypodermic needles lining the inner sides. The sight made Neko look up to Cyrus with uncertain fear. This was the first time Cyrus had seen the intimidating intricacies of the device himself. He began to have doubts.

"I see you've received your gift," Tozen's voice echoed from behind them. Cyrus whipped around to see the familiar figure walking down to the edge of the training ring. Their eyes met as Tozen's knowing smile cut through the air, "Your master really loves you, Neko."

Neko was silent and visibly uncomfortable.

"You should try it on. Like he said," Tozen goaded.

With one final glance at Cyrus, Neko slowly placed his arm, palm-side up, into the gauntlet. Nothing happened for the first few moments. Tozen's eyes were wide as saucers. Then a hard snap shut the gantlet closed around Neko's arm with the ferocity of trap breaking the neck of a starving rodent. The long needles had nowhere to go but deep into Neko's arm. He screamed a terrible sound, a mix of a dying animal and a newborn infant. Cyrus's eye twitched as he watched purplish blood drip from the seams of the joints and drop on the ground. Neko was weeping. Tozen reared his head back and bellowed laughter.

"Well! Now would be a good time to test the capabilities, I'd think," Tozen assessed as me motioned for the two guards that were standing close by.

"What do you say to…three on one?"

Neko looked up with fear. Cyrus turned to Tozen, "What the hell are you trying to do? Sending us three at Neko? He doesn't even know how to use this thing."

"You are wrong, as you have been with increasing frequency as of late, Mr. Santeaux, I was talking about *you.*"

Cyrus watched as the two guards positioned themselves around him, machetes drawn. Neko was still clutching at his arm.

"Do you see my vision now," Tozen asked sarcastically.

The two men charged forward at Cyrus, swinging wild, untrained slashes at his head and chest. He spun his staff and landed crushing blows on his assailants. He did his best to elude them, still managing to squeeze out what little speed he had left in his old and battered frame. He sidestepped another vertical slash, hopped backwards as another passed by his face. He was panting heavily, becoming winded. One guard began to feel himself a bit too much. He charged in overconfidently and was met with a series of quick jabs from the end of Cyrus's staff, hitting various pressure points along his arm. He dropped his machete as his arm went limp.

"Ha ha! The old man still has some left!" Tozen boasted, "Neko. Get up and get in the fight."

"NO," Neko yelled through tears, still seated on the ground.

Tozen's head ripped over to his direction, eyes burning into Neko's face.

"You have no choice in the matter. NOW GET. UP."

Neko, still sniveling, went to wipe his tears and pulled back at the cold metal against his face. That quickly he had forgotten the gauntlet had fused to him. It felt like a part of his body now. He slowly rose to his feet.

"Sensei…I'm…I'm sorry," Neko whimpered softly as he rushed forward.

"Neko," Cyrus yelled, breaking his concentration. A kick to his back came through the small window of opportunity that his lack of focus created. Sharp pain shot down both legs as he stumbled forward, propping himself up weakly on his staff. Tozen stood off to the side with his arms crossed as if watching children play in the yard. The whole ordeal was entertainment, life and death for show. Cyrus wanted to rip his face off. Jerry would have suggested as much. For the first time in his life, Cyrus felt legitimate hatred for another man. If you could even call him that.

Cyrus rolled forward to his feet, surprising everyone. He quickly turned as a guard was slashing forward. He spun inside the guard's outstretched arm and smashed his elbow into the bridge of his nose with a sickening crunch. Blood spurted everywhere as Cyrus swept the guard off his feet with his staff. He caught a glimpse of Tozen's face. Sheer delight. The other guard, with one of his arms still limp, came charging in foolishly with a machete in his off hand. Cyrus took the offensive. He skipped over to the guard and kicked his shin, hopped backwards to knee his face as he was falling in an effortless manner.

"The Black Panther Fist is a *brutal* technique," Tozen said with genuine respect. Cyrus ignored him.

You're time is comin' muthafucka.

Cyrus stood facing Neko, who was already in his Tiger Style stance.

"Neko, you don't have to do this."

The child's catlike eyes were glistening with tears, making them look even more hypnotic.

"Neko. I love you."

Neko's ears perked up a small, warm smile came through the sadness.

"Neko," Tozen called from behind them, dashing their sentimental moment to pieces, "If you ever want a family, if you want ever *anything*, you will do what I say."

"Don't listen to him!" Cyrus pleaded with his pupil.

"But…I want a family," Neko cried back.

"Tozen you son of a bitch. Toying with him like this!"

This time it was Tozen who ignored.

"Fight him. It's the only way. We have to test out that new gift that Mr. Santeaux was so gracious enough to give to you. When all this is done, Mr. Santeaux will become your new father. I will make sure of it."

Neko's eyes darted from person to person. He couldn't discern the genuine love from the fraudulent. Despite his heightened senses, they seemed the same. Neko's eyes swung back to Cyrus. He took a long deep breath.

"Neko!"

With a quick leap Neko was at him. He struck at Cyrus's face and neck, his hands deftly transitioning between clawed fingers and clinched fists. Cyrus struggled to keep up; Neko's blows were starting to land. He was much larger now. And stronger. Cyrus managed to parry a punch and push himself out of the way with his staff. He got enough distance to gather and return to his own stance.

If this is how it has to go down…

Neko turned and charged, this time he was unexpectedly met with a swift back kick. He was fast enough to move before it crushed his face. He slid under Cyrus' outstretched leg and hopped back to his feet. The two reengaged in their fierce fight. Cyrus spun his staff like an airplane propeller around his body, blocking attacks and firing off his own strikes. Tozen was indeed entertained by their viiolent dance, a sage of the Black Panther and the future of the Tiger Style. It was quite the sight to behold. Neko roared as the frustration of glancing blows were starting to mount. Tozen quickly picked up on this and struck like a viper.

"You can't even land one blow! What has all this training been for?! I'm sure Mr. Santeaux is thinking that his *real* son is so much better!"

Cyrus felt Neko's intensity suddenly change. His blows became more unpredictable and ferocious. He was bearing his fangs and spitting animalistic grunts with each miss. Neko shot a jump kick that dislodged the staff from Cyrus's hands. He quickly spun backwards and kicked a Machete off of the ground into his hand just as Neko was charging in. He slapped him across the face with the flat side of the blade. Neko jumped backwards touching his face. He almost seemed surprised that Cyrus didn't kill him.

"Yes! Embrace that," Tozen instigated.

Neko bared his fangs and snarled. It was a low, intimidating murmur. The gold on his gauntlet began to shimmer unnaturally. It looked like the ripples in a pond when a rock is skipped across the surface. Cyrus and Tozen stared with a common feeling of shock and amazement. Neko's eyes were locked on Cyrus. He held out his arm as the gold moved and rolled out, elongating each fingertip into a sharp talon. Neko flexed his hand a couple of times before returning to his stance.

"Wonderful," Tozen excitedly shouted clapping his hands, "Now, FINISH HIM!"

Neko sprung forward, slashing down at Cyrus with his golden gauntlet. It made a slight screeching sound as each finger cut through the very air. Cyrus pulled back and raised his machete, he counterattacked, swinging and poking at Neko.

"He thinks you're weak, Neko! He's not even trying!"

Neko shot forward a series of jump kicks flowing into punches. A three hit combination staggered Cyrus backwards, he swung the machete wildly. Neko slashed upwards with his golden hand, sending pieces of the blade flying through the air. The edges came raining down on them, sticking into the ground around their feet as the battle continued. Cyrus dropped the handle to catch a punch aimed right between his eyes. He could feel the gold metal was warm to the touch as it started to squirm under his hands. The disgusting sensation made him jerk back. Neko danced between fists with somersaults and flips, displaying amazing command of the Tiger Style. The animal instincts added a ferocity to the technique that made it uniquely his own. For whatever reason, the gauntlet on his hand seemed to exacerbate that effect. They both paused for a moment. Cyrus let loose a rare smile. If anything, he had to reluctantly agree with Tozen.

He's ready.

Cyrus jumped backwards a little too late. Neko slashed, claws streaked across Cyrus's chest from shoulder to shoulder. The pain was immediate. Cyrus fell backwards hard, smacking his head into the ground. His eyes were dazed and blurry. He looked down at his chest. Neko's hand cut through everything cleanly. Four precise slashes through his skin and muscle. He could even see where his bone had been cut through his wounds. Like a knife through butter. He panted and coughed blood and thought about his family and his failures as a man and came to the realization that Tozen was right after all. He was going to die here. He could hear Tozen's footsteps approaching. Cyrus glanced up to see the blood splattered on Neko's emotionless face. He assumed the other steps he heard in the distance were more guards. Tozen stood over him, looking down with pity and spite.

"A shame. I was hoping you would stay alive a little bit longer. If everything goes as it should, there was going to be a modest family reunion I'm sure you would have enjoyed," Tozen lamented.

Cyrus stared up at him through bloodshot eyes, gagging. His head fell to the side. Neko was crouched down in a ball, the gravity of all that had transpired was starting to sink in. Tears silently streamed down his face. Each blink casted Cyrus into darkness for increasingly long stretches of time. The other guards had arrived as he shut his eyes and could not force them open again. The last thing he heard was Tozen's command.

"Feed him to Aureus."

CHAPTER TWENTY-TWO
April Fool's Day 2004

You wouldn't believe me if I told you. The dawn that Orion gave me, bro? It's on another level. It's on another level on another planet in another galaxy. It's like eating crappy gas station burritos every night and then getting some filet mignon. You realize how what you had before was absolute shit. This is like that. I can't even believe I was *snorting* it. I look at all the other dumbasses crawling around in base pop like cavemen. Now that I've had a taste of that pure. No way I'm going back to buying bags. Not when I can get whatever I need from Orion.

Orion. That guy is…weird. That gasmask lookin' thing he has on his face is way freaky. Like…some S&M shit or something. But whatever. He's got the goods. And all I have to do is help him with this job that he has to pull. He said, "I'd be well taken care of" so I take that to mean I gotta big payday at the end of this, too. He's already covering all of my expenses. Rent, food, damn video games. Never gotta bonus working in the MCPD, that's for damn sure.

I can get used to this. I've never felt stronger in my life. Last night, ran a mile in three minutes. Maybe less. When I sleep at night, Orion is there and we train. He says that's one of the perks of using The Dawn in its pure form. As if it couldn't get any better? The dreams I had before felt real, but these *are* real. He's been teaching me different fighting styles. Monkey Style, yadda yadda. Fancy hand-to -hand combat stuff that we didn't get at the police academy. I don't know if I got the patience for it. Whatever happened to a good ol' fashioned bar fight? No styles or stances named after animals and shit. Just two hands.

The best part is that time doesn't work the same. We can be in there for days and when I wake up, it's only been an hour. It's crazy, I feel like…I'm not scared of anyone anymore. No zealot, no cop. No one.

Adam was eagerly awaiting the call from Orion. Today was the day of the job. The details were few and far between. Another set of eyes is all that was needed. He wouldn't be doing too much. Though if that was the case, why all the training? Adam didn't let those questions second guess his decision. The only one he could truly make. There was a warrant for his arrest in the Metro corridor. The Mecca was probably on the case now as well. He knew they were looking for him from the bulletins coming through on his comm before they killed his access. He was certain Dunbar's smart ass probably brought that up. He had the tendency to leave no stone unturned. It's what made him so good. At that moment, his personal comm began to gently vibrate. He reached up to his ear to accept the transmission.

"Yeah?"

"We leave now."

Through the darkness they leapt, silhouettes traced with the glow of the Metropolitan Corridor's skyline. Adam felt exhilaration like never before. Leaping from rooftop to rooftop, racing down solar rail tracks. He felt like a superhero. Orion led the way soaring from building to building, streaking up the sides of buildings, surely a blur to any normal person who caught a glimpse. It was strange, Adam thought, that everything seemed so peaceful when they moved around like this. The world swirled around them like a Van Gogh painting in slow motion. They covered huge stretches in mere breaths. It felt like a dream. Adam was unsure if it was or not. They stopped atop a large building belonging to an engineering firm. Orion pulled out a small, cylindrical device that transformed into a telescope. He peered through it before pointing down at a smaller building across the street.

"There. That's my target."

"Okay, so what do I do?"

Orion reached to his utility belt and pulled out another small cylindrical device. It was a remote detonator. Adam looked down at Orion's outstretched hand uncertain, "What? What do you want me to do with this?"

"Thirty seconds from when I make my descent, press it."

"What does it do?"

"It sets off a small EMP bomb that I placed earlier. Electrical signals within at least a five block radius will be killed. My target is quite tech savvy."

"Tech savvy, eh? Reminds me of someone I know."

"Save the sentimental reminiscing and focus on the one task before you," Orion hissed through his mask, his dark black eyes drilling into Adam.

"Gotcha. Thirty seconds," Adam responded using confidence as a front for fear. Orion nodded, turned, and ran towards the edge of the roof. He took a massive leap through the air, drawing his sword as he soared. He stretched out his arm and pierced a glass window with his blade, gracefully going through the surface like an Olympic diver.

26…27…28…29…

Adam pressed down on the detonator and waited. Suddenly there was a loud explosion from down in base pop. He looked over the edge of the building down into the skyscraper lined abyss. There was silence. Then a spherical, blue field began to emerge and grow from the epicenter of the EMP bomb. It steadily grew wider and wider, engulfing everything it touched, turning it to blackness. Adam watched the oddly beautiful display; the bright blue of the EMP field fanning out like a perfectly formed mist providing the only light as it drained the power from everything it touched. The darkness created a perfect canvas for it. Before he could realize it, the EMP field was growing faster, it engulfed the building across the street and continued to swell. Adam took a few steps backwards from the ledge. It crept closer and closer to him. When it was within feet from his face, the field dissipated into the night. Everything within a five block radius, as Orion stated, was pitch black. Adam was impressed with his attention to detail.

"Now what," Adam asked to no one in particular. He paced and waited atop the building.

He only needed me to press a button and be a lookout? I can't even see shit...how am I supposed to be a lookout?

Adam walked back to the edge of the roof. There was an eerie vibe emanating from the gloom. It was similar to standing on a beach and staring into the ocean at night, unsure how deep the depths actually went or what secrets they kept. Adam retrieved a small flashlight from his belt. When he clicked it on, it was a bright star in the mist of the darkness caused by the EMP. The flashlight beamed undiluted across the street as Adam retraced Orion's path into the adjacent building. The broken window was in his sight. His confidence bubbled over, boiling down into hubris.

I can help. Whatever it is, I can do more than just stand here.

Adam walked backwards, turned, and sprinted towards the edge. He jumped into the air with considerably less grace and only his flashlight to guide him. He crashed through the window frame clumsily, landing on the ground with a thud muffled by broken glass. Adam stood and brushed the glass shards off of his clothes.

Now. Now I'll show him what I can do.

CHAPTER TWENTY-THREE

Fourteen Minutes and Thirty Seconds Ago

Shef and Dunbar stood over an elaborately designed plastic maze. There was a small camera attached to the back of a fat, white lab rat who was sniffing at a yellow starting line. Two plastic cages were sitting on an adjacent table. One was empty, the other contained three lab rats.

Why is he separating the specimens? Unless...he's testing the dosage levels If anybody can make the connections he can. Got to be on my stuff today. Just don't make yourself look like an ass, Paul.

Cameras lined around the maze streamed video to monitors on Shef's main rig. Data streamed along one side of the screen.

"So, this chubby guy that you see with the cam strapped to him," Shef said pointing a mechanized finger at the rat.

"Yep. What's his deal?"

"I've been giving him and the gang steady injections of what I've reverse engineered from the street version of dawn. I have it at about 75% accurate by my estimations. Good enough to do this. Shit is trippy, bro."

"Only a difference in injection levels," Dunbar asked.

"Yes, but for a reason. I gave that one triple the amount. I call him Heavy Dosage, or Heavy D for short."

"The overweight lover?"

"Precisely."

He opened the door and the rat took off like he wasn't in a maze at all. He knew every twist and turn to get to the end, which he made it to in no time.

"Okay, so he knows the maze," Dunbar said trying not to sound sarcastic. Shef reached in and retrieved the rat. He held it so that Dunbar could see his face. The eyes were ice blue in a blizzard of white fur. He placed it back in the empty cage. He removed a rat from the adjacent cage and placed it at the start of the maze.

"This lightweight doesn't have nearly the amount as Heavy D," Shef said as he released the door and the rat stumbled into the maze confused. It ran into walls repeatedly, sporadically changing direction and retreading paths. They watched it struggle for a few minutes before it was clear they would be there a long while before this particular rat made it to the finish.

"And this one's a dumbass, I'm waiting for the light bulb moment Mr. Bales," Dunbar stated plainly.

"Now, we get to the good part," Shef replied as walked over to the table and pressed some digital buttons on the side of Heavy D's plastic cage. It slowly started to fill with gas.

"This is a sedative, it's gonna put him into a deep state of sleep. The more I pump in, the deeper he'll go."

Dunbar watched the fat rat stagger around before collapsing. Shef took the normal rat and placed him back at the start of the maze.

"Let all the juices settle for a couple seconds and awaaaay we go," Shef said as he lifted the gate again.

The rat darted through the maze with ease, just as Heavy D had done before his induced nap.

"Wait…what just happened," Dunbar asked perplexed.

Shef retrieved the rat from the maze and held it up so that Dunbar could see again.

"He's…blind?"

"Yep."

"And he ran the maze perfectly after not knowing it at all."

"Yep."

"There's some connection between users such that the heavier user can…communicate when in a near comatose state? How is that possible?"

"Dunbar, there's some crazy shit in this world. Nothing surprises me anymore," Shef lamented as he walked over to his main computer station, sat down, and plugged a USB cord into his robotic arm. Information from the many test results populated various screens. Some hand gestures narrowed down the clutter a bit, but Dunbar still needed Shef to explain what it all meant.

"The light user's vital signs are here. You can see them spike when Heavy D is around. It's a chemical reaction that affects the brain, the senses. Pheromones are released. It's part of the reason dreamers can tell other dreamers. They can smell it on ya."

Dunbar thought about the episode with Adam the night he went AWOL.

"When Heavy D is under, it's like he's able to transmit his thoughts to the others. Each of the three blind mice."

"Three blind mice? See how they run," Dunbar interrupted chuckling.

"My God, you're a cornball. Good thing you're awesome at sciencing. You gotta get some friends. Or get some new ones."

"Yeah," Dunbar said slightly embarrassed, thinking of his friend Adam yet again, "You're right."

"Anyway," Shef continued, "the more users that are present, the effect seems heightened, more potent. They act like beacons."

"Artificially induced telekinesis? As a bonus to all of the other ways it affects the body…"

"Like I said, crazy shit," Shef sighed, "Just looking at Heavy D's brain scans every time I've put him under, the activity is off the charts. It's like he *has* to be in a comatose state in order for his brain to have enough energy to use the bridge that dawn provides."

"This…is amazing stuff," Dunbar marveled.

"Tell me about it, and mine is still not 100% pure. The assholes runnin' around basepop have no clue about this side effect. Now, think for a second, if you got millions of users in the Metro, what could happen if someone knew how to exploit this."

"Jesus," Dunbar responded introspectively.

"Yeah. Literally. Someone could walk around and make people think that, actually *see* that. Whoever is behind dawn is also behind the G8 abductions, we know that much. But even I didn't know that this stuff was *this* bad. The same group behind both…it's scary to think what they could do next."

Dunbar was silent, too scared to agree. Then he realized something.

"Shef, when we were investigating this mass murder, the forb scanned one of the bodies. The marks in his bones reminded me of a prior case. Looked like they were cut with a serrated edge."

Shef's eyes widened, "Orion."

They both eyed each other in mutual disbelief.

"I'm gonna upload all of this into version 2.0 of the forb. It's sitting on the docking station. Shouldn't take too long, take it witcha'," Shef's said getting back to business as usual.

"Sounds good. I want to go over the data in depth."

"Thanks. Seems the more I find out, the more questions spring-"

Shef was interrupted by blaring sirens and a computerized voice. "PERIMETER BREACHED. INTRUDER ALERT."

Dunbar and Shef looked at each other quickly. Next, they heard a loud boom, followed by a slight rumble like a brief earthquake. All electrical devices powered down and the two were plunged into darkness.

"Not good," Shef said unseen, "That's an EMP. A powerful one."

"What? Why?"

"Hell if I know. But anyone setting off an EMP in the middle of the Metro isn't up to any good," he was interrupted by spotlights in the corners illuminating to life. Shef's main station powered on slowly.

"The backup generator should be enough to finish uploading to the forb."

"How long?"

"Maybe ten, fifteen minutes. We're talking about exabytes of information here."

"The faster the better," Dunbar sighed.

"Afraid of the dark," Shef laughed.

"No, I-"

The sound of metal piercing metal rang through the lab. Both men jerked towards Shef's metal emergency doors. A large sword was stuck in the seam. It was retracted quickly.

"Whoa, what the hell?!" Dunbar exclaimed, showing a rare glimpse of emotion.

"Shit...Whoever it is set off the EMP. He knew what he was getting into coming here."

The sword came slicing at the door again, and again, and again, creating more space each and every time.

"He's about to break in," Dunbar yelled panicking, "Can you do something?!"

"If it's who I think it is, oh yeah, I can *definitely* do something," Shef said as he made his way over to a case containing a large sword, an updated version of his traditional blade, and the oni mask he used to wear as a vigilante years ago. He opened the case and pulled the giant meat cleaver out, tossing it in both hands, staring at it lovingly. He slid the mask on, the sound of air escaping hissed out as the mask gently conformed to his face.

"Been waitin' to give this new blade design a run," he said, "Dunbar, go to my seat. Make sure the forb gets all the data from the upload, and put this flash drive in. There's a file called *esleepprep.exe*. Click on it, it'll do the rest.

"Oh...okay," Dunbar replied nervously. Both of their heads jerked around as the sword came slashing down one final time. A pair of gloved hands reached through and pushed the door apart. A tall slender man walked in, his oil-black eyes peered at them from above a crafted breathing apparatus that resembled a painter's mask. It was black to match his outfit, befitting a traditional zealot. Shef noticed that he had some advanced tech on his person, not standard issue by the mecca. Despite the subtle differences, Shef recognized the eyes right away.

"Orion."

"Mr. Bales. Or do you still go by Beam? Either way, it's been a long time."

"Not nearly long enough. I figured it would be hard to drown a fish. Fancy work with the EMP."

Orion laughed lightly, the sound it made coming from his mask was disturbing, like a dog choking on a bone.

"Hmph...I didn't need any of your toys being a nuisance. Efficiency is the goal and time is of the essence so I'll get right to it. Where is Myth?"

Shef calmly readied his weapon. He held the massive blade in his mechanical hand as if it weighed nothing.

"You're crazy if you think I'm telling you anything. We should have stomped your fucking face in. Made sure the job was done."

"Yes. You should have."

Orion dashed forward. Shef met him with steel, swinging glancing slashes that barely missed Orion as he dodged them. The two of them moved around the lab as Dunbar sat at the main rig uploading the information to the forb. He also followed Shef's instructions and initiated the file on his flash drive. Both still had time remaining before they completed their tasks. With the fight going on around him, Dunbar was uncertain if the delicate equipment could hold up. He had a hard time following their movements so there was no way to predict what would happen. An errant kunai would be enough to stop things in their tracks. If one came, there was nothing Dunbar could do to stop it, save diving in front of it. He watched as the two men bounced around the room.

Orion danced between attacks and maneuvered closer. His sword fighting technique was masterful, and the odd way that he moved, smooth but prone to unpredictable jerks, made it even more deadly. Rapid slashes came at Shef in quick succession. He used his huge blade to deflect the onslaught of attacks. His robotic hand swung his sword with ease. Orion took notice. In their prior battle, Shef had to rely on his own muscles to swing such a heavy blade. Now, with his body modifications, he could wield it with one hand, performing counters and parries that he would not have been able to do otherwise. Shef blocked a vertical slash from a jumping Orion and the impact sent him flipping several times in the air. He landed on his feet in fighting position.

"I was always impressed with your engineering acumen, Mr. Bales. It seems I did a favor by taking that arm from you," Orion chided.

"Aye, I'd say so."

"Well, let me assure you, you're not the only one with technology on their side," Orion said as he flipped his wrist up and pulled a small circular tube from it. He connected it to the bottom of his sword's handle. Slowly, indigo colored blood began to flow through. He lifted his sword back up into the low light of the lab.

"The melding of man and machine made possible by Tozen's research. It's quite incredible, actually. Something I'm sure you can appreciate."

Shef watched as the metal of Orion's sword began to shimmer. Slowly, the shape began to morph and change. The blade grew longer, the serrated edge became much more pronounced. The sword now resembled a large saw, with a sharp edge on the opposite side. For the first time all night, Shef was speechless. He was indeed impressed, but he couldn't concede that fact. Instead, he responded with a laugh.

"You'll have to do better than that, Jaws," Shef laughed.

"I plan to," Orion responded, readying his sword, "Before I took your arm...now I'll take your head!"

The two men re-engaged in fierce battle. Shef could feel the increase in power behind each deflected blow, Orion's transformed sword packed a noticeably meaner punch. Sparks flew off of the clashing blades like flint birthing flame. Shef was becoming winded, his shoulder above his mechanical arm began to shoot pain as Orion's unrelenting assault began to wear him down. He was years removed from the peak physical condition he was in during their last encounter. His age began to betray him.

Not sure how much more I can take...

Orion flew in with a jump kick, Shef sidestepped into a devastating swing of Orion's blade, the impact sent Shef sliding backwards. He tossed his sword in the air. The giant cleaver broke into two pieces, transforming into smaller broad swords. Shef's robotic arm split, gears and metal plates turning and sliding. He was left with two, thin robotic arms each with two fingers and an opposable thumb, extending from his elbow. Each new hand snatched the falling broad swords out of the air. Orion paused and marveled. His brow raised in amazement. Dunbar was staring with an equal sense of wonder.

"I call this new blade Blender. Lemme show you how it got the name. "

Shef was on the offensive he threw punches interwoven with lighting quick slashes from his other two robotic arms. Orion struggled to evade and block the blows that were flying at him. He swung his sword down, Shef's robotic arms began to spin like helicopter propellers, throwing Orion and his blade out of the way.

"Dunbar, what's the status!"

"A couple more minutes," Dunbar yelled back nervously watching the battle take place. Just then another shadow appeared through the door that Orion had forced his way through. Everyone in the room turned to see the unexpected guest.

"Heller," Orion yelled with contempt.

"Adam?!"

"Dunbar, you know this asshole," Shef asked through heaving breaths.

"Since you're here, retrieve that device," Orion turned and yelled at Adam, "And kill the other one." Adam looked at Orion, then over at Dunbar, then back at Orion, who was now re-engaged in battle with Shef.

"Adam, what the hell are you doing here," Dunbar screamed over the sound of clashing metal.

"I'm doing what I have to do!"

"You don't know who you're dealing with! I don't know what you're getting into, but this isn't going to last! It can't!"

"Paul…just gimmie the forb!"

Dunbar looked confused, "Man, what are you talking about?! I can't let you take this!"

Adam turned towards Dunbar, the look on his face was considerably more menacing. Even from the distance, Dunbar could see his eyes almost glowing blue.

"Paul, don't do this! I don't want to have to hurt you!"

"What the fuck is wrong with you, man," Dunbar yelled, swearing uncharacteristically, "I don't care about you coming back to the MCPD, but there's gotta be something better than…dealing with this guy! He's an ex-tribunal member. An international terrorist, Adam!"

"What…what?"

"Jesus, you didn't know?!"

Adam stood dumbfounded for a moment. He felt like an idiot. Of course he didn't know, he never bothered to learn anything about the operations at the mecca his entire time as a cop. He felt like it didn't concern him, there was already so much to deal with in basepop he couldn't worry about it anyway. Come to think of it, the name did sound familiar when he first heard it, but that was neither here nor there now. Now, if he expected to get paid, and get more pure dawn, he had a job to do. He charged at Dunbar.

"Ahhh Shit," Shef complained springing to action, Orion stopped him in his path with a vertical slash that smashed into the ground.

"Dunbar, take the forb and get out! Now!"

Shef leapt over the blade and made it over in time to put himself between Adam and Dunbar. Shef was fighting both men now. His robotic arms spun and slashed, clanging against Orion's giant saw blade as he threw punches and kicks at an unarmed, outmatched Adam. For all of the training time spent with Orion, Adam was completely useless in the face of an opponent such as Shef. Orion indeed took notice of this inadequacy.

"Done," Dunbar yelled as he snatched the forb off of the docking station.

"There's an emergency escape elevator in the back. Go! Take it, and get out of here!"

"Shef, what…what are you going to do!?"

"No way I'm making it out of here, bro! Run! Do it! I'm going to make sure this bastard dies this time!"

Dunbar paused as the three continued to battle. Shef kicked Adam hard in the stomach and twisted around. His robotic arm spun and struck at a dizzying rate, slashing Adam's face and chest. He fell backwards over a table.

"Adam!" Dunbar screamed.

Orion saw his opportunity and closed in. Shef reverted back to his previous form, two robotic arms became one, broad swords rejoined as a giant cleaver. With a huge swing, he aimed at the side of Orion's face just seconds too late. Shef looked down at Orion's blade piercing his stomach. The visualization immediately cued the pain. He only felt a brief taste of the intense ripping sensation that was tearing apart his internal organs. Had it not been for the anesthetic gas that his mask began to emit into his airways, he would have passed out then and there. Shef and Dunbar watched Orion quickly turn his wrist 90 degrees and tear the blade out of the side of Shef's body. Blood poured onto the lab floor. Shef knew instantly his spine was severed.

There wasn't much time left. Orion shook the blood off his blade. It spattered across documents and computer screens. With a hiss, the tube connecting his wrist to his sword recoiled back into his arm like a parasitic worm. Slowly his sword returned to its original form. Dunbar turned and ran as fast as he could down a back hallway to an already open elevator door. It was only big enough for one person to go inside and was a seat inside with seatbeat. He sat and buckled one across his lap, then another that went across his chest like a harness. There was only one button on the panel. He pushed it frantically. As the doors slid shut, he watched as Orion slowly paced over to Shef's torn and bloodied body struggling to breath.

"Impressive. I'll grant you that," Orion commended, "But not enough. Not in the face of what's coming. Handing over Everett would have prevented this collateral damage. You may not be the only one that ends up dead because of some…misguided sense of loyalty."

Shef couldn't speak, but he heard every word that was being said. The pain from wanting to get the last word and physically not being able to do so hurt more than his actual wounds.

Just…a….little…longer….

Orion slid his sword back into his sheath and sighed.

"As for you," he said to Adam's unconscious body, "You should have stayed where you were. You almost made a mess of things."

The emergency lights in the room changed from soft yellow to dark red. Orion looked up nervously. Then looked back down into the face of Shef's mask.

"Hmph…I'd think nothing less than you having rigged it to blow," Orion noted without fear.

Shef laid there shivering, numb from his chest down, solemnly waiting to talk with his father. He had so much to ask him. Digital text scrolled across the display in his mask.

It's ready…now…I can say goodbye to this ol' body of mine…

The elevator shot downward so fast Dunbar thought it was free falling. He held the forb close to his chest and made himself as compact as possible. And then he prayed. He felt the chair slowly begin to lean backwards as the speed increased. There was a huge jolt that shook the escape pod, then it was smoothly moving at a steady pace. After around five minutes it slowed to a stop and the doors slid open. Dunbar unlatched himself and threw up over the side. He was a couple blocks removed from the EMP radius. He looked up to Shef's tower to see, the top floor, the lab, engulfed in flames.

"No…"

Explosions rocked each floor all the way to ground level. The blasts looked like they were carefully placed to ensure the building would collapse on itself. Flames lit up the dark sphere of city that was affected by the EMP bomb. Dunbar could feel the vibrations from the explosions under his feet. He watched the tower collapse, the rumble echoed down the streets like an unseen stampede, slowly the light from the flames were extinguished by the rising dust cloud. Dunbar looked on in disbelief. He stared silently for what seemed like an hour, tracing the pile of rubble that used to be Shef's lab with his eyes as they slowly adjusted to the night. He looked down at the forb under his arm. It was a bit bigger than the first version, about the size of a bowling ball. He held it out and pressed the familiar power button. The black orb vibrated gently. A pulsing red light began to circle in two rings around the dark sphere.

Dunbar watched on confused. This must have been something new with the upgrade. The pulsating lights gradually stopped and began to emit the blue color that was associated with activity. Dunbar tossed the forb into the air, expecting it to float. Instead, it hummed and twisted. Small pistons moved and pivoted. The forb transformed into a more humanoid shape. A small robot with arms and legs and a small head. There was a rectangular display where the eyes should be. The robot hovered with what looked to be a jet pack on his back. Dunbar figured it may have been some type of condensed air system that could recycle the air around it, negating the need for fuel. Shef was a genius like that.

"Shef...I can't believe..."

"Believe what? Did it work?"

Dunbar stared at the hovering robot with his jaw dropped. The voice was definitely a slightly digitized version of Shef's.

"Oh shit. It worked."

"What...who...Shef?!"

"We can celebrate later. We don't have a lot of time, Dunbar."

CHAPTER TWENTY-FOUR

The Break

When he opened his eyes, he was greeted by constellations. His whole body felt numb and he could barely move. The fear of paralysis crept in, but the tingling sensations in his extremities were a relief. His surroundings were not. Cyrus let his head fall to one side where his eyes met those of Aureus Rex on the opposite side of the cage. His large eyes were shining in the night. Cyrus continued to look on, wondering what was going through the mind of the beast. Hopefully it wasn't, "I wonder what dark meat taste like."

Gold teeth and a helluva poker face…damn tiger reminds me of some guys I know…

Cyrus didn't have too many options other than wait to see what Aureus would do next. He peeked down at his chest, it was wrapped in gauze that was soaked through with blood. Judging by how he felt, and the last words he heard Tozen say before he passed out, Cyrus realized he was kept alive just enough to watch himself become dinner. Aureus rose to his feet and yawned. His mouth opened wide, tongue flapping out. Moon light ricocheted off of the gold fangs in his mouth. Cyrus imagined the huge jaws clamping down and ripping a substantial chunk out of his already tattered flesh. Aureus began to walk over to Cyrus, his paws crunching against the grass were the only sounds in the night, a methodical countdown to an inevitable death.

Well…so be it…

Cyrus looked straight up into the starry sky. He lived a long life equally filled with accomplishment and regret. What would life been like if Jerry lived and he never took the job to develop Mount Z's training program? He asked himself that question often, seemed like a fitting one to end his life pondering. He could have had the family life he wanted while the world was worse off. He slowly closed his eyes and felt the earth underneath him gently shake as Aureus got closer and closer. Cyrus could hear panting above him, feel the moisture exhalations on his face. A gun shot rang out. Then another. Then another eight. Cyrus instinctively opened his eyes, Aureus looked wildly back and forth before pacing the cage.

What's going on…?

A gauntlet-clad hand slashed off the lock to the cage with ease and swung the door open. Cyrus turned his head to see Neko, dressed in all black, carrying a satchel, a large dufflebag filled presumably with supplies, and Cyrus's familiar walking staff.

"Sensei…we're leaving."

"Neko," Cyrus struggled to say, "I…we…"

"Save your energy sensei, we have to leave now. I've already caused some…minor trouble."

Neko reached into his satchel and pulled a syringe filled with dawn.

"Now, um, I think you do something like this," Neko reasoned out loud. Cyrus's eyes widened as he tried with all of his energy to offer some tips, lest Neko accidentally kill him trying to save him. It was no use, he was hanging on to consciousness by a thread. Mustering words seemed like an insurmountable task. Neko raised his arm and plunged the syringe into Cyrus's heart, through the gauze. The jolt woke Cyrus up enough to yell, "Push…down!"

"Oh, oh yeah," Neko responded seemingly oblivious to the severity of the situation. He turned and looked up at Aureus, "You're coming, too."

The big beast stared at him confused

"C'mon, there's nothing for you here, you know it."

The tiger tilted his head slightly in consideration. Then he plodded over to where both of them stood and licked Neko's face. Neko laughed, "There we go! You mind carrying him on your back for a bit?"

Aureus began to growl in disapproval. Then, he lunged. He went over Cyrus and Neko's heads and swiped his huge paw. When they turned, they saw one of the Lightrays, camouflaged in the night collapse to the ground, blue blood pouring from the chunk of his body that Aureus clawed away. The beast turned to them and nodded. Neko scooped up Cyrus under his arms and helped to lay him on Aureus's back. He strapped the large duffle bag behind him.

"Sensei, try not to move too much. I got some rope, I'm gonna tie you to Aureus."

"No, no I can hold on," Cyrus stated, surprised at his newfound energy. The dawn in its pure form was already setting about healing his body. But how long would it last? Search lights became visible in the distance heading in their direction. Neko looked at Cyrus, then at Aureus. He stared the tiger in the eyes as he rubbed between his ears to earn his last little bit of trust, then Neko bolted out of the cage on all fours. Aureus followed with monstrous strides. Cyrus clutched Aureus's fur so tightly he thought he would rip a handful out. He heard gun shots undoubtedly being fired at them. Bullets landed in their path, kicking up dust and dirt clouds that they ran through on the way to the outskirts of the compound. Cyrus lifted his head to see trucks pulling up into the distance, blocking their escape route.

"Neko, watch out!"

Neko quickly pounced on the first guard stepping out of the driver side of a truck. He shot up out of his low running stance and kicked the door as the guard was stepping out, smashing it against his legs, making him scream in pain. Smoothly, he rolled to the next man standing in their way. He popped up in front of him and sliced his rifle to pieces with his gauntlet. The guard whipped out his machete haphazardly, Neko struck his elbow with an open palm causing the weapon to drop. His use of the Tiger Style to decimate the guards was a sight to behold. He was a blur of slashes and kicks, deftly eluding the guards and parrying attacks moments before they landed.

Precise combinations gracefully dismantled opponents. Neko had indeed grown into a one of a kind fighter. He bared his fangs as he continued to incapacitate foe after foe, leaving tattered and bloodied bodies littering the ground. He turned to see a guard raising a rifle. Aureus rushed the guard and with a swipe of his huge paw, knocked the lower half of the man's face to the ground. He fell over dead seconds later.

Neko looked at Aureus and nodded in thanks. When it was all said and done, 16 men lay dead or dying. Neko looked back at Cyrus and Aureus.

"Shall we?"

The party continued towards the perimeter of the compound until a silhouette appeared in the distance standing between them and freedom. It could only be one person. As they approached, Tozen stood leaning on a katana in its sheath. The blade was much longer than normal, almost matching Tozen in height. As they drew nearer, Cyrus wondered how a person could wield such a thing. Neko and Aureus came to a stop.

"I had to come see this myself. How unfortunate that you've chosen this path, Neko. I had so much faith in you," Tozen said with a disingenuous tone.

Neko didn't respond. His upper lip quivered into a snarl, flashing his fangs every couple of seconds. This was the closest thing to hatred that Cyrus had seen in his eyes since their training began.

Tozen chuckled condescendingly, "You're willing to forfeit everything that I promised you? A family? A life of importance? I took you out of the nothingness, certain death…and gave you purpose!"

"You…are a liar," Neko said sternly. Cyrus was proud of him. It sounded like he had grown a pair, wasn't afraid to stand up to Tozen. Cyrus also thought that this new found bravado could lead to an abrupt end of their escape mission. Tozen turned towards his ex-pet.

"Et tu Aureus Rex?"

The tiger growled menacingly.

"Mr. Santeaux. I beg you reconsider," Tozen said as he slowly pulled the katana from its sheath, "My research is missing one key component. You could lead to that component."

"The Lotus Palm…in order to perfect it you need me somehow," Cyrus reasoned.

Tozen looked absolutely shocked, it gave way to rage.

"You think you can do anything to stop me? You will die. You've been injected with dawn, but that won't be enough. You should know how grave your injuries were. It'll keep you going for a week, possibly two, but when you have no more, nature will take its course. Aureus may end up eating your corpse yet."

"I'll take my chances," Cyrus hopped off of Aureus's back. He felt good, great even. If that was true, what Tozen had said about the dawn, he intended to use this time to leave some marks that he'd be remembered by. He readied his staff. Neko stood alongside him in his Tiger Style stance. Tozen stood before them holding his long sword outstretched to the side. Surprisingly, he was the first to strike. He swung his sword with tremendous skill, causing Neko and Cyrus to quickly elude its shining edge. Neko attacked with his gauntlet, Tozen displayed otherworldly senses, as he quickly blocked both Cyrus and Neko with his sword. The great beast Aureus Rex had seen enough, he entered the fray as well. He ran up on the battle, swiping down on Tozen with his huge paws. Tozen slid out of the way just in time. He quickly parried Cyrus's staff, and attatcked Neko with series of quick elbows and knees. It looked very much like Cyrus's own Black Panther Fist.

He knows that style as well...?

The tense battle raged on. Cyrus didn't know whether he was feeling the effects of the fight, the injuries, or Tozen's technique. It was unbelievable. Despite having another fighter and a damn tiger on his side, they were being boxed into a corner.

How could this man be so skilled...where did he train?

Cyrus moved in. He felt his body moving faster, stronger. All at once, he understood the allure of the dawn. He felt invincible. He rushed Tozen taking the lead. Tozen ducked and spun out of the way of Cyrus's whirling staff. Cyrus dodged Tozen's counterattacks and used his staff to vault over him, Aureus leapt in right behind him, biting at Tozen's jugular. Tozen caught his jaws with his hands, holding them apart.

"Neko! Now!"

Neko ran towards Tozen's back as he struggled with Aureus. He raised his golden hand. As he brought it down, Tozen's long blade deflected the strike, sending sparks into the air and thrusting Neko's arm away. The sword spun back as if on a string and took off Neko's other hand at the wrist.

"Argh!" Neko yelled in pain.

Tozen used both of his hands to throw Aureus to the side, the large tiger flew into the air like a child tossed by his father, and slid to a stop on the ground. Cyrus, Neko, and a dazed Aureus stumbled into a triangle surrounding Tozen. He stood with his arms crossed, his long katana floating in front of him. His eyes were completely blue and they emitted a steam of the same color.

"What the hell type of..."

"Mr. Santeaux," Tozen snarled, "You are witnessing the power of the Lotus Palm. Take word of its majesty to your grave."

Cyrus tried not to look astounded. Neko's face showed otherwise. Even Aureus stared at Tozen, with his sword swaying ominously in front of him, with tremendous awe.

"Impressive. But I know you haven't perfected it yet. The God Fist. If you were truly a master, you wouldn't have this much trouble with us, now would you?"

Tozen shot back a cold glare, "What makes you think I find this troublesome?"

"The uncertainty in your voice," Cyrus responded. Tozen's brow furrowed in anger.

"Sensei, I can hear guards coming, we have to go!"

Cyrus spun his staff into fighting position, "Right!"

Cyrus, Neko, and Aureus ran for the gate. Tozen, displaying speed comparable to a zealot, was in their way in a blink. He fought Neko and Cyrus with hand-to-hand combat, as his sword slashed and swung as if controlled by an invisible handler keeping Aureus at bay. Tozen smashed through Cyrus's staff with a downward chop, he kicked Neko in the stomach and followed up with Snake Style quick strikes to his chest and face.

"Neko!"

Cyrus rushed in, feeling like his young self, he flipped over a low kick and delivered a combination of Black Panther Fist strikes to Tozen's midsection. The impact filled him with adrenaline. Tozen stumbled backwards, his sword came rushing over his head twirling through the air like a deadly marionette. Neko returned to aid in fighting a sword wielded by the wind. Aureus charged at Tozen. He readied himself to take the beast head on. Aureus pounced, trying to bite a chunk out of Tozen's midsection. Tozen brushed off the giant paws swiping at his head and neck with tremendous speed and skill. Aureus stopped and let out a monstrous roar of frustration. It echoed in the night like an avalanche of sound. Then he darted towards the dancing blade and clamped it between his gold fangs, wrestling with it. Cyrus saw this as the last opportunity. Headlights from a caravan of guards were swiftly approaching.

"All of this commotion," Tozen yelled with unexpected excitement. He was definitely taking joy in engaging in such a fierce battle, "You all are making a fatal mistake!"

Neko yanked a smoke bomb from his satchel and tossed it in the air as it erupted into a massive black cloud. Aureus threw the blade to the side, and sprinted over to Cyrus, who hopped onto his back. With Neko close behind, the trio shot out of the smoke cloud and made haste towards the perimeter gate. Neko pulled ahead, with quick slashes he cut an opening through. The three disappeared into the night, concealed by a cloak of foliage.

Tozen walked out of the smoke cloud. He held the sheath while his sword slowly lifted off of the ground and gently slid into it. As he stared off into the darkness, one of the guards appeared next to him.

"Sir, do you want us to follow them?"

"Santeaux won't survive. We'll find Neko. Collect all confidential research. I will give you a list of important personnel to retain. Burn everything and everyone else to the ground. It's time for a change of scenery."

CHAPTER TWENTY-FIVE

The Walk

I think it's been about three days counting by the sunsets. Tozen said the effects of the dawn wouldn't hold me up forever. He was right. I'm starting to feel it. Constant muscle pains. Cold sweats at night. Sleep deprivation. Neko warned me as soon as we left about the dreams and perhaps I should try to stay awake. I thought that was a good idea, just as a means to put as much distance between us and Tozen as possible. I didn't know how bad it actually was. When I finally did fall into a deep sleep, maybe after a couple days or so, I could feel him in my mind. Scratching. Constantly knocking. The amount of the dawn that I had in my body was small in comparison to most, and even still, Tozen found a way in. It's crazy. A perfect dream instantly ruined by seeing his face in a crowd and realizing he's been watching you the whole time. Jarring to say the least. It makes me fear what Neko goes through.

Neko and Cyrus walked through wet jungle, Aureus lumbering behind them. They were headed towards a small village, to let Neko tell it. Cyrus wasn't in any position to argue. There was a reasonably good chance he wouldn't even make it to see their destination. They had to stop more frequently to conserve his rapidly depleting energy.

"Neko, one second," Cyrus said as they slowed to yet another such stop.

"Sensei, are you okay? We really shouldn't waste time. Tozen can't be that far behind and-"

"Just a moment, Neko," Cyrus panted, cutting him off. Neko saw his sensei laboring and walked to him. He helped prop him against a nearby tree. Aureus walked over, stretched, and laid down on the moist ground, seemingly happy to get a break as well.

"I just needed a minute. I think the dawn is wearing off."

"Yeah, I could tell."

"How," Cyrus asked.

"I can smell it. Sense it. It has gotten a lot weaker since we left."

"Yeah…How much longer?"

"Another two or three days, maybe less if we can avoid stopping. With respect, sensei."

"I understand, Neko. Aureus?"

The tiger lifted his head, surprised that Cyrus directly addressed him. He stared at him and blinked hard a couple of times as if to say, "Get on with it."

"You mind carrying me for a bit? We can switch places in a couple hours if you want," Cyrus said as he flashed a weak smile. Neko chuckled. Aureus stood up and snorted.

"I'll take that as a yes. Neko, lead the way."

The day gradually faded into night. As the trio marched on, Cyrus struggled to see through the darkness. Neko and Aureus moved along fine, their eyes having long adjusted to the change in light. Cyrus began to cough spastically. He struggled to hold another one in, but it broke out of his mouth, followed by another one more violent. Aureus was the first to stop, causing Neko to turn around. He walked over and surveyed his teacher's condition. He put his hand on Cyrus's frail shoulder and felt his labored breathing.

"I think we've gone far enough for now."

Neko helped Cyrus down.

"Aureus, could you dig us a place to sleep," Neko asked.

Aureus begrudgingly obliged and began to scratch a small crater into the jungle floor. Neko was reluctant to light fires for fear of giving themselves away, but he had taken to gathering what he could and setting it aflame with a button operated lighter that looked like it came from a lab.

Pretty smart move to grab that, Neko.

Neko flinched away squinting as the flame grew brighter. Aureus walked in a small circle before stretching and lying down comfortably in the hole he had just dug. Neko helped Cyrus to his feet and walked with him to Aureus. He propped him up on the large beast. The fur was soft and his rhythmic breathing was already lulling Cyrus to sleep.

"Neko, I…I'm not too sure I'll wake up."

"Sensei, don't say that. We're another couple days out, once we get there, I'm sure someone will be able to help you," Neko said as he cradled his Cyrus's head and gave him some water out of a flask.

"Yeah," Cyrus answered unsure, "I wanted to ask you about Tozen."

Neko became visibly uncomfortable, even Aureus's ears perked up at the sound of the name

"You've been pretty adamant about not going to sleep, or at least trying to avoid doing so."

"You've seen him in your dreams, no?" Neko asked before Cyrus could continue.

Cyrus watched the flame from their campfire sway in the night for a moment before answering, "Yes, they started at the compound."

"Well, it's good that we left before they got worse. Because they would have gotten much worse."

"Tozen summoned me to a room once, right after I met with…" Cyrus paused, remembering Dr. Singh, "I walked into the room, and he was sitting perfectly still, didn't even look like he was breathing. Yet, somehow, he was able to talk to me and everyone in the room."

"He talked straight to your brain, right" Neko asked, attempting to rationalize the situation in the way a child would.

"Yes. In the science world, that's called telepathy. Probably telekinesis enables Tozen to manipulate his sword as well. But how…how did he learn to do this? How *could* he learn to do this? Is this really what the Lotus Palm grants its true masters?"

Neko let out a yawn that was reminiscent of Aureus, "I dunno sensei. But this might help. I took them from the lab."

Neko went through the satchel and pulled out a folder that was thick with documents. He also pulled out a small tablet computer.

"I'm not too good with computers and things," Neko said, "But I got some stuff for you to read. Maybe this will help?"

He handed him the folder and the tablet pc. Cyrus saw the word *confidential* in large red text on the folder. He flipped through it as a smile crept across his face.

"And Tozen didn't see the point in teaching you how to read," Cyrus laughed. Neko smiled warmly in response. Meanwhile, Aureus was snoring as loud as five grown men.

"Neko, put out the fire. Let's get some rest."

Cyrus knew that he had to keep himself alive at least until they made it to their destination. It was the only chance he had of contacting Xi.

Shortly before dawn the trio restarted their trek with Neko leading the way. Cyrus flipped through documents as they walked. Many of them were case studies concerning test subjects that were injected with the dawn, not unlike the files that Jasper had showed him prior to her murder. The most interesting bits were related to the Lotus Palm Manuscript. This was the most comprehensive set of information he had seen, and even still, it seemed purposely vague. If Tozen had not achieved true mastery of the technique, what did he need to do so? Cyrus was determined to figure that out. Seeing Tozen's capabilities as they were was enough to fear what he could become.

"Sensei, we're getting close."

"I'm sure that's news to your ears, eh," Cyrus said atop Aureus's back. Aureus tilted his head and shot him a side-eyed glance.

Moments later they pushed over a hill and emerged into a clearing. In the distance, they could see small cottages and smoke rising from chimneys. It was a welcome sight to all three of them. As they got closer and closer, they could see people going about their daily lives, only a few noticed as they made their way into the village, some only raising their heads momentarily before returning back to their tasks.

"We should probably find who's in charge here, Neko."

"Sensei," Neko chuckled, "Where do you think we're going?"

The trio continued along the central path of the village. Cyrus noticed little bits of technological advancement here and there; solar panels, people on communicators, a cellular tower.

Odd to find this stuff here…

They arrived at a house that was larger and in much better shape than the rest. As they approached, a short, stocky man wearing round glasses walked out. He had thin strands of hair combed over his bald spot in a feeble attempt to conceal it. Despite his awkward appearance, he immediately gave a warm and inviting smile.

"My goodness…is that you?"

"Hello, Mr. Sahn."

The man walked up to Neko and wrapped his arms around him, giving him a loving embrace.

"It's been so long," he said pulling away from him and giving him a once over. His brow crinkled as he noticed Neko's eyes.

"What…what did he do to you?"

Neko changed the subject quickly, "Mr. Sahn, this is Cyrus Santeaux. He's trained me for a long time now."

Mr. Sahn extended his pudgy hand as Cyrus slowly dismounted from Aureus's back, "Sir, pleased to make your acquaintance."

"Likewise," Cyrus responded politely.

"You should remember him, too," Neko noted.

"Of course! He's gotten so…large," Mr. Sahn said as he walked over to Aureus and wrapped his arms around his neck. Aureus licked his face in delight. Mr. Sahn took his fingers and peeled the tiger's lips back, getting a good look at his golden teeth. He shook his head solemnly.

"Please, you all must be tired. Come in."

They all walked into Mr. Sahn's home where the smell of cooked food made all three salivate. Aureus couldn't control his slobber from dripping onto the floor.

"Ah, famished as well I assume," Mr. Sahn clapped his hands and a young woman appeared from another room, presumably the kitchen.

"Please prepare meals for our guests. A rack of lamb for our four-legged friend." Aureus nodded his head slowly, victorious. Cyrus couldn't do anything but laugh. Neko, Mr. Sahn, and Cyrus all took seats on the carpeted floor cross-legged. An impressive spread of Thai dishes was laid out before them. As Neko obliterated food as if he'd never seen it before, Mr. Sahn and Cyrus engaged in conversation.

"Mr…"

"Santeaux."

"Santeaux, yes. Sounds familiar."

"Does it? I would think that you don't run into too many Santeauxs in this part of the world."

Mr. Sahn took a slow sip of his tea, but his eyes never left Cyrus's, "Indeed."

"Mr. Sahn," Cyrus continued, "I see that you knew Neko previously?"

"Yes, yes I did. He was just a baby then, him and Chairat."

"Chairat?"

Mr. Sahn laughed. The folds under his neck jiggled slightly.

"Yes, that's what we called him before."

"Before? Before what?"

Neko stopped shoveling food in his mouth and looked at both men nervously.

"Before he came," Mr. Sahn said with a sense of dread.

"Tozen."

Mr. Sahn drank his remaining tea, staring into Cyrus's eyes unblinking, "Yes."

"Neko, you should go…check on Aureus."

Neko nodded quickly. He looked worried. He started to get up to leave but came back to quickly stuff his mouth to capacity with food. He bowed his head with comically inflated cheeks and left the room. Mr. Sahn continued to speak.

"They came years ago. We lived a much simpler life prior to that, to put it modestly. Scientists and doctors at first. We had so many that were sick. They built water filtration systems."

Cyrus sipped his tea, "But when Tozen arrived, I assume things started to go badly."

Mr. Sahn sighed, "To say the least. He came in the middle of the night, with armed men. I don't know what the criterion was or how it was determined, but some people were taken…the others were…"

"Killed?"

Mr. Sahn nodded in solemn agreement, "Women. The elderly. The sick. The disabled. Children. My children."

"And Neko? His parents?"

"Killed as well. He was too young to be on his own but old enough to remember the scene, I'm sure. Tozen rounded him up with the others and took him."

"I see," Cyrus said watching the beads of sweat slowly start to form on Mr. Sahn's skin, "So the question I have is: What made him spare you?"

Mr. Sahn was silent for a moment, "I watched Tozen's men medicate Chairat, Aureus as you call him, just enough that he couldn't fight back. Then they pulled each one of his teeth out and replaced them with the ones you see now. I still remember the look in his eyes."

Cyrus leaned backwards in disgust.

"I just didn't want anything else to happen…to anyone else. I agreed to help him in times of need."

"And Mr. Sahn," Cyrus said slowly, "Would you consider our unexpected arrival to fall under one of those times?"

Mr. Sahn sat absolutely still. The two men's eyes were locked.

"They are making their way here. I'm sorry."

"Don't be," Cyrus said sternly, "You had to do what you had to do. If you haven't noticed, sir, my health has been on the decline of late."

Mr. Sahn looked down, "Yes. We have good doctors here, still. They could give you something to help ease your pain."

"That is much appreciated. One last request. I need to get in contact with a friend, can you accommodate that?"

"I will make sure of it. Sleeping quarters will be prepared for you all as well."

"Thank you. I'll go let Neko know the arrangements."

Mr. Sahn politely came over and helped Cyrus to his feet. Aureus's ears perked up when he heard the large doors slide open. Cyrus walked out, where he saw Neko lying in the grass front yard with Aureaus. He was staring at the stars using his palms as pillows.

"Neko. We have to talk."

"This smells bad," Neko said sadly, "what's happening?"

"A place to sleep is being prepared. For me. Listen. You have to leave here."

"What? Why?" Neko asked confused.

"Tozen is just going to keep looking for you. You *know* what he can do. How he can get into your head."

Neko unfortunately knew all about that. Cyrus continued.

"The Lotus Palm has given him great power. Almost…demonic power. We…you…have to do what you can to stop it. I'm going to contact a friend. He will be able to help get you to the corridors. Aureus, your life is out there," Cyrus said nodding towards the darkness of the trees, "It'll be hard enough to get Neko out of here in time. I hated the flight over here, so I could only imagine how you'd feel."

Aureus's lips peeled back in what only could be interpreted as a smile.

Neko looked at Cyrus. His eyes withheld tears.

"What about you? What happens to you?"

Cyrus looked at him deeply, sincerely, and told him the truth.

"I'm not going to make it Neko, you know that. I just want to use what I have left to protect you. Protect Everett."

"Everett?"

"Yes. He's my son. Find him before Tozen does. Please."

"I…will try my best, sensei."

"Leave before dawn. If you can make it to Bangkok, we'll take care of the rest. My colleague will provide you with any information that will help. You can trust him."

Neko, looked down nervously. Cyrus put a hand on his shoulder.

"I'm proud of who you've become, Neko."

Aureus stood up as if on cue. He leaned down so Cyrus could use his massive frame to help himself up off of the ground. Together, they walked towards a smaller, adjacent cottage. Aureus slowed his strides to match Cyrus's as he struggled to walk towards the door.

"Aureus Rex. Or Chairat. You've had it pretty rough yourself, huh?"

Aureus stopped walking and looked at Cyrus with a tilted head, surprised to hear his old name.

Cyrus was now just a few steps from the threshold of the door. He rubbed Aureus between the ears as the large cat licked his face.

"Oh, feeling sentimental are we," Cyrus asked with a laugh.

Aureus turned and began walking away, but not before one last glance in Cyrus's direction. Cyrus nodded at him, turned, and opened the door to his room for the night. It was a comfortable, if not quaint space, with only a bed and a bathroom. Cyrus wasted no time lying down. All of the exhaustion over the last couple of days, the last couple of months truthfully, began to settle on his weakened frame. Every ache and pain and labored breath became more prominent. Thoughts began to rush through his mental. He could see his mother's face right before he left to join the ARU. He could see Everett's first steps as a baby, Tarin's tear soaked face as he told her that he wanted to enroll Everett in the training program at Mount Z. His friend Jerry slumped against a tree, dying. His son as a grown man, dressed as a member of the Metropolitan Corridor Tribunal. Slowly, he faded off into a deep sleep. The footsteps that crept into his quarters went unheard as he lay still. Tozen walked over to the edge of the bed and stood over Cyrus.

"Mr. Santeaux," He said with a soft tone, "You are much smarter than even I have given you credit for."

As he spoke, he held out his hand, which gripped his katana blade. The blade removed itself from its sheath and slowly, silently, floated into position. The pointed tip hung right over Cyrus's heart. Tozen stared coldly as the sword began to push through Cyrus's chest. With a sudden jolt, it pierced through with ease, so fast the blade touched the floor. Blood started too ooze from the wound. Cyrus's chest heaved up and down. Up and down. Up. Down. It didn't lift again. Tears fell from his closed eyes. Tozen smirked as his sword withdrew itself slowly, now glistening with blood. He removed a small handkerchief from his pocket and rubbed it along his sword as it floated through the air, gradually making its way back into its sheath. He walked out into the night, where Orion was awaiting him. Flames engulfed the buildings as Tozen's guard raized the village. Dead bodies were being piled in the center. Mr. Sahn was one of them.

"Mr. Santeaux is no more."

"I thought you sent some of the guards to take care of this?" Orion asked.

"They ran into a certain four-legged complication," Tozen replied, motioning his hand in the direction of a group of dismembered guards. Huge claw marks and bite marks had ripped them to shreds. The paw prints of Aureus lead off into the jungle.

"A shame about Santeaux. I honestly thought that he would become one of our strongest members. I remember the letter I received from him after the attempted siege of the Ark. He seemed…quite enthusiastic. It inspired my commitment."

"As it should have," Tozen responded.

"Neko is gone as well," Orion mentioned.

Tozen was visibly annoyed by that fact, "I figured as much."

"What is the next directive, Tozen? The Corridors are in a tizzy about the recent world events. If we wait too long to act…"

"I don't need to be lectured by you, Orion. Your task is to find and apprehend the Santeaux boy. Something that you *shoud* have done when you failed so miserably obtaining the Ark."

"Understood. I will depart immediately."

"Yes. You will. The final phase begins now."

CHAPTER TWENTY-SIX

The New Cell

Everett snapped out of a nightmare, popping up in his seat. Olu's eyes slowly opened.

"You dreamin' again? Damn, I thought you wouldn't shut up."

Everett rubbed his face with both hands. Olu leaned up in his seat.

"Yo, you good? You bout to throw up or some shit? Actin' like it's yo' first time on a plane."

"I'm fine," Everett said coldly as he stood up, "Besides, this is your first time on a plane like this. Usually, a goon like you wouldn't be able to enjoy all this luxury."

"Nigga all the paper I got you gon' talk to me about luxury? Whatever son." Olu put his headphones back on and let his head lean against the window. They would arrive in New Rouge soon, the capitol city of the Gulf Corridor. This was Everett's first time visiting in person, though he had familiarized himself with the area prior to their departure. The Gulf Corridor surrounded the Gulf of Mexico with huge coastal cities that stretched from the Southeast side of Texas to the Florida panhandle. The Swamp Corridor to most, it was the premier port and shipping destination in the entire United Corridors.

The oil industry, though dwindling because of the advancements in renewable energy, still had a firm hold on the area. The poorer populations that couldn't afford to lace their houses with solar panels or buy cars with hydrogen drives still relied heavily on gas and oil. That fact was, not surprisingly, exploited by the rich CEO's of these companies. Everett was well aware that the Swamp Corridor was known for corruption at all levels. It'd be interesting to see if that corruption permeated the Gulf Corridor Mecca. If a turncoat like Orion could sit on the Metropolitan Corridor Tribunal for so long unchecked it wouldn't be far-fetched to assume the worst.

His target was Zachariah Tomes, the premier of a zealot cell called the Red Dogs. That cell led the Gulf Corridor Mecca in arms acquisitions as well as general arrests. They were known for their infiltration and tracking skills, which were derived from Tomes (callsign: Red Quill). Tomes was a world-class hunter. His weapons of choice were a specially crafted composite bow and a larger than average hunting knife. His fighting style was a combination of Muay Thai and Krav Maga. According to the dossier, Tomes was once suspended for using brutal force on a detained murderer. Conversely, he was also commended for tracking an escaped gun runner for twenty plus miles, on foot, before finally apprehending him. Everett reached for his communicator. It'd probably be a good idea to talk with Shef before he headed in. He placed the call and shortly thereafter, a voice answered. It wasn't Shef's.

"Um, hello? Myth?"

"Yeah. Yo, who is this?"

"This is Dunbar sir, from the MCPD. I've been working with.."

"I know who you are, where's Shef? Put him on."

"I…um…he's a little…uh…"

"Just put him on the damn comm."

"O…ok."

Shortly thereafter, another voice came through. It sounded like Shef, but it was noticeably altered.

"Why do you sound like Roger Troutman, son?"

"Orion. He's back."

"What?" Everett exclaimed, leaning up in his seat. He was so loud it shook Olu out of his sleep. He pealed off his headphones with a disgusted look on his face.

"Nah. How do you know? You sure about this?"

"Bastard showed up at the lab. Him and some other guy."

"What happened?"

"He came in asking about you, we got into some fisticuffs. I blew the lab to hell as a last resort."

"Shit," Everett said solemnly.

"We were lucky to make it out. I wanna believe he died in the explosion, but you know and I know he found a way to slither out."

"Yeah, no doubt. Well, I'm glad you're alive at least."

"Yeah," Shef paused for an unusually long time, "Me and Dunbar were analyzing the dawn. Get a load of this shit."

"That bad?"

"Worse. I have to confirm this but it seems like a heavy user gains, and don't laugh or say any crazy shit, they gain telepathic abilities. They can send messages or commands with their mind, which seem to intensify when the subject is sleep or in some type of meditative state."

"You mean, I have to worry about every fiend in the streets being able to move shit with his mind now?"

"First, that's telekinesis, not telepathy," Shef corrected, "Second, they'd have to be an extremely heavy user. According to my conversions, a grown man would have to abuse it for 8-10 years before he was even capable of doing it and most are totally oblivious to this side effect. I was hoping Orion would let slip who he was working for, but no such luck."

"Yeah, an ex-tribunal member knows better."

"Myth, no time to waste. Now that my lab is a smoking pile of rubble, my research is gonna take a hit. Luckily, I had some gifts prepped for ya'll before your departure. There's a titanium trunk in the back of the jet. It's got some new duds for you and the Anyogu kid."

Everett's eyes looked in Olu's direction, he was wide awake and listening intently on the conversation.

"I'm sure he'll love it," Everett said holding back a grin.

"The Gulf Corridor Tribunal has already been notified of our operations. They provided solar rail access to one of the private entrances to The Preserve. All you have to do is find Tomes. No pussy footin' Myth. The world is on the verge of war and the people behind it are after you."

"It's hard being the popular kid sometimes."

"Keep me posted."

"Myth out."

Everett slid the communicator off of his ear where Olu was waiting to pick up the conversation.

"Who was that?"

"That was Shef. As if the situation wasn't urgent enough, he said the lab was attacked. They were looking for me."

Olu didn't respond.

The dude that broke into my shit...he was probably there...

"Anyway. We land, then head for The Preserve."

"What the hell is that?"

"It's a huge artificial hunting ground," Everett informed, "Kind of a big deal down here."

Olu nodded pretending to care, distracted by another lingering thought.

"We need to suit up. Got some new gear."

Olu glanced back, "Your boy Shef gonna have niggas dressed as Power Rangers?"

"Shef is one of the most brilliant scientific minds in the corridors," Everett responded, "Anything he gives *you* will be an improvement. So shut your ass up and get ready."

Everett watched through the window as the plane began to descend, the fog in the air gave the impression that the clouds stretched from the sky to the street. The lights of the megalopolis began to dully shine through as they landed in the swamp.

CHAPTER TWENTY-SEVEN
The Gulf Corridor

Olu and Myth sat in an empty solar rail car. They were headed for The Preserve, the massive hunting ground created in the face of an expanding cityscape that infringed on the native wild life. Hunting is a way of life in the Gulf Corridor, especially in the New Orleans, New Rouge area. The way of life had to be preserved, hence the name. Shef provided intel on Tomes and the Red Dogs. All they had to do was make contact. That proved to be more difficult than anticipated. The Gulf Corridor Mecca, though cooperative, were just as fruitless in their attempts to contact the Red Dogs as Myth was. It seems that when they went on one of their training excursions in The Preserve they purposefully shut off all communications. The only way would be to find them. A fact neither man was too excited about.

"So, we have to go to this place and find these muthafuckas in a swamp? We don't need none of these cats *this* bad," Olu lamented staring out of the window as swamp forestation sped in dark green blurs past the window.

"He's good at what he does. I'm not a hunter either, trust, but if you need to find someone, anyone, anywhere, he can do it."

"All this technology in this tight ass suit and we *still* need someone to do what? Eat some grass and tell us we're going in the right direction?"

Myth sighed, "All this complaining, I'm wondering how necessary it is to have *you* here."

As the sun began to set, they arrived at The Preserve. Huge concrete walls stretched around the enclosure, for as far as they could both see. There were watchtowers along different points of the wall. The solar rail integrated smoothly into the structure, coming to a stop under a concrete canopy.

"We're here," Myth said.

Myth and Olu both stepped out. Myth snickered as he noticed how uncomfortable Olu was walking in his new Shef-engineered suit, an awkward stride like he sat in something wet. The humor was magnified by how comfortable Myth felt wearing the suit in contrast. The mask was a different story. Olu refused to wear it because he didn't want to cut his beard so he opted to use a black ski mask that he just happened to bring with him. Myth didn't want to waste energy arguing about why he brought it. But he had to ask.

"Really?"

"What?"

"A God damn *ski mask*, Lu?"

"Ay, it's get it how you live. Got these two," he smiled large to reveal an elaborate platinum grill in his mouth. The nearby lights gently bounced off of his shiny teeth. Myth just stared at Olu in disbelief.

"We should get going. Take this," he tossed a device to Olu, "It goes around the back of your head, tighten it so it doesn't slip off."

"What's it do," Olu asked as he fumbled to put it on over his ski mask.

Myth shook his head, "It's a light visor. It'll project a two inch ring display in front of your eyes. Infrared, xray, all that."

Olu clumsily adjusted it into position.

"No, press here," Myth demonstrated. A perfectly symmetrical black band of light pixelated into view, covering his eyes.

Olu nodded in approval and activated his own visor.

"Hard."

"This will make it a hell of a lot easier. You can see what I see in the upper right corner of the display. Might as well scan for footprints first, maybe try to find some heat signatures."

The two began their journey into the grounds of The Preserve. The compound itself seemed like an immense labyrinth. Scaffold walkways connected trees. Concrete tunnels and walkways blended into the wood and wet earth. Myth was busy scanning the environment as Olu trudged closely behind.

"I'm glad we have these visor things on, it's dark as fuck. Why would someone wanna come here for fun?"

"Quiet."

Myth stopped and looked around. He saw animal tracks through his visor outlined in light blue. The sounds of the night filled the air with a variety of noise pollution. Frogs croaked in no particular rhythm against the constant backdrop of insects buzzing. His eyes went to a nearby tree that had faint footprints going up the side towards the canopy. The footprints were from a man.

"Yo, they're trying to stay off the ground. We should do the same, use the bridge system they have integrated into the trees."

Olu sighed, "Now I gotta climb trees an shit?"

Myth held up his arm. He nodded at Olu's. He looked at it confused.

"Okay. Now what? I ain't a zealot, so I ain't hip to this."

"It's not hard, Shef's new design actually made it a bit easier. Point your arm. Shoot. The light on your hand means it's got a sufficient hold of something. Clinch your fist to recoil the cord."

"Man, whatever, I got –OH SHIT!"

Myth watched as Olu zipped out of sight and seconds later come crashing back down to the ground on his chest. The impact knocked the air out of his lungs. Myth couldn't contain his laughter. Olu mumbled curses as he got back up to his feet.

"Alright. We're out for real this time," Myth said.

He zipped up quickly with Olu clumsily following behind him. They went deeper and deeper into the hunting grounds, encountering different animals on the way.

"This place a zoo or hunting grounds," Olu asked as they swiftly made their way through the night, "I coulda sworn I saw a rhino."

"You ain't seen no damn rhino."

"Son, I saw a rhino."

The duo came to a large clearing with a stream separating two banks. They swung down. Myth was impressed with Olu's use of the grapple arm. He caught on quickly even though he complained about it every bit of the way.

"So, any sign of 'em?" Olu asked.

"Nah. Trail is cold. All of the footprints I can see on the trees have faded."

"Faded," Olu said with doubt, "We're in their house. Somethin' tells me they're paintin' the picture they want us to see."

Myth silently agreed with that reasoning. He toggled his visor to night vision mode and scanned the surrounding area. He stared off into the tree line. A fox dashed out into the clearing. Myth continued to scan the wooded area. His eyes drifted upward where he saw a figure in the distance crouched on a high branch. They were definitely being watched.

"Olu. Look up there. See that?"

"Yeah. Yeah I see 'em."

"Just be cool, the others have to be close by."

They stood still, watching and waiting. The unknown pursuer stood equally still in the trees. Myth's head jerked to the right as he saw something flying into his peripheral vision. A flash grenade.

"Olu! Cover your-"

Too late. The grenade exploded with a bright flash, rendering Myth temporarily blind.

Can't front…good move. But if they think that's going to be enough.

He closed his eyes and settled into the Satoichi Fist.

"Lu, you good?"

"Ears ringin' like shit, but I covered my eyes before it went off. The bastard's gone now," Olu said.

Myth listened to the sounds of the night, the slight breeze cutting through tree branches, periodic thumps on wood that were becoming gradually louder. He realized they were footfalls.

"They're moving on our position. Olu, you should switch your visor to pick up heat signatures."

"Man, you know I dunno how to do that shit. That's one of these buttons on the side right here or somethin'?"

"What we got here," an unknown voice came from behind them, "Got some visitors, huh?"

"Seems that way," Another voice confirmed from a different direction.

"Don't think they're poachers, bruh," a third voice wondered aloud.

The three zealots surrounded Myth and Olu. Olu studied all of them carefully, unfazed. Myth was the first one to speak.

"I'm Everett Santeaux. Callsign-"

"Myth," One of the zealots interrupted, "There's not a zealot that goes through Mount Z who don't know 'bout you."

"Well, that'll make this a bit easier. Where's your premier?"

The three laughed loudly. One responded after his chuckling subsided, "Your guess is as good as ours. We been looking for him all night."

"Man, let's cut this bullshit so we can hurry up and get the fuck outta here. All this small talk, psh," Olu snarled.

"You're obviously not a zealot from the looks of things," one of the three observed.

"He's gotta ski mask on for Christ sakes."

The three laughed again, louder this time, a joint cackle like hyenas. Myth didn't need his eyes to see that Olu's temper was rising.

"I need to speak with Red Quill, ASAP. You guys will assist with that," Myth said.

"Oh, we will?"

"E, they look like they tryin' to set it. Just say the word," Olu said, eager for a fight.

"One half-assed zealot and another blinded by a flash grenade. Still can't see can ya?"

Myth didn't respond.

"You need us to find our premier. I don't know about my dogs here, but we're not convinced that you live up to the hype…Myth."

"Now…this is something you don't want to do," Myth said calmly.

All three drew their blades in unison, ruby red katanas with matching hilts. They darted towards Myth and Olu. Myth glided between sword slashes and kicks with ease as two pressed him backwards with their attacks. Olu's awkward means of fighting was proving problematic for his opponent. Sword swings came uncomfortably close to Olu, which did nothing but enrage him, causing him to fight in an even more frenetic, unpredictable manner. He flipped over an incoming attack and landed a vicious combination of punches to his opponent's midsection. The impact made the attacker step backwards to regain his bearings.

"Not bad for an untrained piece of shit. Not good enough, either," he said.

His condescending eyes glared at Olu. They rushed towards each other. Myth smoothly dodged attacks before landing his own. He grabbed the wrist of an errant swipe and planted an open palm into the chest of one of the Red Dogs, sending him falling backwards. Myth leapt into the air, taking out his sword and cutting three arrows out of the night aimed for Olu's back. The pieces pierced the ground around their feet.

"Olu, the premier is here. He's hiding. Let's put these guys down," Myth commanded.

"Yeah, it'd help if you opened your eyes," Olu said angrily.

Myth shrugged, "Both your eyes don't seem to be helping your ass much. I'm the one fighting two of them."

The statement caught the three attackers off guard until one broke the silence.

"What? He's had his eyes closed the whole time?"

"He's a master of Zatoichi Fist. The flash grenade didn't have any effect."

"Fine time for you to say somethin'," his comrade yelled in disgust, "At least he respects us enough to take out his blade now."

"Not quite," Myth said putting his katana away, "Besides, I'm not trying to kill you."

"They sho' look like they tryin' to kill US," Olu said, fists still clinched.

"Holster your weapons, enough of this," Myth commanded.

"We take commands from one premier, and it's not you," one of the Red Dogs shot back.

As soon as his arrogant statement dissolved in the air, Myth was upon them. His Zatoichi Fist gave way to his Long Step Mantis. Swift kicks rapidly fired at the three Red Dogs. They all frantically tried to block his one-man rush. A jumping roundhouse simultaneously disarmed and knocked one of them backwards, his back slammed into a tree. Olu stood back and laughed as he marveled at Myth's skill. The way he skipped and hopped between blades, using his feet as his primary weapon, striking with his hands when needed, all the while exerting minimal effort. It was like watching a maestro conduct a symphony.

When I busted outta Mount Z, he used that blind style on me...almost took me out before I made my move. Son's gotten better. Crazy, but he has.

The remaining two fought back with a sense of desperation. Myth somersaulted out of the lane of strikes meant to do considerable damage. Whilst twisting through the air he fired his grapple arm, hitting an attacking zealot's wrist. He zipped towards him and smashed into his face with a knee. In a flurry, he ripped his blade out once more, slicing a barrage of arrows falling around him as he flipped and cartwheeled back over to Olu's side. The remaining Red Dog tried to capitalize on the opportunity by rushing Myth's back. He swung to take Myth's head off his shoulders. He ducked just in time. When the zealot looked down, he saw Myth's blade pointed up, inches away from his stomach.

"I could spill your whole shit right now," Myth said with his back turned, "Stand down."

"Welp, go on'n listen to the sum'bitch," a voice came from behind the battle. All three zealots re-aligned themselves and put away their weapons. The last of them leapt down from the trees and landed in front of them. He was dressed in a standard zealot uniform with a long red scarf tied around his neck. It flitted in the wind like a ribbon.

"Zachariah Tomes," Myth asked.

"Myth. Heard alotta bout 'cha," Red Quill replied, his southern drawl becoming more apparent with each sentence.

Myth nodded, "You have a new directive. You'll depart with me immediately."

"Premier, what's this dude talkin' about," one of his crew asked from behind. As unruly as the team had seemed during their confrontation with Olu and Myth, now they acted as well behaved as a group of school children.

"The Mecca tol' me this was gon' happen. The G8 abductions makin' people lose their shit, I don't blame 'em. I'ma be takin' off for a bit," Red Quill said, still looking at Myth.

"That was easy, now let's get the hell outta here," Olu said with contempt.

"I ain't neva seen anyone whoop up on my boys like you done," Red Quill said with a laugh. He turned back towards his cell, "If I hadn't lobbed some support from the shadows, one of ya'll assholes woulda ended up dead. Red Fang, you gotta stop thinkin' you can take anyone on. That'll get you killed outchea. Especially against someone like Mr. Santeaux here. Santeaux? You got family from 'round here?"

Myth allowed himself to relax as the tension in the air had all but disappeared.

"No family in the Swamp Corridor. It's rare someone says it correctly on the first try."

"Buddy, I bet. I can only imagine how dem yanks would butcher it," Red Quill said with a laugh.

"I ain't gonna lie, I thought it was Santee-UX," one of his crew said from behind.

"That's why you the dumb one," Red Quill replied, "Apologies to ya'll. This is my cell. The Red Dogs. Red Fang, Red Eye, and Red Hand."

Myth analyzed them as they bowed.

"Oh, now they wanna show some respect," Olu asked angrily.

"And who's this? 'Nother zealot you picked up on the way," Red Quill asked nodding in Olu's direction, "The sum'bitch has a *ski mask* on. Where'd you find this thug?"

"Watch yo' mouth country boy," Olu said stepping in his direction. Myth's arm blocked his path, "We'll be able to discuss the details later. We don't have time to waste."

"Bout damn time. Thought we'd never leave," Olu said as he snatched off his ski mask. Immediately the Red Dogs drew their weapons, including Red Quill. He pulled out his huge hunting knife and held it with a reverse grip.

"What'n the hell is *he* doin' witcha?!"

Myth's face was surprised under his mask, "You know him?"

"Olufemi Anyogu aka Ink aka Lu. One of the biggest crime lords on the East Coast and head of the Ink Boys crime syndicate. He can be linked to a multitude of crimes throughout the entire country, including extortion, embezzlement, money laundering, assault, connections to murders in at least three corridors, and the sale and distribution of dawn."

"You forgot a couple," Olu said unfazed.

"Premier, I think this could go a long way with the tribunal. Brining Anyogu in?"

"Son, you out yo' fuckin' mind," Olu spat more aggressively.

And just like that the tension was turned all the way up.

Myth drew his sword, everyone flinched.

"Nah, Myth. No offense to ya', but me and my dogs would be in a mighty good place if we were to apprehend your friend there."

"How is it even possible for you to have him in your custody outside of the Metro anyway? We should think about bringing *you* in," Red Fang said with enhanced confidence.

"Shut your puppy up while the grown folks are talking," Myth said, "Or I'll do it myself. I want to." The statement caused Red Fang to recoil, remembering the recent battle that put his entire team to shame.

"You have a mission. Tonight," Myth continued, redirecting his gaze to Red Quill.

The Red Dogs exchanged surprised looks.

"How'd you know 'bout that," Red Quill asked.

"Of course I know about that," Myth responded.

"Witcho' stupid ass," Olu added unnecessarily. A quick glare from Myth shut him up.

"We're joining your cell."

Myth's remarks were heard with visible discomfort. Even under masks the dissatisfaction rang clear.

Myth was getting frustrated.

"Let's not get shit twisted, we don't *need* any of your dogs. I think we demonstrated that loud and clear earlier. We're here to help you, make this sting quick. Because trust me, the shit that I'm pulling you *into*, makes all this running around in the woods look real, for lack of a better word…fucking stupid."

"Mmm," Olu added with emphasis like a hypeman.

"Tomes. Trust me when I say that I wouldn't be here if I didn't *need* to be here. I'll brief you on everything you need to know."

Myth put away his weapon swiftly, causing everyone to flinch nervously once more. "We'll be heading back. Please. Join us when you're ready."

Red Quill slid his knife into a side holster, the rest of his team eased up as well. He nodded in silent agreement. Slowly, Myth and Olu disappeared through the trees, leaving the Red Dogs to themselves.

Red Quill turned to his team, "Welp. You heard the man."

"Just like that? Just leave like that," Red Hand's quiet voice asked.

"Myth wasn't jokin' now. There's gotta be a reason for it all. As far as Ink goes…I'll hear what Myth's gotta say 'bout it. But best believe me, I'ma be keepin' my eyes on 'em. My dogs gon' eat if I have anything to do wit' it."

CHAPTER TWENTY-EIGHT

The Seventh Street Wharf

Myth, Olu, and the Red Dogs stood atop a high rise looking down on the Mississippi River. The river's banks were lined with ports and skyscrapers, interconnected with a series of multi-level bridges like a web. There were large ships coming and going. The water purification stations dotted the river between other structures. Myth zoomed in on a particular ship that was unloading at a dock: *The Dancing Blade.*

"There it is," he said more to himself than to anyone else.

"Welp," Red Quill said putting away a small retractable telescope, "let's get on it. Dogs, ya'll descend with Myth. I'll tail, help ya'll out wit' my arrows if I gotta. Find the captain. You got a picture of 'em."

The Red Dogs all looked down at their forearms. Myth noticed the old gear and wondered why they hadn't upgraded. It seemed antiquated to him, spoiled by being in such close proximity to Shef's genius.

"Ya'll gon' down. I'll take out the aerial surveillance cameras from up here." Red Quill took out his composite bow. With a button press, it snapped into full size. His team readied their grapple guns. Olu eyed his grapple arm. Myth walked over to him.

"You scared?"

"Hell nawl!"

"If you scared, say you scared."

"Son. Chill."

"You sure, we kinda high up, you don't really know how to use that, I mean, you said that yourself…"

"Man, I said no!"

Myth shrugged his shoulders, ran towards the building's edge and jumped off. Red Quill looked at his cell and nodded, they all leapt after in quick succession. Olu was still there.

"Somethin' holdin' you back brotha?" Red Quill asked.

"Brotha? Oh you tryin' to talk like you hood now?"

Red Quill laughed and shook his head, "You got me all wrong buddy. Betta hur' up befo' you lose 'em. Wouldn't want to see you smash into one of those metal bridges on the way down."

Olu snorted and took a deep breath. He too, followed Myth's steps off of the building and into the air. He could make out the figures of the ones that had leapt before him, shooting into different directions as they used their grapple guns to avoid bridges and structures on their way down to the banks of the river. He clumsily followed suit, almost killing himself many times over before he landed on a small three story building dwarfed by the other structures. He hit the roof panting heavily but thankful to be standing on it. He glanced up to find Myth's eyes staring at him, filled with childlike delight. Oddly, it made Olu more comfortable as opposed to enrage him.

"Let's hit it. Move fast. Me and Olu have these visors, we'll be able to see through walls," Myth said matter-of-factly.

"Well, no offense Myth, but we won't be needin' any of that. This is what the dogs do," Red Fang said.

"Well then, lead on."

Red Fang nodded to his team mates and they darted in different directions. Myth heard a voice come through his comm. It was Shef."

"Myth?"

"Yeah Shef, what's up?"

"The captain is in that boat somewhere. Whoever sent them is smart. Has them in a uniform so it's hard to tell who's who. Like a boat full of high school janitors."

"So how do we find him?"

"I'd tell ya' that you use the facial recognition software in your visor, but you won't even have to do that. The dogs will find him. It's about what you can learn from him once they do."

"Hm. They're that good, huh?"

"Well, I know how to pick 'em. Just track the one, he's kinda the second in command I guess."

"Red Fang."

"Yeah, whatever. They should be swarming on the captain's location any-"

Shef was interrupted by the distinct sound of gunshots.

"That's the real shit," Olu's voice said through the comm.

"He's right Myth," Shef replied, "that's actual lead. The Metro had you a bit spoiled, the block is a little hotter down here."

"Shit, lots of heat down here! We got a visual on the captain, but they're guarding him pretty good," Red Fang reported through the comm as shots rang off in the background."

Myth and Olu were on their way down without hesitation. The ship was in sight. "Snipers on the boat," Olu yelled.

Myth used his visor to confirm. He zoomed in to see two raising high powered rifles in his direction. Before either man's finger could squeeze the trigger, two arrows crashed through the soft tissue of their necks. They both fell incapacitated.

"Well, get a goddamn move on," Red Quill's voice boomed through the comm. Myth took off with Olu close behind him. They could see through the materials on the boat, the steel and wood that comprised it, warm red outlines of men with guns scurrying about, some blasting random shots.

"I'll illuminate the quickest path," Shef said to both of them as their feet landed on the deck of the ship. Within moments, a light blue series of arrows appeared in their heads up displays. Men that were positioned as lookouts randomly fell about them, punctured with arrows as Red Quill silently watched over them. They burst into a two story storage area filled with large metal crates of cargo. A guard noticed their presence. Olu used his grapple arm to zip over towards them, punching him to the ground with a broken jaw.

"Red Fang, where are they holding him?"

"Myth! Things are getting' outta control here! He's in that back room on the second floor."

"I'm goin'," Myth said.

"Wait," Red Fang yelled through the comm, "There's at least fifteen guys around there, they all have automatic weapons. Real ones! Bullets not some pansy ass stun rounds!"

"Yeah, ya'll not used to seein' too much of this up North, huh," Red Eye said with a hint of disdain, "Ya'll too good for your own good."

"Calm ya'self down Red Eye. Y'all were gettin' pushed back. Nowhere to go but up with him along," Red Fang replied.

"Yeah, so shut the fuck up," Myth said frustrated. Without hesitation he used the shipping containers to jump up to the second floor, dodging shots along the way. Despite Red Eye's chiding, there was some truth to his thinking. The Metropolitan Corridor was different, it was the paramount example. With Myth's lead, the number of illegal firearms had steadily declined. It was rare that they encountered anyone with real lead, and when they did, it wasn't the arsenal that faced them now. This just proved the point that every other corridor was drastically different.

"I gotta visual, moving in."

Myth threw a pair of kunai at the guards in front of him, hitting their hands and forcing them to drop their weapons. He quickly put them to the ground before darting past them. Olu zipped up with his grapple arm and landed close behind him.

"I see you gettin' nice with that shit, boy," Myth said as they ran side by side to engage with another group of guards. The feeling was exhiliarating, something that neither one of them had expected to feel before: fighting side-by-side.   Olu charged ahead, cartwheeling and flipping through bullets, he rolled into a kneeling position and licked off shots from a handgun that he lifted off of one of the bodies Myth dropped moments earlier.

"Whooo shit! That kickback feel good!

"Olu, draw their fire, Red Dogs, flank em."

Shots continued to be sprayed. Hissing and whizzing past them, sparking off of the metal shipping containers.

"Dahhh! One clipped me," Red Eye said, "Gotta fall back!"

Arrows rained on guards shooting from the floor below them. Red Quill had entered the fray. He jumped down, putting his bow away and ripping his hunting knife from his belt. He tore through a crowd with quick rapid fire stabs and Muay Thai style kicks that devastated bones. His long red scarf twisted in the air behind him like a ribbon dancer.

"I'm good down here, keep goin'!"

And so they did, closer and closer to the barricaded room that the captain was in. Myth ran towards them, ripping out his sword. He dipped every shot fired at him. When he got close enough, he severed both men's hands with quick flicks of his blade. Olu knocked them out with a flurry of elbows and fists. An assembly line of pain. Red Fang was on the opposite side of the metal scaffold walkway, his hands were full fighting off guards, Olu was dismantling his opponents, taking their weapons and beating them half to death with their own guns. Myth shot his grapple arm and zoomed over to Red Fang's position as a guard readied an assault rifle.

"Shit, we're not gonna make it," Red Fang cried out.

The guard steadied his aim and began to blast rapid fire shots at Myth and Red Fang. Myth stepped directly in the path of the oncoming bullets. With a quick series of hand gestures on his wrist screen, a blue silhouette pixelated into view in front of Myth's body. He jumped backwards and watched each bullet shoot blue sparks into the air as it entered the shield before falling to the ground harmlessly.

The guard looked stunned, leaving enough time for Olu to creep up behind him and kick him hard in the back of one of his knees. When he collapsed to a kneel, Olu fired a knee to his skull to finish it.

"Shef. You're a fool for that one," Myth said out of breath.

"Worked a lot better than I thought it would, I ain't gonna lie," Shef conceded, "He's in there."

The door to the room was kicked off the hinges. Before the captain could draw his gun, two kunai cut through the air hitting his shoulder and hand. He yelled out in pain. The Red Dogs went to apprehend him. They sat him down and bound his hands. Red Hand ripped out the kunai with little regard for the captain. This caused him to scream out in pain once again.

"Where is this shipment coming from and where is it going," Myth asked calmly.

The captain did not respond.

"This sum'bitch wanna play it the hard way, huh," Red Quill said annoyed.

"I know where they're from. I was able to piece together stuff from you and Olu's video feeds. The containers were loaded in Bangkok."

"Thailand," Myth said out loud intentionally, everyone watched as the captain got visibly more tense, "This is a huge buy," Olu said, "Everybody that push know that the product hits the shores here first. And the people movin' it get a sizeable cut to do what they do. This dude here ain't no different. He gettin' gwop, he don't wanna fuck it up."

Myth was quiet. Olu looked at Myth. He nodded his head, so Olu continued.

"If he was someone workin' for me? I know they getting' paper, cuz you gotta treat the people who work for you with respect like that, feel me? Who's gonna work for a nigga who ain't breakin' bread?"

He walked slowly over to the captain.

"How you balance shit son is you gotta make 'em fear you. Like, if you worked for *me* you'd *know* that I would have no problem murkin' you out. Laugh about it later."

The captain's eyes darted back and forth nervously.

"Dead men don't cash any checks."

The captain looked around. His chest was heaving up and down heavily and sweat dripped from his forehead. He still didn't say a word.

"Oh, fuck this shit," Olu said as he pulled a pen from somewhere on his person, no one was quite sure from where. Only one person knew that the pen contained poison. He knew that his friend had let his nickname in the streets make an appearance. Olu slammed the pen into the captain's neck, he squealed with pain.

"That's poison, son. If you start talkin', we can get you the cure or whateva, whateva. But you don't have a lot of time, maybe like fifteen minutes, if that, for real. So you may wanna start spittin' shit out. Hopefully you'll have enough time to call some family or some shit, tell 'em you love 'em an shit."

"Okay. Okay."

Myth's eyes widened at the voice of the captain.

"We just deliver. Get from one point to the other."

Myth stepped forward, "For who? Who are you moving this for?"

"I'll be damned, if this dumb bastard don' start talkin' I'ma put an arrow straight through his face," Red Quill exploded, quickly removing his bow and loading it with an arrow.

"Chill, we've gotten this far, it'd be good to leave with as much info as possible. Now," Myth said returning his glare to the captain, "Talk."

"A...man. The head of a science group, is what we've been told. Nobody I know believes this. Tozen."

"Tozen, Shef did you get that," Myth asked through his comm.

"Got it, gonna start data minin' now," Shef's voice confirmed.

"Alright, we're done here. Meet us at the extraction point."

"Gotcha, Shef out."

"Let's roll out," Myth said to the group, "Quill. You gotta good cell down here. No doubt. You know what you have to do."

Red Quill nodded, "Welp. Looks like I'll be takin my leave from ya'll. Ya'll be just fine. This'a huge bust, should reflect kindly on all ya'll records. And Myth here is the fuckin' man," Red Quill added comically, "No doubt we don't get this far without him…or Olu."

"Yeah, you saved our asses in there," Red Eye said to Myth.

"No, I saved *your* ass in there," Myth said extending his hand, "You gotta long way to go. Don't get too gassed too early."

"Noted." Red Fang said, gripping Myth's hand with a firm shake.

The voice of the captain cut through the relaxed atmosphere, "What about the antidote for the poison, I'm…"

"Gettin' light headed," Olu asked sarcastically, "Dry mouth? Shortness of breath. Yeah, it's jumpin' off now."

"The…cure," the captain asked spastically coughing.

Olu leaned down towards him, "Yo' dumb ass ain't gettin' no *cure*. You're 'bout to cough to death in like three good minutes. Just needed you to up with a name. It's the weak ones that usually do. No sense of loyalty."

The captain began to violently foam at the mouth, his eyes rolled back into his head. The jerking of his limbs came to a stop. A long awkward silence followed.

"What, we got the name didn't we? Besides, we didn't have time for this bullshit," Olu said shrugging.

"He's right about that," Myth said, "Let's go."

CHAPTER TWENTY-NINE

A Little Later

"You ain't tell me we was takin' the bad ass X-Men jet, bro. The perks of bein' on a tribunal, huh?" Red Quill said.

Everett laughed, "This case is the highest clearance. What did you expect, Tomes?"

"I expected…well, I dunno what I expected. A private jet with a pilot, though?"

"Actually, technically there *is* no pilot. Shef controls it remotely," Myth replied. "You shittin' me? Keeps getting' better."

"Well, soak it up while it last, Tomes."

"You right 'bout that," Red Quill said reclining in his seat, "You can call me Zac."

"Well, Zac, I said you'd get more info, so here goes."

"I'm all ears."

Everett input some commands on a touchscreen embedded in the arm of his chair. Shortly after, Shef's voice came through speakers in each man's head rest.

"Shef you there? We got Zac Tomes with us."

"Good, good. Ya'll movin' ahead of pace. Anyway, the shipping containers definitely were filled with dawn, tons of the stuff. The Gulf Corridor Tribunal is saying it's the top three drug busts to date. Some of that was destined for the Metro. Will put a dent in Olu's pockets no doubt."

"Pssh, it'd take a lot more than that," Olu said dismissively as he pulled a hood over his head and went about staring out the window.

"The name that was given, Tozen, there's no record of anyone with that name, first or last, working for the shipping company or for any of the organizations that contacted the shipping company."

"Probably a fake name," Everett suggested.

"Could be. I'll keep searching. On the world front, they've started special sessions at the U.N. concerning the G8 Incident, that's what they're callin' it now."

"Yeah, what they sayin?"

"They're demanding answers. Every other country is convinced it was an operative from one of the corridors, zealots more than likely, and the longer we can't provide answers the guiltier we look."

"Any word on whether the captive leaders are alive," Everett asked as he reviewed documents on a tablet computer.

"No word yet. No ransom or nothin'. You'd think that with these high profiles involved, you could get a trillion dollars in ransom. So, why not ask for it? Man, when these countries get tired of our beatin' 'round the bush..."

"They'll be trying to start a war. We got the name and we know the same group is behind the drugs and the kidnappings. "

"The same group," Zac asked leaning forward. He looked even younger under the mask than Everett expected.

"Yeah, when I was," Everett stopped short of mentioning his tribunal status in the past tense, "the Metropolitan Corridor Tribunal, with Shef's help, made the connection."

"Trippy shit, man," Zac yawned, "Makes sense why ya'll need me now. If it's 'bout trackin' someone down, I gotcha."

"That's the hope Mr. Tomes, but he may be a bit harder to locate. Hopefully, we'll find out more in the Midwest Corridor," Everett said, "Hopefully...but first there's a quick stop I wanna make, I'm sending the coordinates now," Everett said as he leaned back in his seat.

CHAPTER THIRTY

A Quick Stop

The dawn was breaking over the mountains as they arrived at Mount Z. It had been so long, almost ten years, since Everett set foot here. The training didn't change, the joy of success didn't change, the permanent ripple effect of failure didn't change, only the faces. Mount Z, a massive, chiseled constant swimming with variables. Zac and Olu were asleep in their chairs, trying to get what little rest they could between the legs of the trip. As they began to make their descent, Olu stirred awake when the bright sun forced his eyelids open. He looked agitated. Then, upon gazing out the window, he appeared to grow nervous. The last time Olu was at Mount Z, the circumstances were drastically different. Returning was sure to stir some emotions in the typically stoic gangster.

"Muthafuckin' Mount Z," Olu whispered out loud.

The trio eventually found themselves on the familiar path leading to the entrance. Winter was still in full effect mode up in the mountains. Snow still clung to tree limbs and the breeze carried a cold bite with it. As they approached the intricately carved oak doors, they slowly opened to welcome the prodigal son back again. Overseers standing watch in towers above gazed down, faces largely shrouded in robes. Everett stole a glance at Olu, he was silent, contemplative.

"C'mon. Master Xi should be waiting."

They walked familiar pathways through familiar vistas. Each breath brought with it an increased sense of nostalgia. The distant site of kids lined up at the pole stairs made Everett smile. Students were milling about going from training area to training area, accompanied by overseers. As they followed winding paths, some turned around to catch a glimpse of Everett, Olu, and Zac as they walked. The older ones seemed to recognize Everett. They leaned and whispered to nearby friends, who in turn stole their own quick peeks. Soon enough, more of them were turning around to see him. One had the bravery to call out from his group.

"Hey! Are you Everett Santeaux?"

Everett slowly nodded. The whispers and mumbling grew a bit more raucous, followed by students breaking their ranks to surround him like a celebrity. Truthfully, he was. His record running of the pole stairs still stood after all this time and his exploits after graduating had become legend. To hear the excited kids tell it, he single handedly fought off an army to destroy the Ark. Their eyes were filled with excitement as they reached out hands to give dap, shouting out their own times on the pole stairs and their plans post-graduation. Everett felt a surge of happiness from the adoration, but also the realization that some of these faces may not make it to graduation. Some may not make it to next week. Overseers, seeing the situation getting more unruly ushered the students away as Everett, Olu, and Zac pushed through the mob.

"Damn, brotha," Zac said as they continued down the path headed to Master Xi's dojo, "Yo' legend grows every year seems like."

"Seems like it."

"Don't gas this nigga, man," Olu said with an equal measure of playfulness and spite.

"I came outta Mount Z in 2001. I was here when he ran the pole stairs. I was here when he went to stop *you* from runnin' around like a goddamn lunatic. One of my friends was killed when you decided to quit. An underclassmen who ain't do nothin' but get in the way of a coward who wasn't enough to cut it," Zac shot back at

Olu with venom. Olu's face scrunched up like he smelled something foul.

"What the fuck did you just say," Olu said stopping in his tracks.

"I said," Zac said stepping to him without fear, "that you cut and run outta here cuz you ain't built to be a zealot. Never was. Never will be."

Before the situation escalated, Everett stepped between them.

"Chill. We're not here for this. Olu, you need to try to keep a low profile. Trust g, a new haircut and beard isn't enough to make people forget what you did here. How you left this place. You are an elephant on thin ice. Zac, despite what feelings you may have for him, you gotta tuck that shit away. What's going on is bigger than all of us, dig me?"

Olu and Zac stared at each other unflinching, until the trademark smirk spread across Olu's face.

"White boy's got some balls. I will say that."

"And you ain't too bad a fighter, either. Even though the sun shines on a dog's ass every once in a while," Zac replied with a grin.

After diffusing the situation, the trio walked the rest of the way in silence, each to their own thoughts, until the three stood at the large double doors to the dojo.

"Now this brings back some memories," Everett said aloud.

"Reminds me of gettin' my ass whooped in my initiation match," Zac said with a chuckle.

Everett rapped on the door. Before the echoes from the knocking could dissipate in the air, an overseer opened the door and led them in. In the center of the familiar sparring ring sat Master Xi, legs crossed, with a walking cane across his lap. His eyes were closed in deep meditation. His hair was gray to match his beard. The long braid rested on the ground behind him. Everett was happier to see him than he thought he would be. Xi's eyes slowly opened and a warm smile followed.

"Everett."

"Master Xi," Everett said with a bow of the head.

Xi slowly rose to his feet with the aid of an overseer's outstretched arm. The years had taken a toll on him, a fact that the crow's feet at the corners of his eyes supported. He used his cane to slowly walk towards them. The pronounced limp was impossible to ignore.

"It is indeed a pleasure to see you again, though not totally unexpected," Xi said before turning to Zac.

"Zacariah Tomes. You've found good company to keep, I see. Rising to premier level in about the same time as Everett did. Very impressive what you've done with the Red Dogs in the Gulf Corridor."

"Thank ya master," Zac said, his southern twang making the polite statement sound comical, "I've been recruited for a mission, so I intend to continue doin' what I do."

"I fully expect that, Zacariah. And who is," Master Xi paused, his eyes squinted examining Olu's face, "Bloody hell. You have got some nerve showing your face here, Olufemi."

"And you have a new pimp walk since I beat the shit outta you," Olu replied with no remorse. Xi quickly turned to Everett for an explanation.

"We need him, Master. He can help. He has already helped."

Xi turned back to see a satisfied smirk plastered on Olu's face.

"Him? Help? The only thing Olufemi has ever helped is himself. It's one of the reasons he turned out to be such a profound failure."

Xi's comment visibly got under Olu's skin. His smart-ass smile quickly disappeared.

"Come. Sit. We have much to discuss."

They all walked into a side room that was modestly furnished with an oak table and chair for each man. An overseer stood off to the side. Xi nodded, and the overseer promptly left the room. Everyone took a seat.

"Everett. Recently, I received a message from your father, Cyrus."

Everett's eyes widened. He hadn't spoken to his father in years.

"My dad? Why wouldn't he just contact me directly?"

"Time was of the essence and I could better accommodate his request with the help of my international connections. It was a more sensible route to reach out to me instead. Besides, he was apprehensive having been…estranged for so long."

"What's he doing? Where is he?"

Xi's eyes bounced to the floor and back to Everett's. There was a long, awkward pause.

"You know, he was relentless in the pursuit of new research that would aid in advancing the training program here in the Corridors. He was last in Thailand, working for a man named Tozen."

"What," Everett exclaimed with shocked surprise. Olu and Zac exchanged concerned looks.

"This man," Xi continued, "is despicable. What's worse, he has the Lotus Palm Manuscript and it's given him tremendous power and influence."

"The Lotus Palm, master? I remember sitting here as a kid and you telling us that the shit wasn't even real," Everett said firmly.

"I didn't think it was. I hoped that it wasn't."

"So, what's the big deal wit' the Lotus Palm," Zac inquired.

"The Lotus Palm Manuscript contains the practices and techniques of the Lotus Palm, also called the God Fist. It's believed that every style of martial arts can be traced back to this one. Even the meditation techniques that we incorporate, including the mind-body separation training that we do here, were first explored in the text of that manuscript. From what I've learned over the years, mastery of the style has never been achieved. Even to learn a significant portion took generations to accomplish. Fathers taught sons who taught sons who taught sons and even still, they never achieved *true* mastery."

"What denotes a true master, then," Everett asked.

"Nobody knows, truthfully. It is said that a true master can adapt and learn any style he comes against. He can toe the line between the conscious and unconscious mind, between life and death itself. In doing so he becomes a God."

"Jeeesus," Zac exhaled.

"Nin-Jesus," Olu laughed. No one else did.

Everett sat back and let out a long sigh, "Master, we've found out that this same guy Tozen is the one behind the G8 Incident and the influx of this new drug, The Dawn, into some of the corridors. Further, Crewshef has conducted experiments and concluded that dawn unlocks a kind of…mental strength in the users, to go along with the physical enhancements."

"Mental strength," Xi asked somewhat confused.

"Telepathy, telekinesis. It's hard to believe. But I trust Shef."

Xi solemnly shook his head, "This man is willing to ruin anything in his path to attain his goal. Cyrus's communication from the outside world was cut off at some point during his captivity. He made no mention of the G8 incident and that has to be the reason why. He spoke about dawn and how it was used in Tozen's experiments."

"That's that pure," Olu said flexing his knowledge of the illegal drug, "that shit is hard to come by. The powder that most cats slang and use has been cut. Kinda like makin' crack from cocaine."

"This dude sounds like he doin' everythang under the sun 'cept hidin' under kid's beds like the boogie man," Zac wondered out loud.

"He feared that you were in danger based on what he learned about Tozen's plans," Master Xi continued, "Which is the reason he sent someone to find you. Someone that he had been training in much the same way he trained you, Everett."

Upon hearing this, Olu's eyes widened and his body tensed up.

"Sent someone to find me? Why?"

"There is another layer to this, Everett. Through the information about the Lotus Palm that your father provided, there seems to be a common theme throughout. There has to be a certain innate ability within a person to master the Lotus Palm, a proclivity for the style itself."

Xi looked into Everett's eyes knowingly, "I assume Tozen believes you can be that person."

"At any rate, I'm glad you're safe. It was rather cunning to ensure that you had another set of eyes on you," Xi's gaze turned towards Olu, "You should know more about this, isn't that correct Olufemi?"

"Wha?"

"You heard me. Does your deceit know no bounds?" Master Xi said with disgust.

"What is he talking about Olu," Everett asked with a furrowed brow.

Olu leaned his head back and took a deep breath, "A dude ran up in my shit." "Whoa," Zac interjected under his breath. It was low enough that Olu heard it. Zac tried to hold back laughter. Olu continued.

"I had a guy break into my house before you came and tol' me I had to go with you, before even *you* tol' me I had to go with you. Killed some of my guards. Easily. Even gave me and Big Ax a run for our money before fallin' back. Said he was a messenger or whateva and I was supposed to keep an eye on you or whateva whateva. Or he'd go after my fam."

Everett shook his head, "How long did you plan on sittin' on this?"

"Ay, I wasn't about to let dude go rip my family apart. They don't have nothin' to do with this shit. Had to do what I had to do."

"Like I said," Xi scolded, "He only cares about his own interests. He's helping you, though that never was his intention. With that said, he was never going to harm your family, Olu. You just needed additional motivation, as has always been the case. What I didn't expect was Everett bringing you on this mission. It seems to have worked for the best, as there was another sent on Tozen's behalf to find Everett as well."

"Orion," Everett said.

"Correct," Xi confirmed.

Everett stared at Olu with cold eyes, "What did this messenger look like?"

"An animal. He was a man, kinda, but not really. He had cat eyes, sharp teeth, muthafuckin' tiger stripes, son. Tiger stripes."

"Orion was the same way. When we fought him at the Ark, he was visibly different, mutated," Everett reasoned.

"Tozen has been experimenting with gene splicing and other perversions of science, who knows what else his facility has churned out," Xi replied.

"This is all makin' my head hurt," Zac said.

"That's the first thing you said that I agree wit'," Olu added.

"Master Xi, knowing all of this information, and knowing about my dad, why didn't you rush to tell me anything?"

"Everett, I knew that you would come. I've seen it. Dreamt it. When the time was right, you would arrive. And here you are."

Everett, Zac, and Olu all sat silent, the power of their adversary seeming more and more insurmountable.

"So, is he coming back to the Metro?"

Xi looked sincerely into Everett's eyes, "I'm afraid…his health was ailing when he sent the message. He didn't think that he'd…"

"Understood," Everett said, a lump in his throat choked the words into near silence.

"We're headed to Chicago in the Midwest Corridor. There's a facility there that has been engaging in some questionable activity according to Shef, hopefully we can find out more. Try to figure out a way to stop this."

"That's what I'm afraid of, Everett," Xi said as he slowly stood up with the aid of his cane.

"Maybe there is no way to stop this."

Part II: Dawn Breakers

CHAPTER THIRTY-ONE

The Midwest Corridor

"Sorry to hear about your, dad man. Ya know, Xi doesn't know for sure." Shef said solemnly.

"I appreciate it, Shef, but we can't think about that right now," Myth interrupted, "We touchdown in Chicago soon, what's the deal?"

"The deal is, there's a large science and technology firm, Advanced Gentech Research, that operates in the Midwest Corridor. They have contracts across the world with different agencies, governments. Me and Dunbar here followed up on the shipping manifest, seems like some of the stuff on that boat that ya'll infiltrated in the Swamp was destined for this place."

"What would they need with crates of dawn?"

"I dunno. But you know who's gonna find out?"

Myth's silence acknowledged the obvious.

"This time it'll be a bit easier for ya, knock on wood," Shef continued, "Premier Constantine Alvarez, callsign: Exo, will meet you when you land. You've gone over his dossier. One of the best in the Midwest, no doubt about it. Proficient hacker, too. His cell has been assigned the case for the last month."

"So, help him so that he helps us?" Myth asked.

"Pretty much. He's a bit...prickly. Whether he leaves the Midwest with you is contingent on what he sees."

"Sounds like an arrogant bastard," Myth said.

"You guys should get along just fine, then."

The jet descended into the epicenter of the Midwest Corridor. Huge sky scrapers and eco-apartment complexes stretched up into the clouds as the twisted lines of solar rail tracks wound up and through the skyline like stitches holding together broken flesh. Every structure was built with sharp, sloping angles meant to better optimize the wind that rushed through the corridor, forcing it through locations where it could be harvested for energy. They landed at a private runway near the mecca of the Midwest Corridor.

"Suit up," Myth said shaking Zac awake and slapping Olu's hooded head with the end of his katana.

The door opened and a walkway lowered onto the tarmac. Myth emerged first, followed by Red Quill in his new suit, and Olu lumbering behind rubbing his eyes. In the distance stood an unmasked zealot, arms crossed. From what Myth read, Alvarez always kept a straight face and he was very direct. Members of his cell routinely changed. One of the main complaints being Alvarez was such a hard ass he drove them away. The stoic premier known as Exo had a reputation for being a tough person to gauge. Hardly smiled, hardly laughed, hard to read. A graduate of Mount Z class of 1999, he moved up the ranks swiftly by heading different arms recollection mission across the Midwest Corridor. The numbers didn't lie. There was a steady drop of firearms in the streets and that was largely due to the diligent work of Alvarez. Regardless of who comprised his cell, he led by example. As they approached, Alvarez's dark hair, pulled back into a small pony tail, and dark eyes set in a brown, scarred face became more visible.

"Everett Santeaux. The pleasure is mine."

"Constantine Alvarez, I assume."

"Correct. Call sign: Exo," Alvarez said with a subtle Spanish accent, "If you and your team would follow me. I'll brief you on the matters at hand."

"The reports were right. You are about your business," Myth said.

"I'd think a tribunal member would understand that."

Myth wasn't sure if that was a slight, but he disregarded it in the name of doing what they came to do. No time for petty bickering caused by a bruised ego. They all boarded a small solar rail car and began the brief journey to the Midwest Corridor Mecca. The familiar black pyramid soon came into view. It looked especially majestic overlooking Lake Michigan and the rows of massive wind turbines that the Windy City had become known for.

"Let's head to one of the conference rooms," Exo said stepping off onto a platform with a brisk pace. An uncomfortably silent trip to said conference room followed. Once they were all seated, a large screen descended slowly from the ceiling. Myth noticed the entire conference table was one large touch screen interface. Exo walked over to his seat used the controls on the table to dim the lights.

"Approximately 45 days ago, one of our cells encountered a criminal organization using an advanced technology. This was in addition to the guns they were blasting at us, mind you."

"Still a lot of guns in the streets?"

Exo laughed condescendingly, "It really is true. About you guys being pampered in the Metro. Guns are everywhere here. If feels like a never ending mountain we're climbing. We stop a major trafficker one day, the next day three more pop up."

Exo's tone annoyed Myth, but he disregarded it once again.

"And still, the Midwest is second to the Metro in terms of drop rate, arrests, and successful high level missions."

"Be that as it may," Exo responded quickly, "Even the cells here feel overwhelmed. The police force can only do so much when the perps they're trying to apprehend can outgun them. Easily."

"We see some'a that in the Swamp, too," Zac added, "Cops gettin' fed up. They don't wanna charge into the meat grinder, just call up the mecca and send a cell."

"Exactly," Exo continued, "Zealots these days are a panacea for anything that goes wrong in the corridors. Dawn is turning people into…super powered savages. We're trained to deal with armed adversaries, trained to hunt and recover the guns that are in circulation, but…"

"But?" Myth asked waiting for Exo to finish his thought.

"But I'm not convinced that the police force here, or in the Gulf, or in the Metro, or *anywhere*, are capable of supporting the cells like they should be."

Myth had heard enough.

"Alright, let's just…enough of this dumb shit. We didn't come here to listen to you complain about what cops are or aren't doing in *your* corridor. We have a specific mission and you were chosen for it. We're here, as zealots, to do the jobs that others are not capable of, regardless of what that is. It extends beyond just arms recollection or high level crime. Where we are needed, *when* we are needed, we go. That, I can assure you, I've learned in my time on the tribunal. If you ever wish to ascend to that position, you would do well to remember that. If the job is starting to become a burden to you, Alvarez, then by all means resign."

"Sonned 'em," Olu said through a faux cough.

Exo and Myth stared at each other for a moment. The tension in the room was palpable.

"Duly noted, Santeaux. I won't waste any more of your time. You're here to aid in the ongoing investigation of tech firm, AGR, or Advanced Gentech Research. We've had some undercovers in the police department planted in the company to gather intel. It appears that they ramped up work on some high-level project in recent weeks."

Exo scrolled through pictures with sharp touch commands. They showed documents and blueprints for different devices. Masks that looked like space helmets. Cybernetic limbs, eyes, organs. Different vehicles for different types of terrain. One of the cooler ones was a one man helicopter a little larger in size than a motorcycle.

"That thang sexy," Red Quill blurted out.

"Took the words right outta my mouth," Myth agreed.

"We noticed a spike in dawn-related arrests, as well as arrests for arms trafficking. They all spiked around the time that AGR began its classified project."

"So, what is it," Olu yelled lacking the tact usually associated with these types of meetings.

"If we knew, we wouldn't be in here, criminal," Exo said cutting his eyes in Olu's direction.

"Ohhhh my God, is everyone gonna keep bringin' that up?" Olu replied exasperated.

Myth picked up the conversation that Olu had so easily derailed.

"Send me those files, I'm sure Shef would like to go over them. As far as the facility goes, you have a plan of action?"

"Of course," Exo said as he brought up a blueprint of the building, an 80 story skyscraper, "They have guards by the doors. Our informants say that the classified projects are on the higher floors. I figured we should go in from the top."

"Drop in?"

"Yes. Work our way down. A series of dormant viruses have been installed on key servers in the building. Their activation will coincide with our arrival, allowing us to bypass most of their security systems."

"Most," Red Quill asked, prodding.

"There are guards, likely armed. There's also the possibility that these classified areas house prototype weaponry of some kind." With more swipes and presses of his finger, Exo brought up a video. It was a dashboard mounted camera in a cop car capturing a crime scene.

"This happened a couple weeks ago in basement population. The police are out in force, zealots are there with them, and now, here," As Exo went silent, everyone watched the video. A man picked up a two handed weapon. Rings inside the barrel slowly spun to life as a blue glow pulsated from inside. Then, a quick burst of blue energy resembling a lightning bolt shot out of the weapon, hitting a car causing it to explode. The force sent a shock wave that knocked the camera into darkness, killing the feed.

"What THE fuck, dude," Red Quill whispered.

"Yo...I need that," Olu mused rubbing his beard.

"The real question I have," Myth added, "how in the hell did *that* end up in the streets?"

"Leave that part to me. The grimey shit. I'll get wit some of my connects, see what they talm'bout," Olu suggested. Myth nodded. Exo continued talking.

"It doesn't matter where the guns end up, here is where they start and if we-"

"Whatchu mean it doesn't matter where they end up," Olu asked angrily the tone of his voice was harsh and accusatory. An awkward silence followed. Myth knew that he could diffuse the situation, as he always tended to do, but he wanted to let this ride.

He's saying what I'm thinking. And Alvarez actin' like a bitch anyway...

"Whatchu mean it don't matter? You been in basepop here?"

"Of course. I've been there during operations," Exo said.

"But have you *been* there? Do you even know what it's like to live there? Trust me, I been in yo' streets more than *you* have. People strugglin' outchea. The dawn was just easy money, and it's all these muthafuckas in towers and shit that's buyin' the heaviest anyway!"

Olu was firmly on his soapbox now.

"When you down there in the bottom, you gon' do anything to try to climb up. Anything. Even if that means jackin' a bitch for a lighting shotgun or whateva the hell that thing was."

"So, what's your point?" Exo said sounding annoyed.

"The point is, who are you fightin' for? Yeah, yeah, whateva, I'm the criminal, huh? But the way I move is based on loyalty and respect. I look out for mines. Zealots 'sposed to be the ones comin' down savin' shit. So save it.!"

"I plan to save it," Exo replied smugly.

"Not the city, save your pompous bullshit!"

"Pompous," Myth said aloud, shocked and impressed.

"Yeah, I caught that," Red Quill added.

"If you not fighting for everyone in your corridor, from base pop up, you gon' fail every time. That's real."

There was another long silence. Not awkward this time as much as everyone was silently contemplating Olu's rant. Exo calmly addressed Myth.

"Sleeping arrangements have been prepared for you all. A good meal and some much needed rest, no?"

"Daaamn, straight," Red Quill exhaled.

"I'll send you the details in a format that can be easily uploaded."

"I appreciate that," Myth said while rising. They all walked out of the conference room and into a long hallway. A female operator was waiting for them.

"Gentlemen, follow me."

Red Quill removed his mask. He and Olu exchanged a nod with a similar facial expression: raised brows and a slight, mischievous frown. They began to walk down the hall side by side, jointly ogling the young lady leading the way.

"So, I been meanin' to ask. Your call name or call sign or whateva. Red Quill."

"Whata 'bout it?" Zac asked.

"Why not just go wit' Red Neck. I mean, you the countriest muhfucka I done met."

Zac laughed heartily, "The red scarf kinda represents dat. Red Neck just sounded too..."

"Corny?"

"Yeah, exactly."

"And the Red Dogs? You just pulled that out the air?" Olu continued.

"Nah, bro. That's from a song."

"Yeah? What country song is that?"

Zac laughed again, "Nah. Goodie Mob."

He recited the hook.

"Ohhh shit," Olu said genuinely surprised.

"Told ya', bro. Shouldn't judge a book by its cover."

Exo watched Red Quill and Olu disappear around a corner before turning back to Myth.

"Santeaux, could you wait for a moment please?"

"Yeah, what's up?"

"I...I want to apologize. Things have been hectic as you can imagine," Exo paused, "I'm honestly...concerned about what we'll find."

You should be.

"Nah, I'm sure it'll be routine for the likes of you."

"Made easier by you and your team," Exo looked down, "I will be considered for ascension soon, if the rumors are to be believed. I don't want it to seem like I know it all, because I don't, but I want to...I need to learn."

"Cool story. First rule? Don't listen to rumors."

CHAPTER THIRTY-TWO
The Drop

The black jet came to a stationary hover, shrouded by clouds in the night. Shef's voice came through everyone's comm. Myth, Exo, Red Quill, and Olu were all lined up by the door. Red Quill flipped his hunting knife back and forth in his hands excitedly. Myth placed his light visor on. He tapped a button and it gradually hugged the back of his head, the tiny led lights on each side came to life. A black visor pixelated into view, hiding his eyes from the outside world. On the inside, he was met with a series of displays and granted technologically enhanced visual power. Myth looked at Exo. He seemed nervous if his eyes were to be trusted.

"You good?"

"Yeah. I'm a bit...acrophobic."

"Scared of heights? Wasn't it your idea to drop in?"

Exo hesitated, "I was thinking more along the lines of repelling down from a chopper. Not jumping out of a plane."

Shef's voice came through the team's shared communications, "Be easy, buddy. I designed those uniforms to have gliding capabilities, just deploy before you hit the deadline."

"The deadline?" Exo asked.

"Yeah, if you pass the line without deploying, you'll be dead," Shef said.

"Oh...alright then."

"Don't worry, Exo, it's like riding a bike. Only you have exactly one chance to ride the bike and if you fall off, you die."

"You have a very real knack for being reassuring, Mr. Bales," Exo said less than enthusiastically.

Myth put a firm hand on his shoulder, "Trust me, if Shef designed it, it works."

"Activate your light visors," Myth commanded the crew.

"Looks cool er'ry time," Red Quill marveled as his light visor came to life, covering his eyes.

"Shef, open her up."

"Ten-four."

The doors hissed as they slid open. Wind whipped into the interior, sending Red Quill's red scarf flitting in the air.

"The target landing area is highlighted in ya'll visors. Can't get more obvious than a big red x."

Myth dived out of the plane without a second thought. Red Quill was the next out. Olu looked at Exo.

"I ain't bout to be the last one out. Like an ol' bitch."

He ran and jumped out of the plane. Exo stepped to the side and watched the others streak through the clouds.

"Whatchu waitin' on," Shef's voice chided through Exo's comm.

He took a deep breath and leapt out into the night. Information streamed in his display: the air temperature, the speed at which he was falling, a glowing green line that lead to the red x imposed on the roof of their destination. Exo cut through the air with his hands at his sides. He watched as Myth and the others deployed their gliders, cloth-like membrane extended from hands to waist like kites. Exo input the commands using the touchpad on his forearm and felt the sudden jerk as the air filled his wings. He floated down to the destination where the others were waiting. Once his feet were on solid ground, the wings under his arms retracted into his suit.

"Amazing," Exo said out loud.

"I'll take that as a compliment," Shef replied through the comm, "Exo, the virus your guys put on the servers in the building has gone live. Ya'll got full access, for now. No telling how long it'll be before they start to deploy countermeasures of their own."

"Right. Exo?" Myth said looking in Exo's direction. Exo nodded and pulled an explosive device that resembled a small cube from his utility belt. He placed it on the roof and sprayed a neon substance around it in a circle. Then he stood back a couple of feet.

"There is no direct roof access from inside, which is a red flag for a building of this type. They have to be hiding something. We're punching our way into a top floor lab," Exo said as he activated the explosive device from the touch pad on his forearm. A small flash shook the roof. After the smoke cleared there was a perfect circular hole to drop through.

"Shef, we're in, you seeing this?"

"Yeah Myth, I have a visual."

The large space was filled with lab tables, computer stations, and rooms that were presumably for patients of some sort.

"What would a tech firm be doin' with live patients?" Red Quill wondered aloud.

"Myth, get to a terminal. I'll see if I can hack in. Poke around," Shef suggested.

"I already did," Exo said as he was rapidly typing on his forearm display, "A server room is two floors below us."

"Good. Go pull anything you can, Exo. Red Quill you go with him, head down now. Me and Olu will catch up," Myth ordered.

Exo and Red Quill promptly exited, leaving Olu and Myth to investigate the lab for any additional information.

"These areas look like doctors were performing triage, there's all types of medical equipment here," Myth said as he scanned the room.

"Ayo Shef," Olu asked through his comm, still trying to get a gauge for how the shared channel worked, "How can I do a scan or whateva to see if there's some, some smurf around and shit."

"That's...actually not a totally stupid idea," Myth said turning around, eyes wide with sarcastic shock.

"Sending the commands to you two," Shef replied matter-of-factly.

Myth watched Olu clumsily input the gesture commands. Then he followed suit.

Then they both looked at each other.

"You *see* this shit?" Olu asked to everyone.

They could see remnants of the dawn, or at least blood that had been polluted by the dawn smeared everywhere. The walls, floors, spattered on the ceiling, hand prints across computer monitors. It was a grisly scene hidden in plain sight. Just then, Exo chimed in.

"Myth. We're in the server room. Do you have a visual on this?"

"I see it Myth, that'll work," Shef interjected, "Exo, there's a device in the small compartment of your utility belt," he instructed, "Take it out and plug it into one of the available USB ports. I can sneak in through that."

"Gotcha," Exo took out the device and plugged it in as he was told. A small blinking red light started to flash.

"Okay, it's transmitting. I'm gonna start downloading the interesting bits...uh-oh."

"Uh-oh?"

"Looks like someone knows we're in, backup security systems are coming online," Shef said, sounding a bit worried. Red Quill's voice was next over the shared communication channel.

"Whoa boy, we gonna run into some issues down here."

"Quill, what's goin' on?"

"Myth, the backup security's got the guards downstairs buzzin'. I can feel the vibrations in the floor. Looks like they're about to move."

He can sense them? Incredible.

"Shef, what's good," Myth asked as he instinctively fondled the handle of his katana.

"There's about 20 guards scramblin' right now, moving up the building. Elevators are still down, so they gotta hit the stairs. My suggestion? Make moves."

"Olu, let's hit it."

Myth and Olu hit the door into a hallway.

"Exo, come back."

"Myth, we moved to another terminal. Credit to Mr. Bales for this new tech. Since he's able to see through my visor, he can direct us to points of interest."

"Red Quill here, I confirm dat. Just more empty labs, nothin' to worry 'bout."

"Guys, the guards are picking up the pace, at this rate they'll be muckin' things up in about…fifteen minutes, give or take," Shef informed the squad.

"Shit," Myth muttered.

"Alright, I'm going through the blueprint of the building and some design documents, looks like you guys want to head for the 65th floor."

"Yo, how are you doin' all this shit so fast?" Olu asked genuinely perplexed.

Shef didn't answer that particular question, but he had stumbled upon a new development.

"Myth, what's that doctor's name at Mount Z? The one who does the injection therapy stuff?"

Myth shuddered at the memory of being strapped to that table at Mount Z.

"Aldridge. Dr. Ste-"

"-ven Aldridge," Shef said finishing Myth's statement.

"Doc? At Mount Z?" Red Quill's confused voice added.

"He's on the board of directors, Myth."

Myth got a sick feeling in his stomach. Master Xi always said that was one's intuition and that most times it pointed in the true direction. Myth left the room with Olu following close behind. He went to the emergency stairs and jumped down the middle. The information in his visor streamed how many feet per second he was falling. Heat signatures from the guards coming up the stairs were getting closer. Using his grapple arm, Myth zipped onto the 65th floor.

"Myth, Red Quill here. Looks like we got somethin'."

"I'm coming to your position."

In moments, the cell was reassembled in a spacious store room area. There were large cases containing odd looking weapons.

"That one," Exo gestured, "That one looks exactly like the one from the video."

Shef pulled up the exact clip and displayed the paused frame to everyone's visor.

"No doubt," Myth confirmed.

"Guys. You got company."

They all could hear boots storming up the emergency stairs. The metal doors burst open and guards poured in. They started shooting on sight, causing Myth and his team to scatter for cover.

"Whoa! Shoot first ask questions later, huh?" Red Quill said as he whipped out his composite bow. He loaded up an arrow and fired it. It streaked through the air and exploded into a plume of smoke. Kunai cut through the smoke hitting guards in vital points. They collapsed into unseen hurdles for the guards that followed to stumble over. Light blue shells flew through the air exploding into electrified clouds when they hit a surface. Myth scanned one of the shells on the ground, knowing Shef would be able to pick it apart for information.

"Those aren't your standard stun rounds. No matches in my database. It would be a good idea if ya didn't get hit by one."

To Shef's surprise, everyone burst out in genuine laughter.

"He said *get hit by one*," Red Quill said with playful disbelief.

"I know, right," Myth added chuckling. In an instant they all scattered in different directions. Red Quill's scarf danced between flying bullets like a ribbon.

"If one of you have an EMP, it could work. The weapons look like they're shooting charged bolts of electricity," Shef informed them.

"I got one, but the sum'bitches got me in they're sights, need a window!"

Red Quill spun around, loaded an arrow with an odd shaped head, and was in a kneeling position ready to fire. He flipped backwards right before a giant bolt destroyed the floor in front of him.

"WHOA!"

"Son, there's more comin' in," Olu noted.

"Exo, help Shef with the tech. Empty those drives! Download everything, every file. Olu?"

"Yessir!"

The guards readied their weapons. Myth and Olu charged forward side by side. They ducked and weaved through the oncoming hail of gun fire. Myth skipped from one guard to the next with violent kicks, slashing bullets out of the sky in between. Olu rolled in behind him striking wildly at anyone in arm's reach. His elbows and knees crushed faces and femurs. The two moved in tandem creating elegant mayhem. A yin and yang approach to the decimation of their opponents. Myth: the graceful, precise swordsman, moving between attacks almost preternaturally. Olu: the hitman striking with a brutal, hypnotic rhythm. Myth and Olu stood still in a circle of fallen bodies and severed limbs. Other guards fell back to reload. Their reinforcements with the larger guns, the ones from the video, stepped forward in their place. The strange blue discs in the barrel of the guns began to spin.

"Move!" Shef yelled.

Myth and Olu dived out of the way. The blast blew a hole through the floor and the subsequent floor below it.

"Purp bomb out," Red Quill whispered. He loosed the arrow. As it grew closer to the wave of guards, a bright purple explosion knocked some of them off of their feet. Like Shef thought, their weapons all seemed to power down. Immediately a hail of arrows stopped guards from reaching for knives and swords by pinning their hands to walls, tables, or their own bodies.

"We almost done here or what?!" Red Quill forcefully asked.

"Shef?"

"Gimmie a few more minutes, Myth. Between me and Exo, we should be able to get it all."

"Clearly they don't want that. What's in those files?"

"Dunno. I see some of the classified stuff is encrypted so it might take a lil' while to really get to the dirt."

"Yo, E."

Myth turned to Olu, "What?"

"Yo. Check ol' buddy out."

Myth turned to the guard that Olu had gestured to with a head nod. He pulled a small tube from the back of his head and plugged into the weapon he was holding. A stream of his blood flowed through the tube. Slowly the weapon began to contort and change. The metal melted and crawled up the length of the guard's arm. As the guard visibly grimaced in pain, the process was nearing completion. His arm was encased in metal and his entire hand from the wrist down was replaced with the huge barrel of a cannon. It quickly charged and fired a dense bright blue ball. It was headed towards Exo, who was at a computer terminal behind them. He eluded it just in time. The blast blew a giant hole out of the side of the building, the cold air rushed in as smoke and debris spilled outward.

"Christ!" Red Quill yelled. He dodged the blast with the use of his new grapple arm. He swung and landed near Myth and Olu.

"E, that muthafucka just turned to Mega Man, son," Olu calmly observed amidst the chaos.

"And on that note. Shef, get ready to get us out of here," Myth commanded.

"The quicker the better," Exo added.

The guards kept pouring in. Red Quill fired an arrow. As it got closer to the guards it exploded into a mist. An arrow quickly followed that ignited the mist, sending an arc of white-hot flame outwards. It stopped three guards in their tracks, melting their armor and weapons to their bodies.

"The chariot has arrived," Shef said. Through the gaping hole in the building the team could see the jet come to a hover just outside. The large side door opened.

"We're out! Now!"

The team followed Myth's command, dodging bullets as they whizzed past.

Myth turned his head. The guard was readying another shot with his new arm cannon. Then came the blue glow and high pitched squeal. Myth zoomed in with his visor.

"He's aiming at the plane, Shef!"

The guard used his free hand to steady his aim further. The kickback jerked his shoulder. The cell ran towards the hole in the building while the blue ball zoomed towards the plane like a comet. Shef peeled the jet away as the blast squealed under it in the night. The ball of energy hit an elevated solar rail track and exploded. Large pieces of debris fell downward leaving others to dangle precariously. Myth dived out of the building and shot his grapple arm. It caught on the wing of the plane as it was gaining altitude. He zipped up and into the side door with relative ease.

"Uh…where is everyone?"

Shef was turning the jet around and heading back in the building's direction, "Red Quill hooked onto the opposite side of those solar rail tracks. Exo and Olu both dived down. They're still droppin', Myth, it's too tight for me to get down there!"

"Shit. Shef connect me to Olu's visor."

"Done."

A small rectangle expanded in the upper left corner of his vision. He could see Olu's point of view as he was plunging towards the streets.

"Olu, what's going on!?"

"People are down there, son!"

He was right. People in the streets were scrambling for their lives as huge pieces of concrete and metal fell around them. Olu aimed his grapple arm and fired it into a nearby building. He swung gracefully to the streets. Exo was behind him.

"Everyone get inside of a building now!" Exo screamed at the mob. Olu ran to where a woman was pinned to the street, her leg mangled under a slab of concrete. Olu struggled to lift it off of her as she wept and screamed.

"Another piece of the track is falling!" Red Quill yelled through the comm. The structure began to groan as another piece of the solar rail track snapped off and dropped towards the street. It grazed the top of a smaller building on the way down, creating more falling debris. Exo ran to Olu and helped free the woman. She grabbed onto Exo's arm. The mass of metal and concrete crashed into the street. The mechanical hands of two grapple arms shot out of the dust cloud and latched onto a nearby building, Olu and Exo zipped up and out of harm's way. The woman was crying frantically, still in shock.

"You're going to be fine," Exo said comforting her.

"Shef, call an operator at the Mecca and tell them to stop that train. Olu, Exo, rally to Red Quill's position. Shef, send it to them. We'll swing by and pick you up from there. Let's get the fuck out of here before the Midwest Tribunal tries to bill us for this," Myth said, still exhilarated from watching Olu's exploits.

Looks like he's starting to like this hero shit.

"Done and done," Shef calmly replied

"Train's stoppin'," Red Quill confirmed. He watched it squeal to a hault in the distance.

In moments the jet hovered in the sky over the rendezvous point.

"You guys make your way back up, we're headed out."

"Ten-four, Myth," Exo answered. Exo and Olu prepared to leave.

"Wait," the woman said.

"A medical team will see to your injuries, I've already notified the police department," Exo said.

"No…I wanted…just…thank you. Things down here are so fucked up we don't expect anybody to help. The fact that ya'll saved me when you coulda left me to die…"

"Don't thank me ma'am," Exo said as he glanced over at Olu, "Zealots are responsible for everyone. From base pop up."

The two zipped up and out of sight. The woman looked up just in time to see their ride speeding away in the darkness, climbing higher and higher into the clouds.

Myth removed his mask and took a deep breath. The other members of his cell did the same.

"Hell, that was some fun, huh?" Zac said as he removed his token red scarf.

"Fun? I dunno if that's what I'd call it," Exo said as he took a seat.

"Shef, you there?"

"Yep," Shef's voice came through the cabin's intercom, "Pullin' info out of this massive data dump. Mannn, look."

"Come with it," Everett said eagerly.

"Where do I start? Looks like the weapons that ya'll stumbled on are the results of years of research and development. From what I can tell from schematics and whatnot, it's nanotechnology activated by dawn. Or at least, someone who's usin' the dawn. Not totally sure how it works yet. Pretty incredible, from a strictly scientific perspective, I'll tell ya that. The way the weapons changed, I've seen it before."

"Me too, yo," Olu added.

"When Orion came to the lab, he did something similar. It made his sword change forms in the same way those weapons did. Trippy stuff, brother," Shef said.

"The dude that broke into my crib he had like a golden glove on. When we started getting' into it, that shit changed up all crazy. Started shimmering and changin' shape. I thought I was still high," Olu said.

"So dawn is turning people into…goddamn T-1000s?" Myth asked.

"Classic movie, bro," Zac answered getting sidetracked.

"There's still tons of files to go through. I'll get Dunbar in here ASAP to help. This tech, though. It's a problem."

"Add it to the list," Everett replied.

"We can pick this back up when ya'll are in the air headed to the Pacific Corridor. Ya'll take it back to the Mecca, debrief, and get some rest so we can head out. I hear Redwood Fortress is a sight. Alright, lemme go charge my batteries."

"Do that, Shef," Myth said, "It's about time you got some sleep."

"Yeah…sleep."

CHAPTER THIRTY-THREE

The Pacific Corridor

Everett and his cell sat quietly in their seats. They would arrive in the Pacific Corridor in a little under two hours. After their mission in the Midwest Corridor, Alvarez agreed to join up. Whether it was because he actually wanted to or because he wanted to escape the glare of the Midwest Corridor Tribunal, Everett wasn't sure. They were none too happy at the ruckus that the cell had caused on what was supposed to be a covert operation, negating the fact that they found information that implicated Advanced Gentech Research in a slew of illegal dealings. They all sat, trying to make sense of things. All except Everett. He was thinking about his family, Chance and Simone at home. He wanted to tell them that he loved them, but the mission at hand seemed to always get in the way of that. Then again, that's what his life had become: work punctuated with the ones he loved.

I'll make it up to you both...

Shef's voice snapped him back to the present. Everyone else was staring at him, wondering what took him so long to respond.

"You alright, dude?" Zac asked.

"Yeah...yeah, I'm good. Where we at with it?"

"Dunbar has been going over some of the documents, and he's found some...interesting bits," Shef said.

"Even I know when you say *interesting* you mean somethin' else," Olu said as he rested his head in one hand.

"Well, color you the fast learner," Shef replied sarcastically, "You're right, though. I had a feelin' there was some nanotechnology involved, and everything we're findin' points in that direction. Those connection tubes are a conduit to deliver the dawn in a person's blood to a specific device."

"And that's when the magic happens," Zac added.

"Pretty much," Shef continued, "How that works exactly? We dunno yet. We do know that dawn is the damn gift that keeps on givin'."

"It's crazy. Muhfuckas are just tryin' to get high as shit and have bugged out dreams. If I woulda known this, I coulda made waaaay more money sellin' the shit," Olu said.

"So, for all of the detective work, I feel like we still don't know shit," Everett said exasperated, leaning back in his seat. Everyone could sense his frustration. They nervously eyed one another in silence until Shef's voice broke through.

"I know it's not the ideal position to be in, considering we're behind the 8-ball here, but we are makin' progress. We gotta name in the Swamp to go along with interrupting a massive shipment of dawn. We know that the dawn is being used to further technology used by the same organization behind the G8 Incident."

"And we still don't know *why* they took them, *where* they are, or *if* any of them are still alive. This guy Tozen is said to have some mythical style that makes him a God and he's building an army of drugged up soldiers with advanced tech. Where do we go from here? Someone answer that, where the fuck do we go from here?!"

Everyone was quite with a look of concern, even Olu to a slightly lesser degree.

"Everett," Shef said, "You need to relax a bit man. Just…try to get some shut eye. We'll be in the Pacific Corridor in a little bit. Hopefully things will start to gel soon."

"Take the man's advice," Zac agreed, "You're not lookin' too good. Get some rest."

"I can help go through the info dump, Shef," Alvarez offered.

"Much appreciated. See, Everett? That's why you decided on these guys in the first place. Take it easy for the rest of the flight."

"Yeah...I'll do that."

Everett rose from his seat and walked to the back of the plane where there was a private cabin. Inside there was a bed, across from it a computer workstation. He sat on the bed and initiated a video call to his home. After a minute or two, Simone's face popped up on the screen. She greeted him with a big, warm smile that seemed to melt away all of Everett's anxiety.

"E! How are you? I'm so happy to see that face."

"Hey, what's up?"

"Same ol', same ol'. Being awesome."

They both shared a laugh. Everett had missed hearing her voice.

"Hold on, lemme get your daughter." Simone called out to Chance. The soft rumbling of her tiny feet gradually grew louder and louder until she dived into her mother's arms knocking the wind out of her.

"Chance, look who it is!"

"Daddy!"

"How's my baby girl?"

"Good. When are you coming home, daddy?"

"I don't know Chance, hopefully soon. Hopefully soon."

"I hope so, too. I been practicing."

"Practicing what?" Everett playfully asked.

"Practicing drawing and math and spelling and eating vegetables."

"Wait, how does one *practice* eating vegetables?"

"Like you said, to be good at anything you have to practice. If I want to be good at eating vegetables, I have to practice...because they're gross."

Simone smiled and shook her head as she held her daughter in her lap.

Everett laughed, "You're right. You are right. Well, keep up the good work."

"I will! I love you, dad," Chance said as she reached her hand at the video screen, "I wish I could touch your face."

"I love you, too baby girl."

"K, bye!" Chance hopped down out of her mom's lap and scooted out of the room just as fast as she came in.

"She's been asking about you, E. It's good that you called," Simone said.

"Yeah, I needed to see ya'll, man. Shit's getting hectic."

"The news has been on this G8 shit constantly. Talkin' about Russia is movin' missiles pointing them at the corridors. It's seriously bad, E. I'm scared for you. For everyone, really."

Everett let out a long sigh, "I know. We're trying to figure it out, man."

"Yeah…so, Chance's birthday is, like, in a few days."

"Simone, I'm not trying to argue about this."

"Nah, I mean, I didn't mean it like that. I was just sayin'. If you can maybe make time to give her a call. She's been askin' if you're coming back every day."

"I am coming back."

Simone was silent for a moment. The silence struck Everett as odd.

"I know you are, E. I know."

"Well, then stop with the sad face," Everett said lightening the mood, "Lemme do what I do."

"Which is what?"

"Be awesome."

A smile streaked across Simone's face.

"Well played, my dear."

"Yeah, you know I be on my witty rebuttal shit."

Simone playfully rolled her eyes, "Boy, bye."

"I love you, Simone."

"I love you too, Everett. Get some rest. You look like shit."

Everett followed his wife's advice. He lay back on the bed and, before he knew it, he was sound asleep. He was watching himself from a distance running the pole stairs. Whenever he got to the top, like a video on repeat, he watched his younger self appear back at the bottom to run them again. Everett heard a cacophony of whispers that caused him to whip his head left to right to find the source. "There is nothing left."

"You can't protect them."

"You won't stop this."

Everett felt a hand on his shoulder, an abnormally cold hand. When he turned, it was the man from the previous nightmare he had at his home. He snapped out of his sleep at the sound of pounding on the door, breathing heavily and sweating. He rubbed his face with both hands. The pounding on the door continued.

"Yooo."

Alvarez slid the door open and poked his head in, "We're about to land."

"Yeah. Let's get ready."

CHAPTER THIRTY-FOUR

Redwood Fortress

After landing in Los Angeles, Myth and his cell took a private solar rail train to the second zealot training facility built in the United Corridors. The compound was constructed in the depths of the Redwood Forest, another example of the Pacific Corridor's emphasis on seamlessly blending man-made structures with the environment. The other corridors across the country drew inspiration from the architectural designs that ran up and down the West Coast and Redwood Fortress was the pinnacle of these design ideals. Buildings were constructed high into the tree line, connected with scaffolds, walkways, and a rail system for transportation. Renewable technologies were integrated throughout. Rain water collection systems ran tubes from the tops of the trees to the ground into huge tanks. Some trees had been converted into solar power stations.

The last hand-picked member of Myth's cell was Samson Ashe, callsign: Quake. A graduate of Redwood, he moved up the ranks in much the same manner as the rest. His impeccable record was rewarded with praise and accolades. The Pacific Corridor had active ports up and down the coast, second only to the Gulf corridor in terms of shipments received and maritime traffic. Ashe thwarted major arms shipments in three different cities during his time as a premier. The name Quake began to spread fear amongst the underworld, not just because he was one of the best zealots on the West Coast, but also because he was a behemoth of a man that intimidated everyone who he came into contact with.

The half-Samoan, half-white Ashe stood almost seven feet tall and had the chiseled physique of a statue. He earned his callsign, Quake, early on in his training days at Redwood Fortress. He was halfway through his run of the pole stairs when an earthquake measuring 5.8 on the Richter scale struck. He still managed to finish with the best time in his class, thus his legend was born. Even his blade was unique. It was twice the length and width of a standard issue katana. Over the last few years, he took on the strength and conditioning role at Redwood Fortress, the same position that Chandler Ulysses held at Mount Z. Students called him, "Ashe the Giant".

The solar train rounded a bend and into the sea of massive trees. Everett sat looking out of the window as the sun cut through leaves and branches creating odd shadows in the train car's interior.

"This place looks crazy, like damn high-tech Ewok village," Zac said as he stared out of a window of his own.

"Ya know weed is completely legal in this corridor?" Olu asked the group.

"I was aware of that, though I don't partake myself. While we're on this mission, I suggest you don't either," Alvarez said with the tone of a scolding parent.

"Man, I can't be the only one. Zac? You on dem trees?"

Zac looked at Alvarez who was looking straight back at him. He shook his head no. As soon as Alvarez turned his eyes, Zac looked back at Olu and nodded an emphatic yes. They both snickered. The solar train came to a gradual stop at the docking station, a network of circular buildings that snaked up the trunks of redwoods, all connected with walkways and lifts. The men stepped off onto a platform, where they were greeted by a young woman. She was dressed in a conservative, form-fitting suit. They all recognized her as an operator by her demeanor.

"Premier Santeaux. Follow me. Premier Ashe has a group at the pole stairs. I will take you to him."

They all gathered into a large lift that went further into the depths of the facility. Everett could peer down and see groups of students moving about. Others were descending from their quarters down circular staircases that wrapped around trees. The lift began to descend. The pole stairs were constructed following the exact specifications as the version at Mount Z. They led up to a large platform built around a huge redwood tree, one of the biggest Everett had seen since their arrival. The lift came to a stop. Everett and his crew exited and walked down a small flight of wooden stairs. At the foot of the stairs, they saw Ashe's massive frame. His voice boomed and echoed throughout the forest.

"Focus! If you lose it for one second, you're ass is done!"

As if on cue, a child halfway up the pole stairs misjudged his next jump and fell, grasping feebly at platforms as he bounced down.

"Ah shit, get a medic over to him!" Ashe bellowed.

Zac leaned over to Everett, "Sounds a lot like Ulysses at Mount Z, don't he?"

Everett laughed, "Yeah, he damn sure does."

The operator walked over to Ashe. They exchanged a few words and he glanced over his shoulder at Everett and the rest. He waved his hand and an overseer took his place administering the test, calling the next three students up in line for their run. Ashe took monstrous strides over to where Everett stood, his freakishly massive frame growing with each step closer.

"Who're you?" Ashe's deep voice asked.

Everett hesitated, slightly perturbed by the lack of recognition, before he could answer, Ashe laughed hardily.

"Jokes, Santeaux. Even on the West Coast, we know who you are."

Everett let out a strained smile, "Then, you know why we've come."

"I do. Seems like you already got a cell," Ashe said as he glanced down at the group, towering over them. The height difference made his words seem more condescending than what was actually the case.

"We're lookin' for a center," Olu quipped.

Ashe smiled, "My post game's been vicious since grade school," he turned back to Everett, "I'll have to decline your offer, though."

"Decline?" Everett asked shocked, as if the idea that someone would deny him had never crossed his mind.

"Yeah. Decline. As in, not go."

"Can I ask why you would wanna do that?" Everett asked.

"You see 'em," Ashe said motioning towards the students at the pole stairs, "Those are my guys. I made a choice to come back here. Running the streets gets old. It got old."

"Commendable. But what's more likely is that the nature of your covert operations were compromised by…"

"By what?" Ashe asked forcefully.

"By a seven foot tall zealot. Nothing too *covert* about that," Alvarez finished.

"Well, you know what they say: The bigger they come, the faster they are."

"That…is not at all what they say," Everett noted.

"The decision to come back here was mine and mine alone, trust me. I'm sure I don't have to defend my record. It's what brought you all the way out here, isn't it?'

"No argument there," Everett said.

"So, that's it?"

"Yeah, ain't too much else to say," Everett answered as he turned to leave, "I can't force it. Just know that what we're working on is intense. I need the best."

Ashe stood contemplating in silence for a moment.

"This whole G8 thing, it is getting crazier out there. But, hey, all the more reason to get these guys ready. Who knows what they'll have to deal with when they graduate. I respect that. Well, continued luck here Mr. Ashe," Everett said turning to the rest, "Let's go."

Ashe watched as they all boarded the lift and slowly disappeared back into the trees. Then he turned and walked back over to the pole stairs, barking commands the entire way.

"So that's it?" Olu asked Everett.

"Yup."

"What the fuck, if I knew it was that easy, a nigga woulda still been home chillin'."

"You didn't have a choice or did you forget?"

Olu sat back silent, like a kid who was just told he couldn't go out to play. The silence on the lift was interrupted when Everett received a call to his comm. He reached up to his ear and accepted.

"Santeaux."

"Everett? Get to a TV or something. Right now," Shef's voice sounded frantic.

Everett turned to the operator, "Excuse me, we need to make a detour. Do you have a media center or conference room close?"

"Yes sir, we do. I'll detour the lift now."

They came to a stop at another building nestled in the tree tops. As they emerged from the lift, they saw overseers and students all hustling in the direction they were headed. Everett got a sick feeling in his stomach. When they walked into the room, there were pockets of crowds around monitors that were all displaying the same image. Everett pushed through to get a closer look. A distorted voice was narrating off-screen as the kidnapped leaders from the G8 countries were shown all lined up on their knees, bloodied and blindfolded. In the background was the emblem, a sun rising over a horizontal katana.

"We are the Dawn Breakers. We are initiating the next step of evolution. The so-called leaders before you have resisted us, fought against us, but you cannot fight natural selection. They have done their respective people a disservice. We want to liberate you. Introduce you to the full potential of humanity. The only way to achieve this is to purge the ones who are obstacles to our progress. Once the President of your United Corridors is apprehended, he, along with all of the ones you see before you, will be executed. And thus the dawn will bring a new day."

The transition abruptly ended. News programs quickly picked up the story, trying to decipher the message.

"Shef, what in the hell was that?"

"A pirate broadcast interrupted major news outlets. They're turning up the heat. They must feel you getting closer."

"The President. Where is he now?"

"Zealot Prime and his personal guard are still with him. From what I've gathered, they're headed up to Alaska."

"Get him as far away from the corridors as possible," Everett reasoned.

"Exactly."

"We have to get there. The Prime's guard may not be enough."

"I was thinkin' the same thing."

"Do you have any idea where the broadcast came from?" Everett asked.

"No, but I'm gonna pick apart the video and see what I can find."

"I'll reconnect with you when we're boarded and ready to head out."

"Ten-four, Shef out."

The atmosphere was decidedly different. Everyone seemed nervous, confused, and afraid. Especially afraid. Without saying any words, Everett went back to the lift. The crew followed.

"Take us back to the solar train station right now," Everett directed the operator. She did without hesitation. When they walked off of the lift onto the platform they were met with a surprise. Samson Ashe stood there awaiting them. He looked at Everett and nodded.

"Glad to see you've had a change of heart."

CHAPTER THIRTY-FIVE

The Frozen Vein

"They're on a fourteen-car solar train headed to Eilson Air Force Base in Alaska, taking the Northern Supply Route, which is commonly referred to as the Frozen Vein."

"Wait, we're going right now?" Quake asked.

"I told you it was intense. There's still time to back out," Myth replied as he began gathering his supplies.

"Yeah, we could push you out and show you how the wings work," Olu said as he grabbed his ski mask and light visor. Everyone laughed, except Quake. Exo laughed the hardest, reminiscing about the terror he felt when he jumped out of the jet in Chicago. Shef continued breaking down the mission at hand.

"I'll drop ya'll off over the train. The suits will keep you warm. While in air, don't forget to activate the magnetic grip. This will help you land on the train safely."

"Is there a *safe* way to land on a train going over 200 miles per hour?" Myth asked.

"Yeah, if you follow the damn directions. Oh, and just remember, activate the mag-grip when you're far enough away from the jet. If you're too close, there's a good chance you could get sucked into an engine. Rendezvous with Zealot Prime when you board. From there, ya'll just keep 'em safe and help with the escort."

Myth slid Quake a titanium case.

"That's the best part right there," Red Quill noted.

"What's this?"

"This is your new uniform, designed and created by the voice you here over the intercom," Myth explained, "Don't worry, it'll fit. Like a big ass glove."

"At the current rate, I'll be in position within the hour," Shef informed everyone.

Quake fumbled with his light visor in a comical attempt to put it on. It looked like a Happy Meal toy in his massive hands.

"Watch and learn Yao Ming," Olu said as he demonstrated with his own light visor. Quake mimicked his routine, pressing the button in the middle to make the snake-like metal gently hug the contours of his skull. The visor appeared into view, covering Olu's eyes. Quake marveled at the amount of information at his disposal. When he looked at a member of the cell, their vital signs displayed in a corner.

"This is fucking awesome."

"Wait till we're outside," Red Quill said.

"Fifteen minutes out from the drop location," Shef said through the shared comm.

"Not a bad looking group," Myth mused looking everyone over, "The hillbilly, the goon, Andre the Giant, and Keanu Reeves from Point Break."

"Uploading coordinates to ya'll display," Shef said. Shortly after numeric data appeared in the corner of each man's light visor.

"We are now in the drop zone," Shef said.

"We ready?" Myth asked, looking into each man's eyes. Each one showed a confident fearlessness. It fueled Myth's exhilaration.

"Shef, open the doors."

On cue the side doors slid open, a biting cold swirled inside. Myth didn't hesitate. He jumped out. Everyone gradually fell out behind him leaving Exo and Quake.

"Don't worry, it's like riding a bike," Exo said in an attempt to comfort. He leapt out behind his teammates. Quake took a deep breath. He started towards the door and stopped.

"C'mon big man, the longer you wait, the smaller your window is gonna be."

Quake jumped out. Information began to stream down his display as if it were floating in front of him; the air temperature, the speed at which he was falling, the location of his squad in the air below him. The solar train was approaching. Myth zoomed in on it in the distance. The night was clear, making it easier to see the train softly outlined in lights.

"Deploy gliders."

Everyone followed the command. The air broke their fall as they all began a controlled glide, organized like a flock of birds.

"Three minutes till contact, engage the mag-grips" Shef informed everyone. The cell input the gesture commands into the touchscreens on their forearms. The train seemed to be moving faster as it grew closer, heading directly towards them. Myth and his cell cut through the cold, descending steadily.

"Contact in 5,000 feet," Shef said.

"Shef, I think we were off, the train is coming in too fast!"

The train began to zoom beneath them as they dropped from the air. Myth folded his arms and darted the rest of the distance, he pulled up at the last moment and let the magnetic grips on the bottom of his feet latch onto the top of the speeding train. His cell dropped around him. All except Quake.

"Ohhhhh shit, I'm gonna miss it!" Quake yelled over the comm.

"Quake drop now!" Myth yelled back. Myth and the rest watched from below as the solar train raced under Quake. Quake spun in the air and shot his grapple arm as the last car sped away underneath him.

"I'm…I'm not going to make it!" Quake yelled in a panic.

Olu stood to his feet. The grips made it easier to walk on the roof of the train, but the blistering wind and speed still made him struggle. He stood, firing his own grapple arm towards Quake. Quake missed the train by a few feet, but the mechanical hand on

Olu's grapple arm extended the rest of the distance just in time. They hooked together.

"Got 'em, hold me down!" Olu yelled at the others. They gathered around him, holding on as Quake was reeled in towards the train like a huge fish. He dropped down in the midst of the rest of the cell.

"Jesus Christ!" Quake exhaled.

"See, that wasn't so bad, right?" Myth asked.

"I can't see through the train," Red Quill said.

"It looks like they've built the exterior to prevent anybody from peeking inside, the x-ray and heat sensing capabilities of the visors aren't going to work," Shef reasoned, "There's a service exit that leads to the roof of that train car. You guys should be able to get it open and drop in with no problem."

"I see it," Exo said as he moved to the location. He quickly drew his blade and cut through.

"Good, it's cold as FUCK, outchea," Olu said as he followed Exo through the new opening. The rest of the cell followed shortly behind him. Myth was the last to drop in.

"You guys are in the second to last car. I'll try to establish communications with the Prime while you all make your way up."

"Ten-four," Myth answered.

The interior of the train car itself was strange. It wasn't holding any cargo nor were there any seats. It was a cold, sterile room, a metal, windowless rectangle with sliding doors that led to the adjacent train cars. Another set of sliding doors were on opposite sides to exit the car when it came to a stop.

"Looks really weird in here," Red Quill said.

Everyone else silently agreed.

"Let's keep moving," Myth said.

Just then, Shef's voice came back through the team's shared comm, "Speakin' of weird, I can't patch into any communications. You'll just have to find 'em."

The cell moved from car to car, each one equally as empty as the last.

"This is the fifth section of this train we been in, and it all looks the same. Not to mention, there's nobody on board," Quake said, his deep voice booming in the empty train car. Myth also felt the uneasiness of the situation in his gut. He knew something was wrong. But he and his team were on a solar train speeding through cold, empty land. They couldn't abort now.

Just find Zealot Prime and his guard…

In the next car, Myth and his cell were greeted with a different sight. The interior of the train car was exactly like the televised image they had all seen at Redwood Fortress. The leaders of the G8 all bound, gagged, and blindfolded kneeling against one side of the train car with the emblem of the Dawn Breakers emblazoned on a sheet behind them, hanging on the wall. On the opposite side there was a computer station and video recording devices.

"Red Quill, check their vitals. Exo, see what you can pull off the computers," Myth ordered. Red Quill used his light visor to scan the bodies for injuries while Exo typed ferociously at the workstation.

"They bounced the signal off of proxy servers throughout the corridors, but no mistaking, this is the origin of the broadcast," Exo said under his breath, momentarily forgetting his voice would be heard by the entire squad regardless.

"They're all dead. Puncture wounds through the heart. Myth, there's eight people here," Red Quill said confused, "This one…it's him. It's the President."

Everyone gave the man a once over. Their scanners confirmed his identity.

Myth stood quietly for a second.

Fuck…

"But on the real, what are they doin' on *this* train? This is the same shit we saw at Redwood Fortress, ain't it?" Olu wondered aloud.

The door on the opposite side of the train car hissed open. Everyone's head turned to see who would enter. Myth drew his weapon quickly.

"Who is it?" he yelled.

"At ease gentlemen," a voice said as he stepped onto the train. It was Zealot Prime. He was dressed in the traditional zealot uniform with the stars and bars of his rank emblazoned across his chest. The others stood at attention, except for Olu. He continued to look at Zealot Prime with a sideways glare. It didn't go unnoticed by Myth. He gripped his katana tighter.

"Sir, we saw the pirate transmission from the terrorist group The Dawn Breakers. We had reason to believe that the President and your envoy were in danger. When we got here, we found…this. They're all…"

"Dead?"

"Yes, sir."

"It would seem my personal guard and I have failed in our duty to deliver the President to the safe house without consequence. But, through this failure I have learned that *everything* has consequence," The tone in Zealot Prime's voice was oddly familiar, "As for The Dawn Breakers, I would think *terrorists* is a rather harsh classification."

Myth and his cell stood still with anxiety. Everyone drew their respective weapons.

"This isn't right, Myth," Exo said.

"No, on the contrary. Everything is right," Zealot Prime said as he took off the mask that was covering his face. Myth immediately recognized him. It was the same man from his dreams. He was shocked into silence.

"You…you? Who are you?"

"Yes, I suppose there's no need for this ruse. The President was asking too many questions for his own good. I am many things. Foremost, I'm a determined man with a goal in mind. A goal that

I've been working on for some time. I am the founder and spiritual leader of The Dawn Breakers. My name is Tozen."

"It's him!" Red Quill said, "The guy from the dock dropped his name right before he croaked."

"My name does precede me it seems."

Myth got into fighting position, "You've killed the leaders of the most powerful countries in the world. You're plan is to start a war!"

Tozen laughed heartily, "Oh no. No, no. These countries…without their puppet masters to pull their strings become tantamount to lost children, searching frantically for the next hand to lead them to safety. No. As I said, I've been working on a plan for a very long time. One that your father Cyrus was helping me with."

The statement vacuumed the air out of the room. Myth squinted his eyes, peering at Tozen.

"What are you talking about?"

"I'm talking about your father. You know him? The controlling, egotistical, over-bearing father that forced you to train. Forced you into Mount Z, despite your mother's wishes."

Myth wanted to respond, but couldn't find any words. Tozen saw the mixture of confusion, pain, and doubt in Myth's eyes. It was an opportunity that Tozen made sure to seize.

"Yes, Cyrus Santeaux. Quite brilliant, really. He's responsible for our research taking the leaps and bounds that it did. He will be missed."

Myth pointed his blade at Tozen.

"What did you do to him?!"

"The Dawn Breakers are built on principles. When one of those principles is egregiously violated, a fitting judgment must be rendered. Your father's insubordination proved to be too volatile for our facility. That's why I, after removing my blade from his heart and watching the last gasp of breath flee from his body like a coward from a battle, smiled at the removal of another defective gear in the machine. So to speak."

Myth lunged to attack, to everyone's shock. He hacked and slashed, fueled with anger, as Tozen danced between his attacks with little effort.

"Myth, get a hol' of yourself!" Shef yelled through the comm. Myth didn't respond. His barrage of attacks became overwhelmed by emotion. The combinations were unraveling, becoming less precise. Tozen gracefully evaded attacks. He ducked a slash and advanced. The Black Panther Fist had never appeared so brutal, even when yielded by Myth himself. Sharp elbows rained on him with surprising speed. Consecutive flips put Myth out of harm's way. He was breathing heavily, not from physical exertion, but rather emotional.

Focus…focus.

"So, these people's lives mean nothing to you? What the hell do you want?" Myth asked.

"Everett Santeaux. You're who I want."

"This shit is getting' trippy, bro," Red Quill said with concern.

"For years, decades, I have been studying the Lotus Palm Manuscript. As it stands, I am the only living practitioner of the God Fist."

"Guys, remember, this dude is capable of some wild shit," Shef said, "Stay alert!"

Tozen continued, "The technique is quite difficult to grasp, truth be told. So many moving pieces have to align in order for one to achieve true mastery. Monks used to ingest a serum derived from a particular lotus flower to help obtain a deep meditative state. If a disciple even had a momentary lapse in focus, that deep state would turn comatose. Some never regained consciousness."

"Boorrrrring," Olu said from behind everyone. Tozen ignored him. Olu, being the attention whore that he is, always felt slighted at not being acknowledged.

"The dawn, it has to be your attempt to recreate that same serum," Exo wondered.

"Yes and no. The scientists that I have…recruited over the years have been instrumental in producing something that would work greater than the old disciples could have dreamed. The problem in your corridors can be attributed to the savages that live there. They're taking the key to accelerated evolution and turning it into a common intoxicant. Pathetic, really."

"Myth, he's trying to throw you guys off the scent. Remember, our theory is that his power is amplified when he's around dreamers. He has to know that," Shef said.

Tozen continued, "Masters taught their sons, who taught their sons, who taught their sons, getting ever closer to the apex of true understanding with each generation. You, Everett Santeaux, come from an impressive lineage. Your time spent at the zealot training facility solidified my interest. You may think that you excelled because of hard work and practice. Maybe because of your father driving you or Xi Wang Xi preaching focus. I see something more divine, even if you do not. And that's why I need you. You could be the key to truly mastering the God Fist."

"I'll never come with you willingly. You'd have to kill me first," Myth said sternly.

A wicked grin slithered across Tozen's face, "Exactly."

Tozen disappeared from the door that he had entered. Myth and his cell quickly gave chase into another empty cargo hold. There were three others in the room. One handed Tozen his long katana.

"Oh shit. Myth, that dude in the crazy looking breathing mask? That's-,"

"Orion. I know, Shef."

"Heh, so you do recognize me Santeaux," Orion said drawing his weapon and staring at him with large, black eyes. The sight of his unique blade briefly sent Myth's mind back to the siege of The Ark.

"No water up here Jaws. I'll make sure you die this time," Myth spat.

"Myth, it looks like the mask is a breathing apparatus of some sort, implying that it is difficult for him to exist in normal conditions," Exo analyzed.

The second guardsman stood in silence. The bottom half of his uniform resembled a zealot's, but bandages wrapped his entire upper body like a mummy. Some appeared to be sticky with dark blue stains. His eyes were horrifically blue shot and the skin around them was grotesquely scarred.

"My scans show his entire body under those bandages has been severely burned. We're talking third and fourth degree burns. I don't even know how this guy is breathing, let alone walking around," Exo said.

"Ditto that Myth," Shef added, "Dawn has regenerative qualities, but they're most effective if they are being administered to the body on a consistent basis. This guy was in horrible shape when they found him, the dawn looks like it's the only thing keeping him alive."

"Yo…what type of shit is this?" Olu asked out loud, seemingly out of the blue. He stared at the third member of Tozen's guard in disbelief. Light reflected off of his golden gauntlet. Their eyes met. Neko smirked at Olu exposing one of the sharp fangs in his mouth.

"What the hell are *you* doin' here?!" Olu yelled angrily.

"You should know the answer to that," Neko replied calmly, "Who's the giant?"

Quake stepped up with his katana drawn, "Who's the freak?"

"Freak?" Neko asked with his head slightly tilted.

"I will finish the preparations if you all wouldn't mind entertaining our friends," Tozen instructed as he slinked out of the room.

"Nah, it's not going down like that," Myth bolted after him. Orion threw kunai that peppered the path between Myth and Tozen.

"Now…we'll settle this!"

Their swords met. The clang of their steel was like a starter pistol for everyone in the vicinity. Olu rushed Neko, with Quake next to him. Red Quill flipped backwards and whipped out his composite bow, but the silent member of the guard was on him before he could load an arrow. Orion's assault was merciless. He was much faster this time. Controlled savagery. He looked for openings and slashed with the intent to remove a limb or pierce a major artery. Myth blocked a blow with his sword, the increased force behind Orion's attacks sent harsh vibrations up his arm. Quake's huge katana slashed vertically between the assailaints, Orion hopped backwards, Myth steadied his arm and caught his breath.

"Myth, he's been using the pure form of dawn since The Ark so you can only imagine how much his strength has increased. Be careful! He's got a connection in his wrist. When he links with his sword, it changes. If you can stop him from doing that, it'll make things a helluva lot easier on ya'."

"Bet," Myth said with a weary tone in his voice that made Shef nervous.

"It's too tight on this train, I need some backup if I'm gonna get any arrows off, bruh!" Red Quill yelled frantically. His opponent seemed to be trained, at least to some degree. The technique was sloppy but his strength was otherworldly. Red Quill snatched out his hunting knife, swiping at his opponent's head and neck, switching hands as he transitioned from fists to knife's edge. The knife seemed to hang in the air as Red Quill fired off punch and kick combinations, catching the knife each time before it hit the ground. His mastery wielding the knife would have drawn praise from the rest of his cell had they not been in heated battles of their own. Red Quill attempted a flip, the mummified fighter grabbed a handful of his scarf and slung him into the wall with so much force the entire train car shook violently. Red Quill yelled out in pain, and ducked just before a punch turned the newly formed dent in the metal wall into a gaping hole. Cold air rushed into the train car.

"Quake! Go help Red Quill!"

"But...."

"Do it now!" Myth ordered. Quake moved towards the attacker with huge steps. He swung his massive katana with elegance and power, a dizzying display of swordsmanship from a man of his size. The attacker wrapped in bandages did a handspring to avoid an axe kick. Quake kept the pressure on, allowing Red Quill to get to his feet.

"Shef, man, I'm hurtin' brotha," Red Quill said, breathing heavily.

"Three of your ribs are broken," Shef said, "You can't let him put his hands on you. That goes for all of you! The one in the bandages seems to be the strongest by far!"

Olu evaded slashes from Neko. He ducked and weaved in and out of his attacks, before using every one of his limbs to counterattack. Punches, kicks, elbows, knees, and head butts were dodged or parried. Grappling techniques were easily slipped out of by Neko before they could inflict any real damage. The fight was a stalemate, and Olu was none too happy about it.

"So that's who you've been workin' for this whole time, huh? The one behind all this bullshit?"

Neko didn't respond as he calmly dodged Olu's incoming strikes. Olu feigned a high attack and quickly went into a foot sweep. Neko hopped over his leg but couldn't avoid the roundhouse kick that followed. It hit him in the chest, sending him rolling backwards. He popped up on all fours like an animal. He pounced at Olu, slashing at him with the claws of his gauntlet. Olu began to notice that this fight was different than the previous one. Neko seemed to be moving at a deliberately slower pace than he was capable of. Olu grabbed his golden arm and held Neko face to face as fights raged around them.

"I can't escape Tozen if I wanted to. The dawn has...connected us," Neko whispered.

"Why kick in my door, then?"

"It's difficult to get to a member of your tribunal. Thanks to your sensei, Xi, I found out he was coming to you. If I could make it first, I could ensure an extra set of eyes. I knew you'd keep him safe. You're his friend, even though you don't admit it. I can smell your lies."

Olu was stunned into silence at the brutally honest assessment.

"And Tozen just let you back in the crew? No questions? If he's anything like me, that shit woulda never happened."

"I had to prove my allegiance first."

"By doin' what?" Olu asked.

"I killed Zealot Prime and his guard, at Tozen's request. The bodies were thrown off. The pieces of the bodies, anyway."

"So, we gonna finish this or what?" Olu asked breaking away and putting up his clinched fists.

"Yes, but not the way you think. I owe what I am, what I've become, to Cyrus Santeaux, not Tozen."

"Quake, you're a big target, don't let him land anything!" Shef said.

"This guy must be high out of his mind! His eyes are almost completely blue!" Quake said. He held the flat side of his wide katana in front of his abdomen in an attempt to block an incoming punch. The bandage-wrapped fist smashed through the blade with ease and sent Quake flying to the floor with a thud. Myth sliced his blade through the air, aiming for Orion's wrist.

"Hmph, your friend Mr. Bales must have given you some pointers," Orion sarcastically said, "It won't help."

Orion swatted a flurry of arrows out of the air. He then noticed that three more arrows formed a perfect triangle around him. They shot vertical lasers that criss-crossed paths. Orion flipped out of the way just in time, but not before his arm was singed deeply by a beam. The brief distraction allowed Exo to launch an attack, Myth was close behind. The two were able to keep Orion on the defensive. Quake's attacker slowly walked towards him.

From one knee, Red Quill loaded up an explosive-tipped arrow.

"Get to the other train car, now!" Red Quill yelled to the rest of the cell.

Orion slithered between blades, cutting through the air, before sliding into the next train car. Myth and Exo followed after. Neko dashed out on all fours, with Olu close in tow. Quake left next, with Red Quill aiming his arrow at the man wrapped in bandages, slowly walking towards him. He loosed the bolt. It stuck in the chest of the man and caused him to stumble, Red Quill disappeared into the next car with everyone else. A huge explosion caused the lights on the train to flicker.

"Looks like he, WHOA!" Red Quill's statement was interrupted by a loud bang from the top of the train. Then another as a fist punched through the roof and peeled a hole like a sardine can. The man in bandages dropped in, dark blue blood oozed out of the hole where the arrow had been.

"Sweet Jesus, man!" Red Quill sighed.

"Myth, your team is getting overwhelmed," Orion laughed, "My understudy has proven to be quite the formidable opponent."

"Exo, Quake, Red Quill, focus on that one!" Myth ordered.

"Playing the hero will get everyone killed, Santeaux," Orion hissed.

Myth noticed that during the commotion, Orion had successfully connected to his sword. Myth watched as the sword shimmered and transformed into the giant saw blade that Shef had encountered previously.

"Myth, you can't fight him alone!"

"I'm not alone, Shef. Now show me what other tricks you got in this suit."

"I'm uploading commands now, just listen to me!"

Orion swung his blade. Myth dodged as it ripped a huge chunk out of the wall. The rest of his cell fought hard against the mummy. He was deceptively swift, but between the three of them, they were landing blows with increasing frequency. Exo leapt over Quake's shoulders, bringing his katana down with force. He severed the man's hand midway through his forearm. His indigo colored blood sprayed as his bandaged hand fell to the ground. The man barely blinked, he didn't slow down in the least bit. He just kept fighting. He grabbed Quake's arm and slammed him against the wall like a child.

"Guys! His arm is regenerating!" Shef said.

Sure enough, the stub was beginning to grow out rapidly. The bandaged man swung a punch at Exo with his bloody stump that seemingly wouldn't reach him. Exo misjudged drastically. Bone, muscle, skin, and a clinched fist regenerated in just enough time to smash into the side of Exo's face. His body slid into a corner, lifeless.

"Exo!" Red Quill screamed.

"I'll check his vitals," Shef said trying to calm everyone, "Don't stop now!"

"He crushed my sword, Shef! And Red Quill can barely stand up!" Quake returned.

"Get Exo out! Shef!"

"Roger that Myth, I'm approaching now."

The jet descended from the sky and kept pace over the train. Quake tossed a smoke bomb. The smoke filled the train car. The bandaged man struggled to find an opponent. Quake scooped Exo up and tossed him over his shoulder. With his light visor, he zoomed in on the jet flying above the train. A calculated shot of his grapple arm shortly followed as they both zipped out of the hole in the train and into the side doors of the jet, collapsing on the floor upon entry. Quake laid Exo out on the floor and stood at the threshold of the doors, staring down at the train below. Red Quill stood up as the man wrapped in bandages stared at him with dead eyes.

"Guess it's just me and you, huh?"

He lunged, aiming a punch at Red Quill's face. The three-fingered hand of a grapple arm caught his wrist. As he turned, Quake zipped down and crushed the man's face with a punch.

"Boom motherfucker!" Quake yelled excitedly.

"Alright country boy. Let's finish this dude off."

"Damn right."

"Shef, where is Olu?" Myth asked while frantically parrying Orion's newly formed sword.

"He moved ahead. He's with the kid with the golden arm."

"With? Fuckin' Olu. He's switching sides again?"

"Not quite. I heard some of their conversation over the comm. They're going to confront Tozen. That other guy says he knew your dad."

Myth didn't have time to respond, Orion was attacking with fervor. Myth struggled to keep up. Sparks flew as the pronounced serrated edge of Orion's sword clashed with Myth's katana. Myth slipped into the Long Step Mantis, firing fast kicks at Orion's lower body.

"Myth, follow the commands I've uploaded to your visor."

Myth spun away, quickly following Shef's directions. He felt his body warm. The fingers on his gloves began to glow red.

"The suit stores your kinetic energy. You can release it through your fingertips."

"How?" Myth asked.

"Yeeeeaaah, haven't really tested this out yet, so."

Myth spun his katana and placed it back in its sheath. He readied his hands and settled into Snake Style.

"No weapon? So disrespectful," Orion spat, "Some things never change, I suppose."

Myth took the fight to Orion. He dodged Orion's barrage of sword swings, looking for his opening. When his window opened, Myth threw three quick strikes aimed at Orion's pressure points. Each one that landed felt different, like the kickback from a large gun. The swiftness and force of the impact sent Orion sliding backwards.

"Gah!" He yelled.

"Looks like we're onto something, Shef."

Orion's brow furrowed. He charged back in. Myth noticed Orion's anger was affecting his technique. The two battled throughout the train car, Myth used his agility to bounce around, hopping off of walls and somersaulting over glancing sword slashes. He ducked under a swipe at his head, and countered with the Caterpillar Sting along Orion's outstretched arm.

It won't paralyze him…the dawn has made him too strong…

It loosened Orion's grip on his sword just enough. Myth snatched his katana and severed the connection between Orion and his blade, slashing a chunk out of Orion's wrist in the process. Blue blood poured onto the ground as Orion's blade returned to its original shape.

"Bastard!"

No witty response from Myth, only another supremely executed combination of attacks. He segued between styles like a master twice his senior. Internally, even Orion was impressed by it. The wound on his wrist quickly sealed up. Both men stood across from each other, breathing heavily.

"Even though that piece of your wrist grew back, it covered up your connection. You can't do it anymore."

Orion looked at his wrist.

"I can see why Tozen thinks you're the key to unlocking the full potential of the Lotus Palm. You seem…particularly blessed with talent."

"Never knew you to give out compliments, Orion."

"I only state facts. You can't win, Myth."

Myth shook his head, "Pshh. To think someone like you ever sat on a tribunal."

Orion chuckled, "Makes the whole thing seem ridiculous, doesn't it?"

There was an awkward pause as Myth considered his question. He was unnerved by the fact that he silently agreed. His eyes didn't betray his thoughts as he rubbed the engraved message in his katana's hilt.

I love you, Simone.

Myth put his sword back in its sheath, much to Orion's surprise. His hand never left the handle.

"This technique is called The Never Ending Edge. The next time I remove my sword, I will strike you and you will die."

Orion's black eyes lit up.

"The Never Ending Edge? You are something to have learned that technique. Well, let's see it. Have at you!"

Orion threw a handful of shuriken that Myth easily sidestepped. As Orion lunged, Myth waltzed between every fist, kick, swipe, and slash. He showed no sign of counterattacking, all of his power solely devoted to dancing around Orion's attempts to hit him. Of course, this just made Orion want to hit him more. Myth landed a half-hearted kick that was more of a push on Orion's chest. He stumbled back for a moment then swung wildly in anger. Myth jumped up and came down on the broad side of Orion's sword, pinning it to the ground under his feet. Orion looked in his face. Myth raised an eyebrow before flipping him off and then flipping off. His grip remained tight on the handle of his sword.

"Myth, incoming from behind you!" Shef's voice reported. Soon after a body came crashing through the sliding doors behind them, it slid across the floor, a tattered red scarf slithering along with it. Quake jumped backwards into the car that everyone else was in, the mummified attacker swinging wild punch combinations without showing signs of fatigue.

"Shef, upload those commands to everyone. For the Kinetic Fist!"

"Did you just make that up right now?"

"Yes…Yes, I did. I thought it'd sound cool, does it?"

There was a brief pause before Shef responded.

"Not really, no."

With his free hand, Myth removed a kunai. He used it like a knife to defend himself against Orion's sword. After a few successful parries, he tossed it like a rocket at Orion's face. He leaned back to avoid it. Myth hopped in with a quick barrage of kicks to the mummy's knees and legs, the extra time allowed for Quake to input the necessary commands. His fingertips started to glow red.

"Ok. Now what?"

"Now," Shef said annoyed, "You can focus energy into your fingertips to pack a bit of an extra punch. You can also control the flow from one hand to the other. Even concentrate it in one finger if you wanted. It's finite though, don't last forever!"

"Alright, I don't need you to read me the manual. Let's do this!" Quake dashed over to his opponent with renewed confidence. He landed a punch. Then another. Quake could feel the difference in the damage his attacks were doing. The mummy's body jerked every time a blow landed. Quake's confidence got the best of him, because the next punch that he threw was promptly caught. A straight kick to the stomach sent him reeling. That's when Myth noticed out of the corner of his eye that one of the mummy's arms looked perfectly normal from the middle of the forearm down. He zoomed in on his hand while he eluded Orion's attacks.

"Shef, that enough to ID him?"

"Should be, I'll have Dunbar help me pull the image and cross reference the fingerprints."

Orion laughed, "If I don't make you pull your katana, *he* will."

"This is for you and you only," Myth quickly shot back.

An unfamiliar voice came through the shared comm.

"Um…Myth? This is Dunbar."

"Who?"

"Paul Dunbar? With the MCPD? I've been working with Mr. Bales."

"Awesome. You should kinda speed this along."

"Uh, right, we found a hit on the ID."

"So who is it?"

The bandaged man continued to walk slowly over to Quake. He had to step over Red Quill's body to get there. He rolled Quake over on his back with a foot, and lifted his head off the ground with a hand. He was about to punch a hole through his face when he stopped suddenly at the sound of Myth's voice

"Adam? Detective Adam Heller?"

The man's blue eyes blinked quickly, as if what remained of his consciousness was thrust forward one last time. He turned his head to see where the voice was coming from. Quake in the meantime had been channeling as much energy into his right hand as possible. He pushed the mummy away and threw all of his might into a right hook. There was a huge flash on impact and the resulting energy blast blew a hole through the bandaged man's upper body. He hit the ground as Quake rose to his feet.

"Get out," Myth informed his team, "Take Red Quill back to the jet."

"Myth, we-," Quake started

"That's an order, Quake!" Myth declared.

Quake's eyes were uncertain, but he followed the directions and scooped Red Quill off of the ground in the same manner as he did Exo. He disappeared out of sight.

"Now, shall we continue," Orion asked as he pressed a button on his neck, the breathing apparatus covering his mouth collapsed and revealed Orion's face. His nose was nothing more than two slits in his face. He opened his mouth. It stretched far wider than a normal man's and was filled with rows of sharp teeth. His skin was pale grey. Orion took a deep breath. The mutation had intensified since they last fought, Orion's humanity hung by a shred.

"That thing helps you breathe, you must be desperate to take it off now," Myth said.

"I intend to end this quickly," Orion replied

Orion rushed in, snapping his jaws at Myth while attacking with his blade. It was becoming increasingly difficult for Myth to keep one hand on his sword's handle, but he remained steadfast in his stance, fighting off Orion with one free hand and both legs. The battle increased in speed and ferocity. Myth was evading death blows by the slimmest of margins, escaping razor-sharp teeth within seconds. Orion slashed Myth's thigh, tearing through his flesh. Still he held on. Orion's confidence surged, he leapt forward with a kick, followed by a downward slash. Myth jumped backwards.

Not yet...

Orion rushed in again, smelling blood. A spinning slash raked Myth across his chest.

"Myth what are you waiting for!" Shef yelled.

"Now...die!" Orion screamed maniacally.

A round house kick caught Myth's face. He spun around and, in a blink, the Never-Ending Edge was unleashed. The katana seemed to cut through the air itself. Myth sheathed his weapon immediately after. Orion went to raise his, and then stumbled.

"That...technique. Is...masterful."

Blue blood sprayed from a precise diagonal cut that separated Orion's sword hand from his arm and his head from his shoulders. The metal train car began to groan. Myth's attack extended beyond Orion and cut through the train car as well. It was beginning to pull apart.

"Holy shit!" Shef exclaimed.

Myth dashed into the next car as the solar train raced away from the portion he just severed, he watched it drop. Sparks shot out in the dark. The cars came to a screeching pileup that spilled over the tracks and into the frozen ground below. The jet sped over head in the darkness.

"These guys won't last too long if we don't get them somewhere fast, Myth."

"I'm not leaving."

Shef's voice rose with anger, it sounded digitally distorted. Myth just attributed that to interference over the comm.

"You'll be walking right into what he wants!"

"Once word is out that all these people are dead, the entire world is going to change, Shef. Killing Tozen is the least I can do."

"Before you go, you should see something."

Shef uploaded the video feed from Olu's visor. It was hard to discern what was going on, but Olu looked like he was engaged in battle. With whom, he couldn't make out.

"They're two cars ahead of you. The piece of the solar train that you cut off is causing the remaining cars to drag. This thing might derail any second, Myth!"

Myth picked up something before he left. When he entered and saw Olu and Neko, fighting frantically against a long katana that was floating in the air. Tozen was seated completely still behind them in a meditating position. The sword changed direction as quickly as the wind blew, easily fending off Neko and Olu. Olu's body was riddled with cuts. Neko's body was littered with newly formed scars where the cuts had healed themselves. The sword quickly flew over to Tozen, where it eerily dangled in the air next to him.

"Olu, you good?" Myth asked.

"Mannn, hell nawl I ain't good!" Olu exhaled.

Myth lobbed an object towards where Tozen sat. As it rolled to a stop, Tozen opened his eyes to see it was Orion's severed head, his face permanently stuck in a grotesque final gasp. Tozen quickly floated to his feet without moving his hands.

"And so he arrives."

"I can't let you do any more damage," Myth said as he raised his sword.

"I assure you, we are still in the infantile stages." Tozen replied, unflinching.

"Be careful, Everett. That's why he chose the confines of the train. He can only control his sword from a certain distance. Your father taught me that" Neko said.

Myth looked at Neko, finally taking in his countenance. Young, brown skinned with tiger-striped birthmarks on his exposed face. His eyes were like a cat's and he had fangs to match.

"How do you know my dad?"

Neko looked at Myth sincerely, "He trained me. Taught me a lot about being…a good person."

Dad…

"Well, I hope he taught you how to be a good fighter, too."

"That he did. He was like a father to me. Which makes you like a brother to me. He sent me here to protect you. I told your friend to do the same thing."

Myth looked quickly at Olu. He shot him a head nod.

"What's your name?"

"Neko."

"Neko. Thank you."

"You're welcome. Your father was very proud of you. I can see why."

The words provided a sense of calm. He took a deep breath.

"Thank you, too, son," Myth offered to Olu.

"We haven't done shit as long as ya' mans is still standing. He's not letting us off this train alive."

"Your friend is right," Tozen said as he suddenly got into position.

He held up an outstretched hand, palm facing inward. He had a clinched fist pulled close to his body. Tozen's katana floated over and snapped into position in front of him. Myth dashed in. Tozen stood unmoved as his sword engaged Myth first. It moved swiftly with ultimate precision. Being freed from a human hand seemed to have liberated it. The blade twisted and spun like a leaf in the breeze. It would be impossible for a person to duplicate such movement. It's unusually long length made the chances of landing a fatal blow all the greater. Olu and Neko dived out of the way as it spun towards them like a razor-sharp wheel. Sparks sprayed whenever the blade's edge scraped the metal walls or floor. Myth flipped over the blade and tossed out some smoke bombs. They immediately clouded the air. Myth's light visor projected an outline around his team through the smoke.

Tozen was nowhere to be found, which meant his body temperature had to be extremely low. He was like a reanimated corpse. There was a loud clang and the smoke was quickly vacuumed out of the train car to reveal Tozen's sword had slashed a small opening in the metal wall. Tozen was right in front of Olu. Olu swung first, firing off combinations like a prize fighter. Tozen dodged his entire string of attacks. Neko swiped at Tozen's head with his golden claws and Tozen ducked without looking. He countered with quick punches to Neko's chest and stomach. Myth threw two kunai at Tozen, but his sword swooped down and chopped them out of the air before they hit their mark. Tozen went into a series of flips to create distance between his attackers.

"Neko, you are becoming a bit bothersome with all this back and forth. So predictable. You can't fight this, no one can. You know I'll always be able to find you."

"You can't find me if you're dead," Neko purred confidently.

"So sure of yourself these days," Tozen replied with disgust.

Tozen got back into his stance and slowly walked towards Myth, Olu, and Neko. Neko pounced at him, with Olu close behind. Neko's gauntlet reflected light as he slashed with his Tiger Style, Olu filled in the gaps peppering in punches and kicks whenever the opportunity presented itself. Tozen fought off the three men with relative ease, his sword weaving in and out of the fight. Sometimes, he would grab it out of the air and wield it himself, others times he would use it as a step to launch a kick. No one came close to landing a hit on Tozen. It started to seem like he was just toying with them

"These guys are in bad shape up here, Myth," Shef said, "I have to get 'em some real medical help. Quick."

Myth was too focused on blocking attacks from Tozen. He quickly sheathed his sword and rushed forward with his Black Panther Fist. Tozen parried at the last second, turning for a moment to look Myth in the eyes before counterattacking using the same style. Each move Myth was about to make, Tozen beat him to it.   A series of elbows stung Myth's upper body. Neko jumped in, thrusting his pointed fingers towards Tozen's stomach. He spun inside and hit Neko in the face with an elbow.   Neko gathered himself and, with both hands, reset his jaw back in his socket with a sickening snap. He spit out blue blood. Tozen stood across from the three with a condescending grin smeared across his face. Myth stood thinking of some semblance of a strategy.

It's like he knows our shit before we even make a move to attack...

"Shef, upload the commands for the Kinetic Fist to Olu's display."

"The who what now?" Olu asked confused.

"Enter the sequence on your arm screen," Myth commanded.

Olu did what he was told and used his two fingers to draw a pattern onto his arm-mounted screen. Red lines began to glow in the seams of his suit down to the fingertips of his gloved hands.

"Olu. Go in. Don't think. Just...hurt him," Myth commanded. Tozen's head tilted to the side, wondering what Myth had up his sleeve.

Olu stepped forward. He folded his fingers and cracked his knuckles. Orange sparks flew out, coinciding with the sound.

"I got that."

Olu took a large step, which blended into a series of flips and cartwheels. Tozen stood unfazed, arms crossed as his blade sliced through the air in an attempt to cut Olu down. It looked like a calculated breakdance routine the way Olu easily evaded it. He started to throw punches and kicks from all directions. Tozen's grin disintegrated as he found it increasingly difficult to keep up. Olu fought with what looked like a bastard son of capoeira and prize fighting, deftly evading Tozen's fists and blade. He rolled forward and struck Tozen's upper thigh, the energy being provided through his suit packed an extra punch. The jolt sent Tozen jumping backwards.

"Seems like my man is giving you a bit of trouble," Myth scoffed.

"This miscreant? As soon as I decipher his style, it will be over for him," Tozen spat back, uncharacteristically frustrated.

Myth, Neko, and Olu burst out into laughter. It enraged Tozen.

"Decipher his style? Good luck with that," Neko added.

Olu rushed in again. He was charging his kicks and punches using the Kinetic Fist technology. His limbs left faint orange trails in the air as he twisted around Tozen, stinging him with blows that he could not predict. A vicious uppercut thrown out of a footsweep caught Tozen off guard.

"Neko."

Neko nodded, and pounced forward on all fours. The blade whirled around to stop him. He deflected it with his gauntlet. It spun back towards him like a boomerang, whistling through the air. Tozen frantically fought off both Olu and Neko. Olu charged through the air with the force of a jagged rock thrown from the hand of a petulant child. Neko pounced and slashed with his golden claws, a delicate balance of animalistic savagery and the grace of a master. Myth jumped into the fray with his Long Step Mantis, firing kicks quicker than Tozen could guard. He landed one to Tozen's ribs and felt them snap from the impact of his foot. Four fingers raked across Tozen's face, leaving hideous gashes. He fought Neko back with Tiger Style, hitting his stomach and chest with a quick string of powerful punches. Neko crumpled to the ground. He tried to rise again, but his knees buckled and he fell over face first.

"I've been a master of Tiger Style long before you were even a thought in someone's head. *SPECIMEN 415*," Tozen said angrily as he jumped backwards. He smiled while both eyes turned completely blue. A mist of the same color began to emit from them, rising into the air like smoke from a chimney.

"Oh shit," Olu let slip, amazed with fear.

"Myth, ya'll will be at the air base soon. I'm starting to take anti-air fire, I gotta pull back!" Shef yelled.

Myth ignored him. He could feel the train slowing as it neared its destination. Time was running out. Myth attacked furiously. Olu came in behind him, aiding in the assault. He threw a charged punch with his Kinetic Fist. Tozen leapt to avoid it. The resulting blast blew a hole through the side of the train car. Tozen was moving faster than he had been previously, fending off both men like a father playfully fighting off his sons. It made Myth realize that Tozen was capable of this power the entire time, a sobering jolt to reality. Even Olu's attempts were thwarted easily, as Tozen was moving so quickly it was hard to predict where he'd be next. He tossed Olu's attacks to the side and delivered his own with ease. Olu stumbled backwards, clutching his chest and coughing up blood. Myth scanned Olu's body.

He collapsed his lung…shit…Olu…

Tozen smiled maniacally. Shef yelled over the comm to abort, escape. He screamed something else about the air composition, but they didn't hear it. They were fighting for their lives and in too far to stop now. It wasn't how they were built.

"And so, this farce comes to the inevitable conclusion," Tozen said as he folded his arms watching Myth, Neko, and Olu all struggle to their feet. The blue aura now surrounded his entire body. Myth took a deep breath and charged forward, displaying every style that he had in his repertoire. Nothing so much as grazed Tozen. Myth swung his sword, Tozen caught it with his bare hands allowing the blade to cut into his palm without worry. Every time Myth blinked he was within moments of being killed by an attack from Tozen. It was dizzying, like a strobe light was on. Neko and Olu shared similar experiences as they all fought, unaware that the other was also fighting the same man. Even Shef's technology couldn't decipher what was taking place before them. He observed through the cell's network of light visors in silence, stunned that even he couldn't follow Tozen's movements.

Tozen smiled wide before unleashing a string of attacks from multiple different styles. Every animal style Myth could think of.

He finished with a vicious Crane Style kick that sent Myth tumbling backwards. Olu took out the short sword that he had tucked. He flipped it in his hands and instantly attacked. The addition of a blade, even a short one, was enough to prove problematic. Olu found himself internally amazed. Shef felt the same sensation as he watched it unfold. Olu slashed wild and unpredictable. He surprisingly punched the floor, leaving a dent and rocking the train car. It made Tozen stumble and that was enough. Olu rolled forward and pierced his stomach with his short sword, dragging it across his belly. Blue blood poured onto the ground. Myth watched in horror, barely hanging on to consciousness as Tozen grabbed the hand that held the knife, twisted Olu's arm in his socket, and delivered a crushing blow to his elbow that made his limb bend in a grotesque manner. Olu cried out in pain before dropping to his knees. Tozen ripped off his ski mask and stood over him. His bleeding had already stopped. Olu looked at Myth, eyes droopy with fatigue.

"Yo...E...I'm sorry...for everything. Looks like you're gonna watch me die afterall."

Olu smiled slightly. Tozen reached down and grabbed his neck. He squeezed slowly, deliberately, until the sound of Olu's gagging while his throat was being crushed was the only audible sound. His body went limp as he collapsed into a heap at Tozen's feet, finger indentations on his neck. Myth's eyes were wide with shock. Shef's words over the comm sounded like nonsensical gibberish.

No...no...

Tozen's sword rose from the ground. It was now that Myth noticed it had been in its sheath for some time. The train came to a stop. Tozen stared at Myth unflinchingly. Neko jumped in one last desperate attempt to catch Tozen with his back turned. Tozen whipped around and stung Neko's pressure points with precise finger jabs. He grabbed him by his hair as his body went limp and slapped him with the back of his hand, just to add more disgrace to his defeat.

"I'm not sure whether to kill you and rid myself of the nuisance or let you live and ensure each day you suffer more than the last."

Neko's golden fingers twitched.

"Ah yes, the dawn in your veins is repairing the nerve damage as we speak. I suppose I need to make a decision," Tozen said slyly, the gashes on his face finished healing right then and there, as if Neko's attack had never happened. Neko bared his fangs angrily. Myth touched the hilt of his sword's engraved message. He got to one knee. Tozen's eyes turned towards him.

"I told you. You have no chance."

Myth laughed at the irony.

Simone…Baby Girl…I love you.

He used the remaining energy reserves in his suit to fire his stored kinetic energy through the bottoms of his feet, causing him to dash forward with a flash. Tozen tossed Neko's body at him. Everything moved in slow motion as Neko's body came hurtling towards him. Tozen's long katana flew into view, resting in the air horizontally in front of Tozen. Myth watched as he held out two fingers over his blade, the blue aura around him surging like flame, and flicked his hand like a symphony conductor. Myth's body hit the floor and slid. He saw Neko's body hit the floor as well, followed by his legs. Myth's light visor fizzled and disappeared. His eyes dropped to the side, as a steady stream of tears fell down his face. A huge gash ran diagonally down the length of his chest, his arm and shoulder were barely connected to his body. As hideous as the injury was, he felt no pain.

Then everything went white.

CHAPTER THIRTY-SIX

The Delivery

"Xi, we've escorted the package here. Should be arriving at the main entrance shortly," Shef said.

"Excellent. It was imperative we moved swiftly," Xi replied through his comm. It looked awkward on his old frame.

"Yeah. You're absolutely sure about this?" Shef asked, still uncertain.

"Absolutely? No. I'm only piecing together what I've gathered from various tomes and sources. I would say that this is a very real possibility," Xi responded as he navigated through the halls of Mount Z.

"Why doesn't Tozen know about this yet?"

"That I don't know. But rest assured he will find out. He will. And when he does, he will come."

"I just dunno, Xi, I mean," Shef started before Xi forcefully interrupted.

"What other choice do we have Mr. Bales? Please, inform me. We know that Tozen isn't going to stop until he gets what he wants. He will NOT stop. If this can just temporarily slow him, that will have to be enough. You've seen what he can do. Saw what he did to-"

"No need to remind me. If he just woulda been listenin'…"

Shef's voice sounded distorted. Tears would have formed in his eyes if he still had them.

"So then, you agree?"

"Yeah. Yeah, I agree. Lemme ask you somethin' Xi. What did you read that made you think of this in the first place?"

"The Lotus Palm, it's said to be the ultimate technique, a bridge between life and death, the conscious and the subconscious. There was an interesting bit that I uncovered. When translated it stated that only a bringer of life can truly become a master of the Lotus Palm. A closer translation isn't *bringer*…it's *giver*. The lotus itself represents this idea in certain Asian cultures."

"Sorry man, I'm not too well versed on my ancient Asian cultures," Shef lamented.

"Well, I will put it succinctly for you: to master the Lotus Palm, you have to be a woman."

Xi stood at the main entrance flanked by overseers. Another group of overseers opened the large wooden doors. Xi stepped outside. He was greeted by an interesting group. One was a miniature humanoid robot floating in the air.

"Master Xi," it said. Lights where the mouth should have been pulsated as the words came out.

"Mr…Bales? Not quite what I was expecting."

"Trust me, this is better than the alternative," Shef said.

Xi turned to the other visitor, "I know this is difficult for you, I'm glad you made this decision," he said softly.

"I…I know. If it's the only way to make sure she's safe."

"You are welcome to stay. Typical protocol has been thrown out of the window at this point," Xi said with a laugh trying to ease the tension to no avail. Everyone's face held a distress that nothing could mask. Xi bent down.

"Hello there."

"Hi."

"My name is Master Xi. What's your name?"

"My name is Chance. Chance Santeaux."

"Chance. Welcome to Mount Z."

To be concluded in

Part III:

Revenge by Chance

Part II: Dawn Breakers